ENTRANCING THE EARL

SCHOOL OF MAGIC, BOOK 5

PATRICIA RICE

Book View Café

ONE

"How does one choose a wife?" Gerard, Earl of Ives and Wystan gazed upon the choicest maidens in northern England waltzing about in acres of colorful silk and lace. Castle Yates wasn't London, by any means, but the duke's dazzling ballroom sported the same hazards for a man avoiding matrimony.

His friend, unfortunately, could no longer avoid it.

"Amenable disposition, I suppose." Jasper, Marquess of Rainford, resplendent in his usual tailored aloofness, frowned at the buffet of femininity imported just for his selection. "Beauty doesn't last. A modicum of intelligence would be pleasing."

Having given up his mistress some months past for lack of funds, Gerard was studying the vast array of non-virginal chaperones. "It's a shame we can't test for enthusiasm in bedplay."

That response produced an unrefined snort from the normally proper Rainford. "I suppose I could look among widows if intercourse mattered for more than the production of heirs. But I'm fairly certain my father did not invite the impure for my selection. He wants an heir of his own blood, however unstable that blood might be."

Gerard hid a wince. The duke's clan had a strong strain of what must be called *eccentric*, even more so than the usual Malcolm family aberrations. Concealing his own weirdness was difficult enough, but Gerard hadn't the wealth to take it to extremes, as Rainford's family did.

He juggled the medallion in his pocket, the one that whispered to him of treasure to be found at Wystan. "At least you don't have to choose a wife for her fortune. If I'm to keep Wystan, I'll have to find gold or marry a bank account."

Should he ever make the mistake of mentioning that he was listening to treasure-seeking voices in coins, any income from a political future was doomed—as well as any chance of marrying wealth.

Thankfully, he didn't actually *see* spirits. He simply heard them speak when he touched a propitious object.

As a scientific, logical man of the world, he had too much cynicism to believe legions of penniless Ives would have overlooked any treasure buried in Wystan.

But beneath his pessimism lurked a flicker of hope. What if he was actually hearing the spirit of an ancient Roman who may have buried treasure on his estate? Even a small store of coins might stave off the decision between marrying for wealth or heaving his female relations from a crumbling castle he could no longer maintain.

The spirit voices had been correct, if less than useful, in the past. He'd learned his lesson as a lad when he'd told his hosts they had a body buried in the cellar. Hysteria and skeletons only achieved notoriety. These days, Gerard favored tactful diplomacy and kept the voices to himself.

Until these past weeks, he'd never had an artifact mention buried treasure. He feared it might be his desperation speaking.

"Marry, invest your wife's fortune in improving Wystan's assets, and you'll have wealth enough to live on," said the lord with more gold than Croesus and the imagination of an accountant.

Gerard shrugged. "I'll inherit the marquisate one day. My future is fated. Before I must retire to dry responsibility for a few dozen intractable Ives and their families, I'd rather not tie myself down to one woman."

"And you want to see sunny climes and foreign maidens," Rainford added knowingly.

Well, yes, Gerard had always wanted to take his gift and explore real Roman ruins in Italy, but his pockets had always been to let.

He retaliated by pounding the slender marquess on the back. "And you're procrastinating on joining the assembly where all those mamas are regarding you hungrily, and the demure maidens your father has chosen are surreptitiously watching you from under their lashes, judging you as husband material. Go forth and match-make."

"You should do the same, if funding is what you need. My father invited the wealthiest, most respectable damsels to be found in this part of the kingdom."

"On the theory that London ladies would not wish to languish in rural Yorkshire, even if this estate is large enough for a small town?"

"On the theory that I have rejected everyone in the south. You take the right hand side. I'll take the left. We'll see if we find any likely prospects and meet in the middle." Rainford stalked off.

Thanking all that was holy that his own father wasn't pushing for an heir since the family had more relations than the marquess could afford already, Gerard ignored the young lovelies and aimed for Lady Alice, a widowed chaperone. He'd known Alice since infancy. She had a wicked tongue, a prosperous father, and put the *merry* in merry widow. She'd be better sport than simpering virgins.

"You should dance," Iona Malcolm Ross advised her companion as they studied the marquess's splendiferous ballroom.

The music was heavenly, as one would expect from the wealthy and generous Winchesters. The floral arrangements—sent Iona into sensory overload. Had she not wished to remain invisible, she'd dance from bouquet to bouquet, deliriously sniffing the fragrances.

Unfortunately, the price of her freedom was a great deal of constraint, an irony she did not appreciate.

The dancers were a portrait in elegant blacks, colorful silks, and scents of excitement and agitation that Iona itched to escape. "Do not let my research hold you back," she encouraged her companion. "I can find the library on my own."

Lydia Ives, the Calder Castle librarian, gazed dubiously at the gliding dancers. "I might manage a reel or two, but even if Max is as light-footed as an angel, he couldn't make me float the way they do."

Iona almost managed a grin at the image. "The two of you would clear the dance floor in your magnificence. None could compare. Just picture it. Make it happen!"

The librarian and her husband were not small people. They towered taller than most of the gentlemen, and while they were young and athletic, they were not light on their feet. But they were splendid in their fine array and happiness with each other.

Lydia smiled a little. "Perhaps we should try a reel or two. Who knows when I may escape my library again, especially after the little one arrives." She caressed the barely noticeable bulge beneath her frilled apron-front bodice.

"Look, your husband has seen you. I'll leave now. And again, thank you a thousand times for bringing me here. I've been longing to see this library ever since I heard of it." Iona retreated into the shadows.

Lydia pinned her with a knowing gaze. "Your sister is invaluable to me. I'd like to hear your story one day."

Iona chilled. No one must know that she had a sister. The librarian was too perceptive. "Maybe after I'm dead. You'll have my journal then."

She hurried away before Lydia could interrogate her. Iona looked too much like her twin, which was why Isobel had dyed her blond hair, and Iona had cut hers. Then Isobel had gone to Edinburgh and Iona now hid in the wilds of Northumberland. Small and mousy when dressed as servants, they normally went unseen by wealthy aristocrats.

But in her eagerness to finally lay her hands on the bee book, Iona had stolen this opportunity to leave her hiding place, even knowing the risk. Now she knew why the Calder Librarian had taken the time to help a humble beekeeper—Lydia had recognized Iona's resemblance to her steward back in Scotland, despite their disguises.

Iona didn't have time to worry about consequences. She'd jeopardized her safety to make this trip. She needed to find the book.

Leaving the lights and music, she hurried down the backstairs, away from any guest who might notice her. Once inside the darkened library, Iona lit a gas sconce by the door. Yates Castle wasn't a library of Malcolm journals, but a real, honest-to-gosh library with every book known to mankind collected by the duke's family over the centuries. It smelled like heaven should smell—of polish, leather, and wisdom.

The duke's library was immense, a palace of knowledge as well as beauty. It extended the entire length of this wing, with two-story stacks along the walls, more accessible ones in the center, and a ceiling painted by some long-gone artist. To Iona, it was a church and university all rolled into one.

Apparently influenced by his journal-collecting Malcolm ancestors, the duke paid a full-time librarian who catalogued and labeled each bookcase by topic. Lydia had vouched for Iona and obtained a key for her. Iona had already made inquiries and knew exactly which shelf she needed.

Carrying an oil lamp placed at the entrance, she wandered through the shadowed stacks, reading the labels. She located the area on beekeeping with a sigh of satisfaction.

Langstroth on the Hive and the Honey-Bee: A Bee Keeper's Manual, finally. She lifted it from the shelf with reverence. She had begged her stepfather for this book since her eighth birthday, a few years after the book had been published. It had taken fifteen years to finally hold a copy in her hand.

One did not find many books on beekeeping in the Highlands and certainly not in her stepfather's non-existent library. And now that she had escaped his hold, she had no money to buy books.

Everything she knew, she had learned from her mother, but those methods were primitive. Few real beekeepers used skeps these days. Burning out a colony to cut out the honey was too destructive. She'd been perusing the books in the Wystan library, but Malcolm journals were equally outdated on the subject.

In her one brief visit to London when she'd been sixteen, she'd been able to find a few pamphlets on modern beekeeping and learned how to build a movable comb. It had been imperative that she learn to do so. Now, finally, she was ready to advance her skills in honey collection and hive construction.

A descendant of generations of Malcolm queen bees, her queen required the best care available. If she could never go home to her other hives, Iona had to protect this one.

She found a table and took a notepad and pencil from her pocket.

Lost in the intricacies of building wooden hives with movable frames, she didn't hear the intruders enter. Only when the scents of lust and duplicity wafted back to the stacks, followed by a lady's moan, did she register the intrusion.

Curling her lip in disgust, Iona tried to determine which door they'd entered by—the one she'd left unlocked, of course. Shame on her. She simply hadn't thought anyone would be interested in a cellar library when there was a ball in the glorious ballroom above. She could see the door but not past the center shelves to where the amorous couple must have availed themselves of an empty table.

The duke's librarian did not like to have his books removed from the library. Iona respected that. But she might not have another chance to read this manual. She had to leave for Wystan on the morrow.

Did the fools not notice her lamp? Probably not, she realized. The library was immense and if the shelves hid the couple, then they hid her and her small light.

She could remain—she'd simply have to listen to passionate moaning or draw attention to her presence so they would leave. She couldn't *think* with all that going on, but being noticed wasn't safe. Removing the book was her only choice.

Quietly, she tucked away her pad and pencil and blew out her lamp. She had already determined all the other exits. She'd simply take the one on the end opposite the intruders. She doubted they'd notice.

Discreetly gathering up her unfashionable ankle-length skirt and single petticoat, Iona mentally apologized to the librarian and vowed to return the book before he knew it was gone. She lifted the volume and slipped toward the exit.

The woman screamed.

Iona halted.

"Pardon me," a male voice said in puzzlement. "Did I hurt you?"

The scent of lust died out, replaced by that of suspicion.

"You beast," the woman cried. "How could you?" In the echoing silence of the enormous library, ripping fabric resounded loudly.

"Alice, don't play insane," the gentleman said firmly. "You know me. I'm the worst possible choice for your schemes. Being a countess isn't all you might think."

"You rake," the woman cried, disdaining the gentleman's logic. "Taking advantage of a helpless widow!"

Iona sighed. She recognized the woman's scent now. She'd only met Lady Alice yesterday but had smelled her fear and worry and recognized her predicament. The lady's father was a wealthy baron hoping to rise in rank. He would not appreciate his widowed daughter bearing a bastard.

Crying rape to force an—earl?—into marriage was not the solution. What did she do now? She owed nothing to either of the couple, but that poor unborn child deserved better than this.

Hiding in plain sight was a tight-rope Iona walked every day. It was simpler in Wystan, where everyone accepted her as the beekeeper and knew better than to question. She'd risked her invisibility by stepping too close to society, but the book was worth it.

Now, she had to deal with the consequences. Circumstances might force her to hide, but hers wasn't a naturally retiring nature.

Donning her best simple-minded servant expression, Iona hastened toward the couple, calling herself every kind of fool but knowing she couldn't allow this scene to carry out to its inevitable conclusion. She might have been a wallflower in London all those years ago, but she'd learned a lot since.

"May I help, my lady?" she inquired, interrupting a dramatic scene where the lady in her ripped bodice clung to the gentleman's lapel with one hand and beat him with the other.

Tall, dark, and possibly handsome if he hadn't been scowling fiercely enough to terrify a phantom, the gentleman warily glanced at her. "The lady has been taken by a fit, I believe. Would you have smelling salts?"

"No, but if you smacked her, she might come around," Iona responded cheekily. "If you are too gentlemanly to do so, shall I try?" She knew she looked small and weak, but helpless, she was not. The lady reeked of duplicity, and the gentleman. . . among other things. . . exuded incredulity.

The lady shrieked a protest. "He has assaulted—" She shut up when she recognized Iona as the librarian's companion.

If she'd actually recognized *Iona*, there'd be hell to pay, but Iona was fairly certain she'd never met Lady Alice before this week. The world was full of people she'd never met, including the gentleman.

Iona crossed her hands over the book at her waist and applied her best domestic-servant expression. "Perhaps I could find your maid, my lady?"

The gentleman's fury had reached the level of a smoldering fire. She could swear she heard him growl. He towered over her, which was annoying. He was excessively large across the shoulders, but his beautifully fitted tailed coat clung neatly over narrow hips. From the way he backed off once released, she gathered he had muscles on top of muscles that he'd courteously restrained while being assailed.

"I can fetch a footman to find the maid," he said stiffly, with that slight rumble still in his voice to indicate his displeasure.

"That would be best," Iona advised, doing her best to hide in the larger lady's shadow. The flickering of the one gas sconce should render her dull gray gown and pale features nicely invisible beneath her servant's cap. Lady Alice wept and didn't protest as Iona steered her toward the door.

"Go to Wystan," Iona advised in a low voice as she led the lady to the main staircase. "The ladies there understand. You and the child will be safe."

Pretending she had not heard, the lady lifted her chin and grasped the polished mahogany banister, dismissing Iona. The frilled train of her fashionable, ebony silk gown swished as she climbed the curving stairway, leaving Iona behind to take the service door.

The gentleman's smoldering scent lingered in the wide corridor. She could hear him speaking with a footman. The servants' network would find the maid. All was as well as it could be. Hugging the precious book to her bosom, she headed for the back stairs where dozens of servants scurried up and down to the ballroom.

Even when she heard the gentleman shout after her, she kept going. In her mind, she donned a cloak of invisibility and vanished behind the baize-covered door. He would forget her by tomorrow, and then she'd be gone. She couldn't risk being seen again.

TWO

Disgusted with himself, with society, and the world in general, Gerard pushed his gelding hard on the last stretch of the journey to Wystan *Castle*.

"Ridiculous name for an old stone keep and watchtower," he told the spirit lingering in his head. "It looks nothing like a castle."

The heart of his earldom dated back to a thirteenth century barony, when the fortress probably was grand for the times. The keep had originally been owned by Malcolms and called Malcolm Castle. After the first earl of Ives and Wystan breached the walls, he'd apparently liked the idea of owning a castle. So he renamed it after himself and turned it into a rambling monstrosity.

Life is in the soil, not the architecture, the spirit in his pocket reminded him, in Latin, of course. The damned soldier must have been a philosopher, but he was right, in his way. One side or the other of Gerard's family had lived here since before the dark ages. They were attached to this land, heart and soul.

He couldn't be the one to lose it.

The journals in the immense Malcolm library housed in the castle mentioned a wooden fortress prior to the stone one. And Gerard didn't doubt there had been a druidic village prior to the Roman invasion. The locals still placed offerings at a pagan shrine in a spring in the oak grove. Wystan had been isolated much too long to move into the modern world with any speed.

Which was why Gerard had put off this visit. When he came north, he preferred lingering in more civilized environs. In Edinburgh and at Rainford's home, he'd had the opportunity to discuss business with worldly men like his engineering cousin, Max Ives, as well as inventors and investors. Although, after the encounter with traitorous Lady Alice, he had to be assured that she had fled on the first train out before he'd lingered with Rainford's company.

"I'm usually not wrong about ladies who are ripe for a romp," he muttered, as much to himself as to the indifferent spirit in his head. Lady Alice had given him the impression that she was interested. They'd dallied occasionally over the years without drama. He didn't know what had come over her.

Women require protection, the spirit said wearily, as if that were obvious.

"Well, if she's in dire financial straits, she certainly made a poor choice in me. I have no funds, and hers aren't sufficient to dig me out. Besides, they'd have to hold me at gunpoint before I'd marry the deceptive wench, and then I'd abandon her at Wystan to fend for herself."

And you'd bolt for the continent, the spirit agreed, almost with amusement, using a crude form of English that Gerard understood without translation.

"So maybe she had the wrong impression of me, too." He knew his faults. He didn't need dead Romans to remind him.

The intriguing part of that whole episode had been the well-spoken servant carrying a library tome who'd saved his hide. Her tongue had been waspish, and her suggestion that he smack the lady had appealed to his sense of the absurd and tapped down his fury. He'd wanted to thank her, but she'd vanished in a puff of smoke. He hadn't seen her again. She was probably a lady's companion and had left with the rest of the guests. Companions tended to be impoverished women of quality. He'd not inquired after her.

He was a practical man. He didn't dally with needy maidens and spinsters who expected marriage. Should he ever hobble his freedom with the wedded state, it would be for wealth. It might come to that if he did not find an additional source of income—or a pot of gold—soon.

Entering the wood surrounding his home, Gerard let his mount rest and breathed deeply of damp autumn leaves and pine needles. The journey from Rainford's castle in York to Wystan in Northumberland would have taken two or three days by horse, but the train up the coast cut the time in half. He kept a horse stabled at the nearest station so he could ride in whenever he wished without notifying anyone of his arrival.

You like annoying the women, his spirit voice concluded.

"I don't want anyone going to extra trouble for me," Gerard corrected. But yes, he liked frustrating the schemes of the castle's meddling inhabitants as well.

The meddling inhabitants were one cause for his desperation.

The train, unfortunately, had been filthy with coal dust. Gerard wanted a hot bath before he must contend with his houseful of interfering old witches. The *witches* part wasn't a euphemism. Wystan had been a Malcolm stronghold since before the arrival of the Normans, maybe longer. The women were quite convinced their first journals recorded the oral traditions of their druidic ancestors. Since his mother was a Malcolm, as well as many of his relations, he knew all about their very odd abilities—and his own.

His father hadn't handed over the estate to Gerard out of generosity. The marquess had done it so he didn't have to deal with the failing fortunes of a monstrously expensive castle inhabited by psychic women under some trust agreement written a century ago. The castle really should be closed up or demolished—except it housed an immense and ancient library.

The medallion's spirit fell silent, presumably in admiration of the rambling structure they approached.

Once the all-male Ives family had taken control of the old keep, practical amenities had been added—and escape hatches. Riding into the yard, Gerard left his gelding with a stable boy and took the cobble-stone path between the old stone walls to the derelict watchtower in the rear. The women had been forbidden this part of the castle, so it hadn't been adorned with roses, padded with wall-coverings and tapestries, or filled with gilded furniture. It was stark cold stone and formidable.

Using his private entrance, he took the worn sandstone stairs down to the former kitchen. Since he never traveled with a valet, he had to pull the water from the pump himself. It sluiced directly into a bath large enough for a male frame. He lit the gas heating element and let the water warm as the tub filled. He didn't know which of his inventive relations had created this luxury but he was grateful for it.

After scrubbing off coal dust and horse stench, he donned a robe, climbed the stairs to his tower rooms, and foraged in the countrified wardrobe he left there. He didn't need to be fashionable in the wilds of Northumberland. Tweed, leather, and boots sufficed, unless he was bored enough to go to dinner. His trunks would catch up with him before that happened.

What he wanted to do was explore his fields for any sign of a Roman ruin where treasure might be buried. It was September. He had a few hours of daylight left. He just needed food.

By now the entire household had been alerted to his arrival, and the women would be bustling all over, stirring the servants into a tumult.

He rang the bell. A footman arrived instantly, no doubt told to wait for the earl's command. Gerard had to admit to appreciating the efficiency of a household that catered to his every wish—as long as it didn't interfere with anyone else's. He ordered food to take with him.

He knew the ladies' helpfulness wasn't in gratitude for a roof over their heads. They had that whether or not he wished it. What they wanted was his presence, for reasons he never cared to understand.

While waiting, he flipped through the invoices and correspondence left on his desk. Avery, the estate's agent, sent important business to Gerard's man in London. He'd already seen Avery's professional assessment of the prohibitive expense of continuing to operate the enormous castle and the aging orchards. He could save a fortune by closing down the deteriorating structure and investing the savings by clearing the ancient orchard and turning it to crops and cattle.

Removing the ladies and their library would be no mean feat.

Once he had his food in hand, Gerard gnawed at an apple from the first crop off the trees and jogged down the stairs to the back gate again.

He could expect to find the women anywhere from the herb and rose gardens to the pigsty, but for now, the yard appeared empty. Maybe they were holding a meeting.

Swinging the leather pack and walking stick over his shoulder, he finished his apple and started on a thick sandwich of cheese from his dairy. He fingered the medallion in his pocket, hoping for inspiration as to where to search, but the damnable spirit had retreated. His Malcolm gift was essentially useless except for amusement—and possibly edification should he ever take up archeological explorations. He had no control over the voices he heard—other than leaving a haunted object behind if he found it objectionable.

With no better direction, he set off on foot for the orchard. The trees were one of the oldest plantings on the grounds and an excellent place to start searching for Roman treasure.

He frowned as he strolled brown strips of what appeared to be frost-bitten weeds where there used to be well-worn paths for carts. Had the gardeners not been scything? He'd have to ask Avery about the unsightly crop. The steward hadn't mentioned any labor problems.

The September sun was still warm enough to be pleasant. The hum of bees reminded Gerard of milder seasons in his family's home in the south. Until now, he'd always visited Wystan in the chilly harvest time of October or November.

The medallion in his pocket remained silent. Perhaps he'd misinterpreted the voice in his head. It wouldn't be the first time. He was inured to disappointment. Hunting for treasure had about the same chance of success as gold at the end of rainbows. But he was desperate for a means of keeping the estate operational and his allowance intact, and he had to visit sometime anyway.

A puff of smoke caught his attention. He didn't think the weather had been particularly dry this year, but any fire could be dangerous if not monitored. He followed the wind through the trees and into a clearing. More weeds, although not as tall as the ones in the orchard. A few still bloomed a startling red.

At one end of the clearing the women had apparently rebuilt the old-fashioned bee skeps and hackles. A figure in veiled hat and ankle-length gray skirt—with what appeared to be trousers and boots beneath—moved among the hives, waving a smoking pot.

He'd had rather nasty reactions to bee stings in the past. He preferred to avoid one now. Assured that the smoke wasn't a problem, he strode in a different direction, only to see a tawny blur of motion fleeing the trees, heading directly for the hives. At a woman's shriek, Gerard grabbed the walking stick attached to his pack and ran to stop the animal.

The beast howled as it leapt on one of the cone-shaped straw hackles. Screaming with what sounded like anguish, the woman swung her iron smoke pot at the animal. Gerard shouted at her to stand back, but she apparently didn't hear. Skep and hackle toppled into the woman's skirt. Bees swarmed while the smoke pot slammed into the dog. The animal bayed and lunged at the woman, knocking her off her feet. The dog was nearly as large as she was.

At least he thought it was a dog. Swinging his stick—more of a cudgel than a polite gentleman's accessory—Gerard whacked the howling animal's flanks, beating it off the weeping woman on the ground.

He could swear she was keening over the swarming bees and not from fear.

Chased by angry insects, unwilling to confront a swinging cudgel, the dog fled.

Gerard cursed as the stinging pests turned on him. He ought to leave the accursed woman to her creatures, but he had to see if she'd been hurt.

He held out his hand for her to take. She was a slight creature. The huge beast could have caused injury. "Are you hurt? I can send someone to clean up. You shouldn't be out here if there's a wild dog in the vicinity."

He could swear the furious swarm of bees formed a protective cloud, but he was more concerned with the woman—who ignored his proffered hand.

"Help me right this." She scrambled to her feet on her own. "I don't think all the combs are sealed yet, and they'll be losing their winter food."

Gerard grimaced as one of the bees landed on his glove. But idiot gentleman that he was, he grabbed the sticky straw and hauled the hive beneath upright. Bees hummed angrily.

The woman appeared to be singing under her breath, swinging the pot and smoking him as if he were a ham butt. He winced and swatted at an itch on his jaw, slowly backing off from the weird scene.

"We need to send Avery and his men out to hunt for that dog," Gerard warned. "Bees aren't worth your life."

"Bees *are* my life," she retorted. The heavy veil muffled her voice as well as the words of her song as she returned to soothing the insects with her chant.

With the hive righted, Gerard backed off. Another bee crawled under his cuff and took a piece of his wrist. He slapped at it.

The woman glared and all but snarled at him. "The workers are only doing what they're bred to do—protect the hive. Don't blame them. And that dog isn't wild. Its deranged owner trained it to eat honey to harass me. Go beat the owner."

"And who might the owner be?" Sucking at the wound on his wrist, Gerard backed off to a safer distance.

He could see little of her face through the thick veil, but the scorn in her voice said her expression wouldn't be a friendly one. The sting on his jaw was already raising a welt. Angry pain traveled up his cheek.

"The animal belongs to Wystan's estate agent. If you don't know that, then you don't belong here. Who are you?"

"Wystan's owner," he replied equally curtly—and hoarsely. He rubbed his throat and tried to take a deeper breath. "And if my agent is keeping a dangerous dog, then it must be for a reason."

He waited to see how she reacted to his identity. Earls were few and far between in these rural environs. Most people groveled—except the Malcolm ladies, naturally.

"Avery doesn't like bees, he doesn't like me, and he doesn't like what we've done to his orchards, even if we improved his crop." She returned to soothing her insects.

So much for groveling. She was one of *them*. He'd known it anyway. Normal women did not hover over bee hives as if they were children. Nausea welled, and he could feel his throat closing up. He fought against the reaction, refusing to allow a bee to bring him down.

"I was about to order the gardeners to scythe that shambles," he croaked. "You're the one responsible? Why?"

"Scythe it now, and you'll lose the seeds that will replant the borders in the spring. Flowers attract bees. Bees pollinate your trees. They may also deter harmful insects. But Avery lacks imagination and refuses to study the effect of natural planting."

She sighed and stepped away from the hives. "I'll not gather honey today. I might as well—"

Gasping for air, Gerard tried not to crumple. He failed.

IONA GASPED AS THE BIG MAN FELL TO HIS KNEES, HOLDING HIS THROAT. Muttering curses, she threw back her veil so she could see better. She hadn't *wanted* to look at her landlord—or for him to see her. She didn't think they'd ever met, but she hated taking any more risks, and there was always the chance he'd seen her twin, as Lydia had.

But needs must—she kneeled and loosened his shirt collar. Noting the swelling on his jaw, she removed her gloves, rubbed her fingers over the rising welt, and brushed off the stinger. She helped him lie flat on the ground and left him wheezing for air.

Picking up her skirt, she ran back to the hives, and with her bare hand, scooped up wax and honey. Holding the salve in her palm, she returned and wiped a little on his jaw, then pried open his teeth to put honey on his tongue.

The Earl of Ives and Wystan was so damned *large*. As he panted, she daringly began inspecting other places she knew bees could invade. The heavy tweed coat should keep stings off his back, and his wool vest should have protected his chest, thank all that was holy. A sting over his heart. . .

She could have killed an earl! Fitting justice she supposed, killing the one who unknowingly gave her safe haven—when the earl she *wished* to kill would never die. Her life was like that.

Her queen commiserated and urged her to keep looking for more stings.

Iona pulled off his lordship's gloves and pried back his cuffs so she could examine his wrists—always a vulnerable spot. Sure enough, a big welt was turning an angry red on his left wrist. He had thick arms, rippling with tendons and muscle, but wrists were mostly bone and blood vessels, even on the strongest of men. She couldn't find a stinger, so she applied the honey salve. She had no idea if it would work. It was a remedy her mother had taught her—and her queen insisted would work.

Communicating with bees was seldom helpful, but she trusted hers.

The earl's other wrist seemed fine. He was wearing good leather boots, protecting his vulnerable ankles. She didn't think there was any way a bee could have entered his leather trousers—again, thank the goddesses.

While her innocent victim gasped for air, Iona hastily removed his collar and cravat, exposing an attractive brown neck and a curl of hair at the top of his shirt. She couldn't lift him to check the back of his neck but ran her hand wherever she could reach. No hot spots or swelling that she could find. She'd never touched a man's neck before. Were they all this solid and sinewy? Touching him intimately stirred odd longings best ignored.

She breathed deeply, testing the air—male sweat, a hint of fear, more than a hint of. . . anger? Resentment? She could empathize. He'd hate showing weakness.

Beneath that lingered an appealing masculine musk mixed with a vaguely familiar whiff of lime—*oh dear*. She sat back and examined the wheezing earl with panic. Tall, wide-shouldered, dark and glowering. . . most definitely the man from the library.

She prayed he didn't remember her.

What did she do now? Run back to the house? She hated abandoning him here, especially near her hives if he was sensitive to stings. He'd swat at any bees investigating him—causing them to swarm. With his sensitivity, that would be deadly.

She couldn't possibly lift him. She might trust her queen, but even a bee queen couldn't control all her workers. He had to be guarded.

She settled on the grass, holding her breath in anxiety while she listened to his rattily breathing. The asthmatic reaction usually eased after a bit, and he seemed large enough to fight it. He hadn't vomited yet. She didn't know if that was a good sign. She hummed under her breath, and her queen hummed back. Her stepfather claimed she was insane, but he'd said the same about her mother and grandmother, and Iona had always thought them the wisest people she'd ever met.

They simply talked to bees. It seemed perfectly natural to her.

"You'll be all right," she reassured the earl, holding his hand and examining his wrist. Had she ever held a man's bare hand? Doubtful. Her own father had died before she was old enough to know him. Her stepfather had sent her and Isobel off to a girls' boarding school in England when they'd been six. Men were foreign creatures to be feared.

She'd learned a little better since, but she remained wary of the gender. Still, she didn't want to helplessly watch a man die.

The welt on his wrist didn't seem quite as angry now. She started to withdraw her hand, but his strong brown fingers caught hers. Not dead then.

"Can you stand?" she asked, watching his chest rise and fall. His breath didn't seem quite so raspy.

"Who are you?" he demanded, rubbing the swelling on his jaw.

"Nan, the beekeeper. The pain will go down if we can pour some willow bark tea into you. I can't carry you back to the house, but I can't leave you here in pain." She tried to tug her hand free. He held it tighter.

"Nan what?" His voice was still raspy.

"Nan Malcolm, of course." The beauty of being part of a large clan was that she could use her name and live in plain sight and no one would know the difference. That her small world knew her as Lady Iona Malcolm Ross mattered little.

"Of course," he said dryly. "Let's see if I can stand without toppling again."

"You topple verra politely," she assured him, rising up on her knees. "If you'll use your walking stick and my shoulder, we might haul you up."

Dubiously, he studied her slender frame, but Iona was accustomed to being dismissed as weak. He followed her advice and used his stick as a brace to sit up. "Do I detect a Highland lilt?"

She bit back a frown. Her boarding school accent normally disguised her origins. She must be more upset than she realized. She ignored his question and aided him in rising. Assured that he could stand without her aid, she turned toward the house. "I'll go ahead and let the others know. Winifred will have better remedies than mine."

"Don't," he called after her. "You have no way of fighting off that dog. I don't need physicking. Walk with me."

Iona hesitated, watched as he used his stick to steady himself and noted his color returning. A big man like that could fight off adverse reactions more easily than others, she reasoned.

She preferred her usual strategy of avoidance. It was imperative for her safety and that of her sister and all the people at home who relied on her.

She flipped her veil back in place. "On the contrary, my lord, you will be safer without my presence."

With that she began to hum. As she walked away, a steady stream of bees rose from the hives and followed her, keeping her safe from rampaging animals and reducing the numbers who might attack him.

THREE

G<small>ERARD CURSED THE BEEKEEPER, CURSED HIS HOUSEHOLD OF WITCHES,</small>
cursed whatever malady caused him to topple from a damned bee sting.
By the time he dragged himself back to the castle, the yard had filled
with anxious women waiting to coddle him.

"Begone, the lot of you," he shouted, like some curmudgeon from a
ha'penny novel.

He was trained in courtesy. He never talked to anyone like that, much
less his poor relations.

The beekeeper was nowhere to be seen. Neither was the dog or his
agent. His Great-Aunt Winifred, garbed in unfashionable full crinoline
and a widow's black, gestured for the others to depart. "Have the tea
and poultices carried to his lordship's chambers."

"I don't want any damned blasted tea and poultices. I'm not an octo-
genarian." He stalked toward the privacy of his tower keep.

"Then suffer through the night," his aunt said without sympathy. "I
can see you are breathing. We can hope you won't strangle in your
sleep."

"I'm not an invalid. Tell Avery I want to see him." He didn't break
stride.

"I'm not your housekeeper," she called after him.

"I was under no illusion that you were," he shouted back. "I thought you wanted to help. Sending for Avery is how you can do it." *Not by hovering*, he muttered to himself.

She probably sniffed in disapproval, but he was too far away to hear.

Coming to Wystan was almost always a disaster. His estate was self-sufficient, but it was one of his many duties to oversee it. Theoretically, he supplemented his meager allowance with the profits, but the income was less each year, and he'd found no miracles to change that. Riches simply couldn't be had from rocky fells and dales.

Soon, he'd have to become a lawyer just to buy clothes—except he'd have to work at night when his duties to his father's extensive business and political affairs didn't interfere.

In his suite, Gerard drank the nasty tea they sent. Despite his protest, he slapped the unwanted poultice on his swollen wounds, then picked at his dinner. He opened and closed the fingers the beekeeper had touched, fighting the notion that he'd almost felt her fear. His gift was for objects, not people. The last thing he needed in his life was *people* invading his head. He dismissed the thought as part of the pain he'd suffered.

He wasn't normally an early to bed, early to rise sort of person, but what the hell was there to do in the country once the sun set?

He could study the stars through the old-fashioned telescope in the observatory, but he had little interest in places he couldn't reach. He stored his other live artifacts up there though. He'd introduce the new one to them, see what happened. Did spirits talk to each other? They'd never done so to his knowledge.

He tried to recall the beekeeper's face, but his eyes had been watering and nearly swollen shut and the memory was a blur. He was pretty certain she had been talking to the bees, though. And judging by the swarm that had followed her, they were listening.

Very little a Malcolm did could surprise him. More often, the know-it-alls irritated him. He made a mental note not to marry a Malcolm.

His question to Rainford about what to look for in a wife now haunted him. *Wealthy* and *not a Malcolm* didn't encompass it all, but it certainly eliminated everyone here.

The topmost floor of the tower had been renovated with real windows for his great-great-grandfather, who had studied astronomy over a century ago. It was almost a museum of Ives' hobbies. Gerard had boxed up a fair number of them to clear a table for his own collection.

He set the Roman medallion next to a crude replica of a horse carved from limestone. He'd kept the horse because it contained the memories of its previous owner riding free and bareback across green hills and through thick forests. There hadn't been forests like that in England in centuries.

He picked up the small silver toothpick, but the old Georgian philosopher who'd once used it had nothing to say tonight. He set it on the other side of the medallion.

"Talk to each other," he said dryly. "Let me know if I deserve to find treasure. Otherwise I may marry and give you over to the housekeepers, who will box you up and store you in the dungeon."

Was that a ghostly *hmpf* he heard? He sat down to make notes in his journal, but his thoughts kept returning to the beekeeper, especially the part where she ran her hands over him. She had a lady's tender skin, not a farm worker's, but then, she was a Malcolm. They generally came from aristocratic families.

The bell he'd installed at the back exit rang. It allowed the few men on the estate to reach him without going through a protective cordon of females.

After finishing the meat pie the kitchen had sent up with the tea, Gerard clambered down the stairs to his ground floor office. If he was inclined to stay here for any length of time, he would hire a manservant to handle this sort of thing.

Having no servants in the tower encouraged him to move on before winter.

Avery waited outside. An educated man of good family, Avery had the thick shoulders and torso of a bull. The middle-aged estate agent dressed better than Gerard in rich tweeds and tailored doeskin. But then, the old bachelor lived on the estate and didn't have anyone or anything eating up his pay.

Gerard gestured at the usual chair in his office and took his oak one behind the desk. "That was prompt. I didn't mean to convey urgency."

The steward propped his wool cap on his knee. "The ladies work themselves into a lather elsewise."

Gerard acknowledged the truth of that. "Am I wrong in thinking they object to your dog?"

"We have badgers digging up the orchard, a fox after the henhouse, and rabbits gnawing their way through the early crops. The dog's good at routing them. Makes a good guard dog as well. Don't know why they've taken a dislike to the creature."

"I gather the animal takes his reward in honey. The beekeeper right-fully objects. The animal needs to be trained to stay away from the skeps." Feeling the ache in his jaw and wrist, Gerard thought it a pity the beast didn't learn from the pain of bee stings.

"Your beekeeper is an over-reaching harridan," Avery said with unusual anger. "She had the orchard dug up for flower beds while I was away at market. And now she's demanding the carpenter build some new-fangled hives to coddle the insects, instead of burning them out the way it's always been done."

Appeasing the tension between his excellent, but traditionalist agent, and the castle's more open-minded tenants had always been a problem.

"You should know by now that the ladies have my father's full support. They do not take on projects at a whim. I'm certain the beekeeper met with a committee of the ladies to discuss what she can do to aid the estate."

Although Gerard was well aware that, to his tenants, providing bouquets for the hall would qualify as reason to dig up unused ground and plant flowers. But honey was a valuable crop and so they weren't being unreasonable.

"I tell you, the beekeeper is a trouble maker. You'll regret encour-aging her. I can't keep the hound out of the orchard without a fence." Avery scowled. Caught by surprise at Gerard's unexpected arrival, he apparently hadn't had time to visit a barber. His shaggy brown hair hung down his neck and his ferocious mustache bristled.

"A fence around the hives wouldn't hurt," Gerard agreed without rancor, although he mentally winced at the additional cost. "The lady is out there alone and unprotected. If she's contributing to the estate's welfare, then we should provide what she needs. Keep the dog leashed until then. I don't want to have to right more skeps while I'm here."

"Aye, will do," Avery said grumpily. "You want me back in the morning to go over the books?"

"I realize I'm too early for the harvest to be in. Give me time to study where we are. The day after tomorrow, perhaps?" He placated the man, knowing he was good at what he did.

Rising, he escorted Avery to the door. As the agent strode off, Gerard noticed one of the women tending a rose bed in the evening gloom. Her gray gown almost disappeared in the shadows. He thought it might be the beekeeper, but she glanced up and vanished into deeper darkness.

Hell, maybe she was a ghost. Weirder things had happened.

Bored, he finally headed for the main house to greet the occupants of his *castle*.

Finally, a spirit voice whispered. And he wasn't even carrying the medallion. That sent a shiver down his spine.

IONA SET THE BOUQUET OF LATE ROSES IN A PORCELAIN VASE ON THE entrance table, where the fragrance of sun and happiness would permeate the old hall.

Winifred, the healer who mothered them all, bustled down the stairs. "To the hall," she cried merrily. "He's headed this way."

"I am not needed, am I? I should draw up diagrams for the Langstroth boxes so the carpenter knows what to do." Iona knew the flaw in that argument, but she hoped there were enough people vying for the earl's interest that she wouldn't be missed.

"You cannot expect any of us to explain why you need new hives," Winifred said in exasperation, finding the flaw immediately. "Now come along or we'll spend the evening listening to Grace prose on about the lost art of spinning."

"Her woolens really are works of art," Iona protested, falling in beside the castle's queen bee. The older woman was much the same height as she but considerably heavier. If Iona sat behind her, she might blend into her shadow. . .

Except Winifred took the chair in front of the fireplace, near the gas sconces so she was illuminated from all sides. Iona searched for a distant corner where the light didn't reach. She wasn't much of one for needle-work, but she could jot the day's notes while the others talked. More light would be nice, but her need for invisibility reigned over neat hand-writing.

"The spirts are restless," Simone announced in puzzlement, sweeping in behind them in a swish of summery fabrics and transparent shawls more suited to a hot July day. "Has something stirred them?"

After the isolation of Craigmore, Iona appreciated the various person-alities populating Wystan. It wasn't the same as her sister's company, of course, but it kept her from being too lonely. They didn't require that she do anything except listen, which she'd learned to do in long summers at her mother's knee.

Even after all these years, she missed her mother fiercely.

Some of the older women were already gathered in their favorite seats. Iona didn't usually try to disappear with this group, but if the earl meant to grace them with his presence—

She carried a small chair to a corner near the dark windows, behind a hanging basket of ferns.

The huge hall they used as a drawing room was large enough to hold a village, so the ladies didn't precisely fill it with numbers so much as *presence*. Their lively chatter dispelled the gloom. Iona could sense their joy and anticipation and smiled at their eagerness. Sometimes, rural soli-tude could be tedious. Iona was well accustomed to it.

"Where is Lady Alice?" Winifred called sharply.

"She was not feeling well and has gone to bed," one of the younger women replied.

After the debacle in the duke's library, Iona could see that Lady Alice might find seeing the earl a trifle awkward. Still, she was glad the desperate lady had taken up the offer of Wystan's shelter. The Malcolm women had no difficulty embracing Alice and her scandalous condition. They were already preparing a nursery for an event almost seven months in the future.

An almost visible sigh whispered around the room as his lordship entered.

In a sea of feminine perfumes and rustling skirts, Lord Ives forged an imposing masculine presence. He wasn't a bulky man like his agent, but elegantly muscled, filling out the shoulders of his coat to perfection. He was still wearing old tweed and leather, but his collar was stark white against his sun-browned features, and his cravat was correct in all ways.

Iona studied him for the infamous Ives traits, but his dark eyes appeared more midnight blue than black. His nose was sharp and long but fitted well with stark cheekbones and square jaw. His hair was certainly Ives black with a hint of curl. He wore it off his collar in back, but a swathe fell across his high forehead. Trimmed sideburns softened the harshness of his jaw.

He was formidably masculine. Iona ducked her head when his gaze swept the room.

"AUNT WINIFRED." GERARD ACKNOWLEDGED HIS AUNT ON HER THRONE. "You are looking delightful, as always."

He greeted distant cousins and was introduced to newcomers who made their presence known in the dimly-lit chamber. None of the people introduced appeared to be the beekeeper.

"The wool this spring was very fine."

He thought the speaker, Grace, might be related to the wife of one of his uncles. The Ives side of his family had a distressing habit of marrying into the multitudinous Malcolms, probably due to proximity.

To make reparations for his earlier ill behavior, he complimented her on the beauty of the woven blanket in his chamber. He praised the cheese made by another of the ladies and inquired about the herb garden tended by a different aunt. The women didn't hesitate to mention improvements that should be made or ideas for new projects of interest.

They were good women, he knew. They fed and clothed the poor with their efforts and employed a village with their projects. They did everything his wife might be expected to do—except share his bed, of course. He didn't dare dip his wick in Wystan or the preacher would be at the door the next day.

He had just discovered the slight feminine shadow in a distant corner of the hall when an unearthly moan echoed from above.

One of his widowed cousins murmured "Oh, dear," and turned to Winifred. "We had best see to Lady Alice."

Lady Alice? Gerard suffered a moment of pure panic at the thought of the deceitful widow talking to his female relations. Alice was *here*? In his home? *Why?*

And what the hell was that keening—a banshee?

Winifred was already on her feet and out the door. The herbalist cousin followed, along with the widow who apparently translated spectral howls.

"Have a seat, Ives," another aunt suggested tartly. "You needn't hover. Tell us what you've been frivoling your time on."

"I'd rather know what the commotion is about." He should have put the medallion back in his pocket. He'd like a spirit's opinion of his haunted household.

The wails had ceased as soon as the haunt had their attention.

"We call the banshee Ceridwen. We haven't heard her in ages. The last time was when one of the kitchen maids miscarried. There's nothing you can do. Have a seat."

If he translated woman-speak—Lady Alice was *miscarrying*? That explained a great deal. He yanked at his collar to loosen it. If Lady Alice had been angling for a husband to hide her disgrace, he owed the mysterious interfering servant in Rainford's library more than he realized.

He needed to get the hell out of here. He felt as out of place as a stallion in a cow herd.

"I don't believe you've met Nan yet?" Grace asked, interrupting his panic.

Formal names were meaningless where so many were related in one manner or another and all called themselves Malcolm, regardless of married names. Gerard was fine with that. It prevented him from sorting one female from another and their rank in the pecking order.

But if the beekeeper was one of his many maternal or in-law cousins, he wasn't aware of it. He waited expectantly for Nan to step into existence.

Instead, a quiet voice spoke from the far corner by the windows. "We've met, Grace, thank you."

Gerard bowed in that general direction. "I've ordered Avery to build a fence around your skeps. He's to keep his beast tied up until then."

He waited for her to step into the light, curtsy in appreciation, anything that any normal young lady would do. She didn't.

"A fence large enough to keep out that monster will need to wait until we build the new hives." Despite the soft tones, her voice contained the confidence he was starting to associate with her. "The Langstroth hives will be larger and require more space than the current hives occupy. I wonder if a flowering hedge with a gate might not be better."

He hated talking with an anonymous shadow. He might as well be addressing the banshee. "Do none of our journals make recommendations?"

He referred to the library that had expanded to a gallery built on the upper level of this hall. If he looked up, he wouldn't see enormous paintings of his ancestors but row upon row of book-filled shelves and oak railing. The narrow staircase to access the gallery had to be difficult for women in billowing crinolines and trailing skirts, but as he recalled, the elderly librarian was small and dressed like a servant.

"I prefer to consult my queen on a matter of this importance," the hidden Iona replied in all seriousness.

Her queen? Vicki wasn't likely to know a thing about bees—

"Do you speak her language?" one of the younger women asked with interest.

The *queen of bees*, of course. Gerard rubbed at the welt on his jaw. He'd do well to stay on the right side of a female who commanded bees. She could quite possibly kill him.

FOUR

THE NEXT MORNING, IONA SETTLED IN THE MASCULINE STUDY TO ATTEMPT TO sketch from memory the box she needed. She wished she had Langstroth's book and not just her notes. She was so frustrated with her efforts by the time Mrs. Merriweather interrupted that she greeted the slender lady in relief.

"Letters from Calder Castle! Lydia forwarded a missive from your sister," the librarian said cheerfully, waving a sealed envelope.

Shock rippled through her, but Iona maintained her pretense by rubbing at a wrinkle of puzzlement on her brow. "My sister?"

"Don't be foolish," the librarian admonished. "Lydia worked it out as soon as she met you. We are librarians, after all. We have records of every Malcolm ever born."

Iona had been dismayed to learn that the various librarians visited each other. Before she'd come here, she'd heard that the Calder Castle librarian was a recluse. She had thought Isobel would be safe there. But the recluse had died and sociable Lydia had taken over.

Worse, the new Calder librarian was from Northumberland. Lydia had visited her family, then stopped at Wystan to see if she might have her child in the Malcolm stronghold most beneficial to births. That was when she had met Iona and put two and two together.

Iona should have stayed out of sight, but the desire to read the Langstroth book had been too strong. She had made a serious error in judgment in asking about the book.

"Lydia plays games," Iona asserted, hoping to make Mrs. Merriweather doubt her conclusion.

"Oh, I don't think so, but librarians are sworn to keep your secrets, so you needn't worry about us—even if we do worry about you. We're here to help."

That was a generous offer, too generous. Iona didn't intend to endanger anyone else in her private matters.

Without confirming the librarian's suspicion, she accepted the letter with a frisson of fear. Isobel would never have taken a chance on revealing their connection unless it was urgent. But she wouldn't tear open the seal while the librarian watched.

"Thank you, Mrs. Merriweather. I'm sure Lydia told her steward about my hives, and that's all this is about. Does the earl ever order books for the library? I know you keep the Malcolm journals, but surely he must require a reference book occasionally?" She didn't even know if it was possible to buy an almost twenty-year-old book. She'd only set foot in a bookstore once, when she'd been sixteen and had no coin.

"Oh, his lordship never stays long enough to read. He lives in London most of the year and has access to all sorts of libraries elsewhere. The journals by other beekeepers aren't sufficient?" she asked in concern, diverted from the letter.

"They tell me a great deal on how to use my gift and what they learned about bees, thank you, but they lack a scientific approach to hive building. I understand Langstroth's concept, but I do not have the ability to diagram it."

"Oh, ask Lord Ives, then. He's quite skilled at sketching all sorts of things. I'll show you." Apparently forgetting the letter, the librarian scurried off to find examples of his lordship's work.

Iona couldn't very well shut and lock the study door so she could read her letter. Afraid of interruption, she waited impatiently. When Mrs. Merriweather didn't return, she gathered her materials and fled upstairs.

The castle was a warren of chambers, old and new, spacious and small, elegant and neglected. She'd chosen one of the small, neglected ones—near the back stairs, with a window overlooking a sturdy trellis.

She liked having multiple escape exits. She refused to be found and caught.

Once safely behind a locked door, Iona pried open the seal on her letter with shaky hands. Just the act of risking this communication meant Isobel must be frightened. That meant her twin's normally cautious nature would escalate to the ridiculous—like concealing code under the envelope flap.

Iona read the obvious script first—Isobel wrote as steward of Calder Castle, inquiring into the best means of protecting their hives over winter. Had Mrs. Merriweather opened the missive, she'd have seen nothing extraordinary.

Lighting a candle, Iona ran the paper over the heat. Yes, there it was, their childhood code. She wrote out the numbers that appeared, then finding the letter "L" on the inside flap, worked out the code with "L" as the number one. It was a basic code, but it had fooled their stepfather and his minions for years.

The coded message was brief and horrifying: ARTHUR IN E'BGH.

Dread clutched at her throat. The American was only a few hours away from Isobel.

They'd been so *careful* in covering their trail. They'd traveled separately from Craigmore, wearing a variety of disguises—being twins made traveling together too dangerous. Isobel had even dyed her honey-blond hair black. They had only the funds they'd skimmed from the household budget and sale of their mother's pearls. They'd each found rooms in different cities. Once hidden, they'd written to the School of Malcolms and to Mrs. Merriweather under their Malcolm names, looking for positions.

It had taken well over a month to establish their new identities and safe havens. It had been almost six months since their escape. Surely their trail was cold.

But Arthur Winter was a wealthy man accustomed to having his way. With the encouragement of her stepfather, Mr. Winter would think himself a hero in scouring the kingdom in his pursuit of the twins and a title. It wasn't the self-absorbed American who frightened her. It was her desperately bankrupt stepfather.

Iona shuddered and burned the letter.

What did they do now?

"Oh, there you are, my lord! I thought we had some of your sketches tucked away in the specimen cabinet, but I can't find them. I'd like to show them to Nan." Mrs. Merriweather bustled across the courtyard.

Damn, he should have known he couldn't escape easily. Quelling his impatience, Gerard waited outside the stable for the elderly librarian to approach. "What sketches?"

"The ones you drew when you were younger, the ones of Roman soldiers and knights and fortresses, remember? They were quite informative." The little librarian practically unfurled like a blossom under his regard.

Gerard didn't want her blossoming or remembering his childish attempts to draw what he'd seen in his head. He simply wanted to examine his fields and hope the medallion in his pocket told him where to find a treasure that might postpone closing the castle.

"I thought those were tossed long ago. I can't imagine anyone keeping them," he said dismissively. "They were just idle fribbles. Why would you want them?"

"I wanted to show Nan that you're quite capable of drawing the diagrams she needs for the hives. It seems we lack the book that might show the carpenter how to build them, and she's drawing it herself." The Librarian smiled expectantly.

His first reaction was *hell, no.* And then he remembered the enigmatic beekeeper avoiding him at every turn, and his curiosity kicked in. The curse of the Ives, curiosity.

"I'll see what she needs," he promised the lady. He didn't think the librarian was any direct relation, just the Malcolm who understood journals. Apparently, it was a calling.

What would happen to the library if he closed the castle and sent all these women—where?

"It's hard to find her," she warned. "She might still be in the study, if you hurry."

Gerard found this admonition a trifle odd. Generally, the women stalked *him*. If the beekeeper wanted his help, she had to wait in line.

It almost sounded as if Mrs. Merriweather was saying he had to wait on his beekeeper.

Amused that the slip of a female had gained so much authority since he'd visited last year—he knew she hadn't been here the last time he was —he postponed his ride. He wasn't much inclined to learn about his tenants, but this one teased his memory.

She wasn't in the study. No one was in the drafty great hall on a brisk day like this. He checked the small withdrawing room where Grace was always spinning. None of the ladies there had seen Nan.

Nan. Surely no Malcolm had ever named her daughter so tersely. He couldn't even recall an Ann or Nancy anywhere on the family tree. Adwin or Aranwen or some other Celtic saint would be more likely, although *Anne* also qualified, he supposed. His family just didn't do simple.

He stomped up the stairs to see if he could see anyone in the bedroom corridors, but after the unfortunate incident with Lady Alice in Rainford's library, the proximity to women and beds made him anxious. He preferred choosing his own wife, not having one forced on him.

Which reminded him that Lady Alice was here somewhere. He'd had his breakfast delivered to his rooms and so hadn't heard any gossip about how she was doing. He supposed he should inquire, if only to know whether he ought to be riding out immediately. But that could wait.

He loped down the back corridor, to the stairs leading down to the garden. He suspected the elusive beekeeper would use these instead of the main staircase, but no shadows moved. Oh well, that gave him time to examine the fields.

He was about to head down when one of the doors opened in front of him—and the beekeeper emerged, just donning an old-fashioned bonnet.

He wasn't even certain why he knew it was her. He'd only briefly seen her face through swollen eyes. He just *knew*. . . Perhaps it was her air of quiet authority, the way she stood straight and tall, although the top of her head barely reached his chin.

At sight of him, she ducked beneath the wide brim, but in that brief moment when he'd seen her face, she looked startled and. . . frightened?

"You needed me to sketch a hive?" he asked, recovering his equilibrium faster than she recovered hers.

He'd finally caught a glimpse of her light brown hair. It had golden highlights—rather like a bee. And for some unwholesome reason, she'd cut it. Instead of forming an enormous pouf, her hair formed short waves and curls around a face small enough to be called pixieish.

"Ummm, yes," she said uncertainly, glancing back to her room as if prepared to retreat. Then apparently strengthening her courage, she nodded briskly. "Yes, if I may fetch my notes?" She darted into the room before he could agree.

She left him breathless—rather like a bee sting.

She also left him pondering her vague familiarity, but she was back before he could take his thoughts too far.

"I am not good at math and measurements," she was saying, holding a sheaf of papers and hurrying down the corridor, apparently expecting him to follow like an obedient servant. "Langstroth observed that bees won't build in a space tighter than one centimeter. How do I convey that? The frames must be exactly one centimeter apart and away from the walls so they won't stick to each other."

Gerard caught up with her and removed the papers from her hands. "You convey that with numbers," he said dryly. "Carpenters can read. Let us go to the music room. There are usually drawing utensils there."

"In the music room?" she asked, her voice lilting as melodically as any instrument.

"It should probably be called the hobby room. It has accumulated everything from oil paints to lutes over the years. I believe balls of string appeared at one time, and a collection of framed moths." He took the steps down two at a time, then realized he was almost running away and slowed down.

She hadn't removed her hat and wasn't wearing the acres of skirts and petticoats more fashionable women wore. In her plain gray gown, she easily kept up with his longer strides, while still looking elegant.

How the hell did she manage that? If his sisters had worn that rag, they'd look like frumpy dowds.

"Oh, you must mean the sewing room. It's currently filled with yarns and threads and fabrics, but I do remember a harp and a spinet. There are drawing materials? I fear I've been wasting your stationery." At the bottom of the wide front stairs, she took a right turn and led the way.

Gerard almost grinned his amusement. Avery was right. This one was an imperious little witch, and she seemed completely unconscious of being so.

Which roused his curiosity. He knew women. His marchioness mother was a Malcolm. So were any number of his aunts and cousins and of course, his sisters. Women abounded in his life. Very few Malcolms adopted the imperiousness of a queen, including his mother.

In his experience, women got their way by being pleasant and making suggestions or dimpling up and flapping eyelashes. They did not take command and charge ahead. Men did that.

Gerard allowed the beekeeper to precede him into the music room. As always, it had one or two women engaged in gossip and playing at needles—he wasn't certain they ever finished anything. They stared at his entrance. Gerard ignored them and aimed for a cabinet where he'd last seen drawing papers and pens.

His inclination was to take the supplies to the study and shut the door, but he'd learned his lesson there. No more intimate meetings with marriageable females. He needed to return to London where he could find women more interested in his coin and bed than his meaningless title. Every woman in his set wanted to be a countess, it seemed.

He laid the sketchpad down and gestured for Nan to take a seat. She studied the layout warily, then removed her bonnet, leaving her pixie features looking young and vulnerable. She took a seat on the opposite side of the table from him. Fair enough.

"Now tell me what you have in mind." He sprawled his long legs under the narrow table, brushing her skirts, as he took a seat. He sorted through the various pens, inks, and pencils in the box. Most of them had probably dried up.

She showed him a rough sketch of a rectangle with what looked like thin drawers. "I want to be able to pull the frames from the hive without them sticking to each other. And then there needs to be a special cover between the bottom box and the frames on top to keep the queen from laying her eggs in the upper part of the hive. That way I will only be harvesting the excess honey. I won't have to burn out the colony or leave them hungry over winter."

Using her sketch as a guide, he applied rulers to draft a rudimentary box with several layers of frames. Her notes didn't quite explain the cover needed to prevent the larger queen from moving into the upper frames. He frowned as he tried to work out how to draw what he'd never seen.

"You need the book," he said in frustration.

"I know," she agreed sadly. "If I'd had time, I could have traced all the sketches and taken better notes. But I didn't have the luxury."

"Then why not just order the book? Give me the author and title, and I'll write the bookshop. It might take a while to reach here. How soon do you need these?" Gerard glanced up and caught a look of such blatant longing on her face, that it almost knocked him backward.

"I've wanted that book since childhood." She sounded much dreamier than the automaton who had been dictating measurements to him. "It's that easy? The book must be twenty years old."

"If it hasn't been reprinted, the shop will look in the secondhand stores or buy it from a lending library or the publisher's inventory. There's bound to be more than one in the kingdom," he said, concealing his amusement that she blossomed at a book and not him. "But if you're in a hurry. . ."

She pensively nibbled on a finger. "I've not had enough experience in this climate to know when the bees will settle in for the winter. I'd really wanted the hives done by now. But I suppose we could start in the spring. It's just. . . we'd have to start building a fence or hedge now to protect the hives we have."

"Or Avery will have to train his beast better," Gerard agreed.

"Nettles," she said in dry amusement. "I should start a nettle hedge."

And that was the moment he recognized her. . . *the tart-tongued servant who had saved his life in Rainford's library.*

FIVE

"You!" THE EARL EXCLAIMED OUT OF THE CLEAR BLUE SKY.

Startled and frightened, Iona pushed her chair away from the table. *Did he recognize her? How?* She'd been so absorbed in the drawing appearing beneath his talented fingers that she hadn't paid attention. . . always a danger. She wasn't prepared to flee, but her thoughts were already doing mental leaps and bounds.

"*You're* the one who brought Lady Alice here," he grumbled in a slightly lower voice. "Why the hell did you do that?"

Iona tried to slow her panicked response to read his scent, but beneath his usual façade of indifference, he was so many layers of confusion that she couldn't sort him out fast enough. He only recognized her from that night? If she didn't have to run again. . . She could breathe a little easier.

"She needed help?" A simple response seemed to be her only option.

"Not *my* help." He shoved back his chair.

The other ladies were discreetly staring at them over their handiwork.

Unaccustomed to dealing with more than bees and servants, Iona floundered. She couldn't order an earl to sit down and shut up. She wasn't even entirely certain why he was. . . what? Angry at *her*? Definitely upset but not exactly angry, she decided.

And then she recognized the problem. He was angry because she'd brought Lady Alice here, to his home. He must have learned about her delicate condition. Since she'd seen him in a compromising position with the lady. . .

She stood up so the earl wasn't glaring down at her so much. "I did not know who you were at the time," she reminded him. "We weren't introduced. I had no idea I was bringing her to your home. I was bringing her to *Winifred*. She's a midwife."

He ran his hand through his hair and growled under his breath. *That* was frustration, she could tell. He was big, but she was pretty certain he wouldn't strike her. She wasn't afraid of men any longer. Men toppled like rose canes when she cut them off in the right places.

"Fine. I'll stay in my tower, out of the way. I'll order that book for you." The Earl of Ives and Wystan strode off, tall, lean, and the most handsome man she'd ever met.

Probably also the most confusing—not that she knew many men for comparison.

Iona sighed. It would be lovely to be normal and attend balls and learn to attract the attention of handsome men. She'd be a doddering old spinster before her stepfather died, though.

She could marry, she supposed. She had just never given it much thought after the disaster her mother had made of the wedded state. And then her own circumstances had made hiding more essential than looking for a husband.

"The earl is temperamental," Simone said reassuringly, looking up from her crochet. "Stifling one's gifts leads to frustration."

Iona put away the drawing materials and nodded as if she understood. If the earl had a gift, it was for upsetting women, it seemed.

"How is Lady Alice this morning?" she asked. Had the earl thought she'd brought the lady here because she believed the child was *his*? Or maybe it was. Who knew?

"I don't believe she mourns the child," Simone said curtly. "We'll keep her away from the earl."

Iona almost smiled at that. It was amazing how the women here understood each other so well. "I think he'll appreciate that."

Lady Alice was apparently a conniving woman of loose morals, but women lacked the opportunities available to men. She'd not judge.

But now that husbands and marriage had occurred to her, Iona couldn't stop thinking about them. She returned upstairs for her beekeeping habit, gathered her equipment from the shed, and set out for the orchard.

Instead of worrying about honey and hedges, however, she realized that if she married, Arthur would leave her alone. He might go after Isobel. . . But a powerful husband could go to court and prove Iona was the eldest. He'd want her to petition the court for her grandfather's title, but. . .

She couldn't go past that thought. Her mother had refused to allow her second husband to use her title and look what had become of that.

She should have been a queen bee, Iona thought wryly as she watched a few worker bees return to the hive with their late summer harvest. Mate once a year, lay a thousand eggs, and let the male die and blow away at the end of the season.

Except human children took a little longer to raise than a season— which was where her mother had succumbed to weakness and married again.

Iona hummed as she worked, soothing the bees and letting them settle down for their long winter's rest. She had only been able to bring one queen with her when she'd fled, but that one would pass on her wisdom to her offspring. They would recognize Iona.

"Next year, you'll have newer, nicer homes," she assured the queen as she worked. "It's warmer here, isn't it? Just think of all the honey the apple blossoms will produce. It will pay for our new homes in no time."

The queen hummed in appreciation. Bee wisdom was limited.

"I may trade some of your honey for hedge roots so you'll have your own fortress. Blackthorn, maybe, they'll provide lovely flowers in spring and we can make gin from the fruit. I think we'll be happy here." She added the last part for herself.

It was hard to be completely happy when others suffered, but at least now that she was free, she could plan. While she'd been trapped, she had only been able to suffer along with everyone else.

She wished she had someone more knowledgeable to plan with. Girls' boarding schools did not teach law.

WITH HIS TREASURE-PROMISING ARTIFACT IN HIS POCKET, GERARD RODE THE well-worn paths of his estate. The cultivated fields were easily studied. He'd already been told it had been a poor year for apples but a good year for sheep.

The medallion didn't acknowledge field or orchard.

Wystan's boundaries did not reach the Roman wall in the south. That seemed a more likely place to find soldiers' loot then a rocky fell.

"I need a little more direction than just *Wystan*," Gerard complained as he rode to the edge of the grain field and gazed glumly upon the rolling hills where the sheep fed.

Treasure is not always buried, the spirit in his head finally deigned to reply—with his usual world-weary cynicism.

"So you don't know where it is!" Disgusted, mostly at himself, he turned his mount toward home. The sun was setting, and he was half starved. "I bet you were simply a common foot soldier guarding the wall and thought this old keep looked wealthy and welcoming."

You would lose.

Gerard imagined he heard amusement in the spirit's voice. Sometimes, he thought he imagined it all. He'd like proof that his gift was useful and not insane.

Not insane, the spirit voice said wearily. *Stulti et caeca.*

"*Blind and stupid*, thanks for that." Gerard had plenty of proof that he wasn't stupid. He'd studied law to better understand the exalted position he'd one day inherit. He'd spent his youthful summers learning agriculture from his father's estate agents. He could read contracts and calculate profits better than most solicitors—which made him his father's unpaid errand boy.

Stupid, the voice muttered.

"I can shove you in a box," Gerard muttered back.

A dog's barking and a woman's shout had him spurring his mount into a gallop, heading downhill at a breakneck pace. The action felt good. The reason for it—was probably stupid. Dogs barked. Women yelled.

But he couldn't erase the image of the slender beekeeper weeping over a fallen hive. Women should be *safe* at Wystan.

Galloping into the courtyard, Gerard recognized the screams as fury. The damned beast was leaping on the beekeeper, attempting to reach the pails she held above her head. The dog probably weighed more than she did.

Women poured from the house, armed with their weapons of choice —knitting needles, scissors, rolling pins—none of which would hold off a determined animal. Sliding his stick from his saddle pack, Gerard spurred his horse into the fray.

The woman with the pails sensibly froze as he galloped close, swinging the stick at the animal's haunches. The dog yelped and stood down long enough for Gerard to place his horse between the dog and the beekeeper.

Sending him an uninterpretable look, she scurried off to safety with her pails of honey. Her short gray skirt swayed, revealing trousers and boots and not ankles.

Gerard dismounted and regarded the stupid beast deprived of his treat. He almost sympathized. The beekeeper was a tempting morsel. "C'mon, hound, you're mine now."

He grabbed its collar and dragged the reluctant animal toward the stable. More mastiff than hound, Gerard concluded, wrestling with the animal. A stable lad ran out to take the reins of his gelding so he could employ both hands.

"Pen this beast up until I find a chain," he told the next lad emerging from the stable. "He lacks proper training."

Gerard had trained horses. He could probably train the dog. He would just have to stay longer than he'd anticipated.

"Miss Mike is good with animals," the stable boy suggested.

Of course she was. An orphaned cousin, Mary Michaela hadn't taken well to society—probably because she preferred women to men. She'd brought her maid to Wystan a decade ago and the two had settled in happily. Where would they go if he closed the castle?

"Have her train this creature to behave," Gerard ordered, as if the lad wouldn't have done so on his own. He wasn't so stupid as to know when he wasn't needed.

Blind, his spirit voice added.

Once in his rooms, Gerard threw the medallion on his desk. He'd add it to the other useless artifacts upstairs later. He stripped off his confining coat, and in waistcoat and leather riding breeches, sat down at his desk.

He'd finish going over the books in the morning, consult with Avery in the afternoon, and be gone the next day. Maybe he could sell his artifacts to a collector and stretch his income another year. He wasn't *stupidly* searching for imaginary treasure any longer.

The bell rang before he could even open a book. "Damn it all to perdition." Usually, his tenants left him alone unless it was important. He took the stairs down again.

A footman waited. "We have guests, my lord. The ladies request your presence at dinner."

"Do they now? I don't suppose they told you who the guests are?"

The footman held out a card. *Rainford.*

"Did he bring a retinue with him?" Gerard asked in resignation. A duke's heir never traveled alone.

"Several gentlemen and their servants, my lord. They're stabling the horses now." The footman stood at attention like a good soldier.

"And the ladies are in more of a lather than the horses, I imagine. Very well. I'll dress and be there shortly."

The footman relaxed in relief and ran off to deliver his happy news.

What the hell was Rainford doing here? Wasn't he supposed to be wooing a bride? It wasn't as if this desolate outpost was on the path to anywhere, so the marquess had to be here for a reason.

He was just drawing his bath when the bell rang again. Grateful he hadn't stripped to his drawers, Gerard climbed back to his small foyer.

A gnarled gnome of a man stood on the step. "The ladies said you might need a valet, my lord. The marquess has given me a reference." He held out Rainford's familiar stationery.

Gerard wanted to disabuse the ladies of that idiotic notion, but instinct said to read the reference first.

Lowell is a former batman, a crack shot, and saved the life of a friend. Hire him.

Gerard snorted at the peremptory command. Rain didn't believe in long explanations. He'd hear the story later.

"Looks like you're hired, Lowell. I don't have much in the way of fine attire here, but I'm sure you'll make yourself useful."

Lowell relaxed his stiff stance. "Thank you, my lord. Shall I draw your bath and lay out your evening attire?"

"Aye, and you can tell me why the marquess has shown up at my door unannounced." Gerard led him downstairs to show him the bath.

"There's a tumult about missing heiresses and a reward but I've not heard more." Lowell admired the bath and plumbing. "Heated water, amazing."

"Thought Northumberland would be the wilderness, did you? I can use a shave and trim, if you've a talent for that." Gerard generally wasn't interested in gossip, but his mind chased around the news of a reward.

If a scoundrel had run off with an heiress, he could track him through Northumberland easily. He knew the land, knew all the innkeepers, as well as the railway men.

He also knew the only likely place for a runaway heiress anywhere about was Wystan.

SIX

"No, I have no interest in meeting a marquess," Iona assured Winifred when asked to join the company. She'd avoided meeting Rainford in his own home. Surely she could avoid it here. "I'd much rather put up the honey so the kitchen can concentrate on dinner."

"Don't be foolish, child. A lady in the kitchen will just fret them. If you don't have a proper gown, I'm sure we can find one. We have wardrobes of—"

"Is it a requirement that I attend?" Iona held her voice steady and met Winifred's gaze with the assurance she'd had to learn after her mother's death.

The older woman refused to back down and lectured instead. "No, of course not, but sometimes, knowledge of the outside world is more important than hiding from it. I think Lady Alice brought enough crinoline for an entire household. I'll ask her maid if there's one you can borrow." She swept off.

Iona didn't *want* knowledge of the outside world if it meant exposing herself to it.

But the ladies asked very little of her. She supposed it wouldn't hurt to sit at a large table with a crowd of people. She'd simply perform her invisible act. Over the years, she had become very adept at not being seen.

She'd only packed one semi-decent dinner gown, made over from her one season in London. It wasn't as if her stepfather entertained or that they'd had coins to buy better. She had vaguely hoped she might be able to buy a few stiff petticoats in a secondhand shop, but she hadn't really needed a crinoline here. Few of the ladies were wealthy enough, or cared enough, to be fashionable.

But they did know how to put on a show, Iona learned when she joined the party gathering in the great hall.

She was wearing a modest gold-and-brown merino over the half-crinoline borrowed from Lady Alice. The gown was old-fashioned, without a bodice apron or train or even a modified bustle, but the colors suited her. She drew her best shawl over her nearly bare shoulders and stood in the shadows, admiring the colorful array of company. Her gold-threaded shawl and flowered coronet disguising her false chignon paled in comparison.

Even Iona knew most of the gowns sweeping about the hall were terribly out of date, but the rainbow of silky fabrics, swathes of lace, feathered hair ornaments, and puffs of curls adorned in diadems appeared the height of splendor to her rural eyes.

"Do we have any notion why Rainford is here?" Lady Alice asked, joining her in the dark corner.

Iona surreptitiously studied the lady. She looked wan but had rouged her cheeks and lips to give the appearance of health, despite the miscarriage.

"I thought he was simply visiting. Isn't that done?" Iona found the tall, silver-blond, smartly tailored marquess in the hall's center, surrounded by ladies.

"No one visits Northumberland if it can be avoided," the lady said sourly. "I think I'll find someone willing to offer me a ride anywhere else but here. Surely they must have a baggage cart."

She drifted away in a cloud of French perfume, anxiety, and dissatisfaction. Iona felt rather sorry for her. Black was not the lady's best color, and she did not seem to be mourning the loss of a child.

Iona entertained herself watching her new friends practice long-abandoned flirting skills with the marquess and cadre of young gentlemen. Like the earl, Rainford had assumed a courtesy title from his father and had little actual power beyond that of his wealth and connections. But society gravitated toward titles, wealth, and beauty. With his icy blond good-looks, the marquess possessed all three.

With twice as many women as men attending, there could be no formal pairing off into the dining room. When dinner was called, all precedence was abandoned under Malcolm insistence on equality. Iona drifted into the dining hall alone.

Winifred had obviously set the name cards, Iona decided, finding her name at the earl's right hand at the head of the table. She cursed herself for not slipping in here earlier and rearranging the cards. She'd become accustomed to taking a seat in the middle and had simply assumed her anonymity would be honored. She glanced longingly at the epergne she preferred to hide behind.

"I have never understood how ladies arrange to have so much hair, but yours looks lovely tonight, Miss Malcolm." Using formal address, the earl skeptically eyed her fake coiffure. He'd seen her without bonnet or chignon.

"When we cut our hair, we stuff it in netting," Simone explained matter-of-factly from his left side. "I suppose it's less expensive than buying hats and lace and tiaras."

Iona's lips twitched. She wouldn't have to say a word all evening with Simone sitting across from her. Winifred was an evil planner.

As if summoned from Iona's thoughts, Winifred clinked her silverware against her crystal wine glass and called, "Quiet everyone."

While the soup was served, Iona glanced down the table to find the older lady had elected to sit at the right hand of the marquess on the opposite end.

"Rainford is about to tell us of the missing children," Winifred announced.

Missing children? Iona waited for explanation.

"The description did not give age," Rainford corrected. "I have telegraphed friends in Edinburgh for more details. *Young heiresses* is all I know, and that they're Malcolms. So we thought you should know."

Iona chilled but pretended interest in her soup.

"Surely there is more, my lord," Winifred demanded. "*Heiress* and *Malcolm* are often synonymous."

"My informant only mentions blond and blue-eyed daughters of the Earl of Craigmore."

Iona's stomach rebelled against the little soup she'd imbibed. Still, even in her fear, she noticed the error. Her stepfather—or Arthur—didn't even know what color their eyes were.

The marquess continued. "I thought Ives might be interested in the reward of ten thousand pounds."

Ten thousand pounds? The entire house, land, and contents of Craigmore weren't worth ten thousand pounds. She was an heiress in title only.

Iona longed to sink lower in her chair as every head turned in the earl's direction. Instead, she sipped her water and watched the Earl of Ives and Wystan like everyone else.

Her host merely shrugged. "Blond, blue-eyed, and female describes almost every Malcolm in existence."

Which was why, when they first set out, Isobel had dyed her hair black and Iona had trimmed hers short enough to cover with a cap and pretend she was a boy. It had grown out a little since then, but no sun touched it under her old-fashioned bonnets, leaving it mostly light brown.

She and Isobel didn't have to change eye colors. They had their father's golden-brown instead of their mother's blue. So, maybe the old goat had remembered his wife had blue eyes and assumed her daughters did also.

"Were they abducted? Is there a ransom note?" the earl asked. "Are they old enough to run off with suitors? Is Craigmore a drunkard to lose his daughters?"

"Oh, the famed Ives cynicism," one of the gentlemen at mid-table said. "If they're Malcolms, won't the Malcolm genealogy tell us more?"

"Not ours," Mrs. Merriweather, the loyal librarian, said serenely. "Craigmore is a Highland estate. They've established their own library, although I can write Lady Abbott and inquire."

How long would it take for all the pieces of the puzzle to fall in place? Worse yet, where could she run when they did?

And a *reward*? That had to be the American's doing. She should have killed him when she had the chance, but she'd not thought him much of a threat then.

"If you would write, Mrs. Merriweather, that would be appreciated," Ives said with his usual indifference. "I do not like the thought of two innocents in the hands of scoundrels. But if they've merely run off with suitors, I want no part in it."

Iona sensed a whiff of interest, but the earl truly was cynical and not particularly worried.

"Your own mother ran off, did she not?" Rainford inquired. "Malcolm women are known to be headstrong."

Iona had known the earl had a Malcolm mother but had not considered the ramifications. No wonder he wasn't too concerned about the missing heiresses. She almost smiled at his confidence that they could take care of themselves.

"Only because so many men are weak," Winifred retorted. "If you find those children, I insist that you bring them here, where we can assure they're safe. Children do not normally run away without reason."

"They may have been abducted," the marquess insisted. "We don't know yet."

Ignoring any suggestion that a Malcolm might be abducted, Simone spoke. "Has anyone inquired of the ladies at the School of Malcolms? Edinburgh is much closer to Craigmore than here."

"I've wired Max and his librarian wife for more information," the marquess said. "They'll inquire at the school."

So much for hiding in plain sight, Iona thought, mind racing. Could she disappear into the company and hope whoever searched here wouldn't notice her? Surely, they'd be looking for twins?

"But you rode for Wystan instead of finding out the details—why?" the earl asked, finishing his soup.

"Rain's sisters were on the way," one of the other gentlemen answered.

Beside Iona, the earl snorted inelegantly. In his starched white shirt and formal attire, he looked the part of imposing earl—or what Iona imagined one should be. Her stepfather did not count.

"Do you hide your sisters from your friends or protect your friends from your sisters?" Ives asked in amusement.

"Both, most likely," Rainford admitted in resignation. "My youngest sister wishes to have a séance. I trust that will not be the evening's entertainment here?"

"We have ghosts," Mary Mike declared. A tall, tastefully tailored lady in her thirties, her dark hair more brutally cut than Iona's, she did not often speak. "The original keep is six hundred years old. It's unavoidable."

"But the old ones mostly wink in and out," Simone said reassuringly. "Only Ceridwen still speaks, and that's only in emergencies. Really, after millennia of human habitation, the world is an ocean of spirits. Hunting for just one is foolish."

"Malcolms have come to Wystan for centuries to ensure the safety of their childbirth and in hopes the infant will be born with the spirit of their ancestors," Grace, the spinner, said with odd formality.

Lady Alice wasn't a Malcolm. Iona glanced in her direction, but the lady sipped her wine with a jaded air of disinterest.

"Oh yes, Ives, that's how the legend says your great-grandfather finally sired a son," Mrs. Merriweather chirped. "Your great-grandmother wrote that a spirit entered her, and she bore the first Malcolm boy in a century."

"Because my grandfather was an Ives, and Ives only had sons at the time," the earl said in boredom. "I know the legend well. It doesn't appear to have carried forward since I have only sisters. I doubt spirits have a great deal to do with conception."

"Enough," Winifred declared. "Our concern should be for these missing children. We should have a plan."

The discussion of spirits and childbirth and conception rendered Iona uneasy, but listening to the company plot her capture put her off food entirely.

SEVEN

RAINFORD'S GROUP HAD RIDDEN HARD ALL DAY AND PLANNED TO RIDE ON IN the morning, so the dinner party broke up shortly after the ladies left the table. Even then, when the men joined the ladies to say their good-nights, half of the ladies had already gone to their own beds.

Gerard didn't see the little beekeeper among the women who remained—but Lady Alice was waiting like a spider to pounce. He excused himself and left Rainford to her delicate claws.

The beekeeper—*Nan*—had been remarkably quiet all evening. He supposed she might be unaccustomed to dinner parties. He would ask about her, except that would indicate interest—always dangerous in this crowd. No, he should ride with Rainford in the morning and make his escape while he could.

But he had the appointment with Avery to hold him back. He'd wait for additional information before searching for heiresses. If he'd been told they were the daughters of one of his servants, he'd be out all night searching. But these were the wealthy daughters of an earl and *Malcolms*. They'd most likely be found in the house of friends or family a thousand miles from here. He remembered one of his cousins, at six, following some whim, catching a ride with a neighbor, and ending up almost fifty miles away by sheer force of personality.

He wasn't terribly worried about heiresses, but the talk of ghosts and ancestry had left him restless. He was past thirty and aware that his duty was to settle down, marry, have children, and run for one of his father's minor boroughs.

He had no particular interest in children, but the thought of conceiving them. . .

Made him restless. He needed a willing woman to work off his frustration, but not here. Lord help him, but the family legends would put him off even bringing a *bride* here. He should be back in London in a week or so. He could wait.

Silver moonlight spilled across the courtyard, illuminating a slender figure gliding through the garden gate. Gerard halted to watch her vanish to the other side.

What did a beekeeper do in the middle of the night? Didn't bees sleep? Without giving thought to what he did, Gerard strolled past his tower and followed.

She had changed into a more sensible gown than the one that had kept him distracted all evening with the sight of creamy, rounded shoulders. For someone so slender, her breasts mounded nicely above the bodice.

He had no right to be thinking like that.

Treasure, the spirit voice murmured tauntingly

"What the devil are you doing here?" Gerard located the ancient piece in his waistcoat pocket where he most definitely had not put it. "I'm tempted to fling you into the pigsty."

But he didn't.

And then, more ominously, the voice added, *Danger!*

"What the devil does that mean?" he asked. The voice didn't answer.

Gerard would normally abandon the foolishness of treasure and danger, only the talk of missing heiresses and a reward almost verified the spirit's admonitions. What did he know about the beekeeper? Nothing, except she called herself Malcolm and wasn't immediate family. She could be lying, but her behavior with the bees said otherwise.

He couldn't let a female wander alone at night, he told himself. He didn't even bother rationalizing why he didn't call out to her.

She settled in the clover she'd no doubt planted as a tasty carpet for the bees. A stone fence behind the hives provided shelter from the prevailing wind, but the night breeze still lifted her cropped, honey-colored hair. She'd removed the heavy chignon. He preferred her bare, slender nape.

Feeling like a voyeur, Gerard leaned against the trunk of an apple tree and listened. She was *talking* to the bees.

Treasure, the spirit repeated in satisfaction.

Gerard snorted his disgust for listening to pieces of silver and concentrated on the whispers on the wind.

"It will be winter soon," she told the bees. "I need to leave before travel becomes difficult."

Gerard frowned. *Leave?* Why?

She seemed to listen to the breeze or maybe the bees. He hoped the bees were smarter than spirits.

"I don't *want* to leave you," she said mournfully. "I don't know if I'll ever be able to return."

Why the devil would she leave? Had one of Rain's men insulted her? Or made her an offer she couldn't refuse? If she were that kind of woman, he'd happily offer more. He was aroused just watching her, which was patently insane and proved Wystan's weird magic was sapping his wits.

He lifted his shoulder from the tree and prepared to turn away.

"Isobel must be frantic," she continued, tensely. "I have to send word to her. If only we'd had time to earn the fare for Canada!"

Gerard froze. There were *two of them*—Nan and Isobel?

She was running away. And they were *afraid.*

"If I let them find me elsewhere, you'll be safe here." That sounded like a promise. "And maybe I can come back someday. He only wants the title, after all."

Gerard couldn't bear it. With a disgruntled sigh, he entered the moonlit clearing, feeling a bit of a fool in his dinner clothes. "Who is *he* and doesn't he understand how titles are passed on?"

He was almost certain Joan of Arc had the same expression when she was captured—facing the inevitable with sorrow and relief.

"My lord," she said stiffly. "You had no right to listen to a private conversation."

"You're talking to bees, for pity's sake." When she didn't rise, he was forced to sit beside her. In his dinner clothes. His new valet would be rightfully appalled. "If you're one of the heiresses, tell me."

He didn't know where that had come from—except the warnings in his head.

Now she really looked alarmed. Her eyes were more golden-brown than Malcolm blue. So maybe he had it wrong. Or maybe the idiot offering the reward did.

"I am no heiress," she said with venom.

He'd best beware of bee stings.

He nodded, accepting her declaration. "And you're a Malcolm living in Wystan, so that makes you doubly safe from me. As one of my tenants, you are protected. Why run?"

She narrowed her pretty eyes in suspicion. "I smelled your interest in the reward. It's a fortune."

He considered that. "You *smelled* my avarice?"

"And your lust," she added. "You should have chosen Lady Alice for your attentions."

Ouch. She knew he lusted after her? That was a trifle humiliating but nothing unexpected in his family. He wanted to ask if she lusted after him, but that was asking for a slap. "I'm civilized," he insisted, wondering if that was the truth. He wanted her—very badly, in all sense of the phrase. "I can control myself. Curiosity, unfortunately, is my beset-ting sin. Who do you flee?"

"My stepfather and the hapless fool he wants me to marry." With resignation, she turned to face the hives again. "My queen understands. If you'll have someone treat her with respect, I'll try to pay you back, but I'm in no position for promises."

"I told you, you are safe here," he said with a trace of the anger he usually hid.

"No, I'll never be safe as long as my stepfather lives. I don't suppose you could loan me a pistol?" She rose and brushed off her skirt.

≈

THE RESTLESS UNEASE IONA HAD SUFFERED SINCE DINNER ONLY ESCALATED with the earl's presence. Despite his outward aloofness—or perhaps because of it—she found him much too attractive, and his offer of shelter weakened her defenses. Now that he knew her secret, though, she itched to escape. Men had a bad habit of taking control without understanding the complexity of a situation.

"No, I will not loan you a pistol," the earl said firmly, standing and tugging her hand through the crook of his arm as if they were going into dinner. "Killing people isn't a solution."

"Of course it is," she replied belligerently, because she was terrified, angry, and reacting to his desire like any foolish woman. And he was behaving like every other man in the universe—taking charge without understanding. "If a man attacks me, I am helpless against his strength unless I have a weapon."

The earl's proximity didn't help clear her thinking. She was actually thinking about *kissing* him! She longed to know what it would be like to be kissed by an attractive man who actually desired her. She tried to tug her hand away but his hold was solid.

"You'll be worse than helpless if they send you to prison. The better solution is not to put yourself in jeopardy. I could have been an itinerant stranger just now. Perhaps you should learn to make friends with the dog. At least he'd be some protection."

She frowned and kicked a clod of dirt. "I never had pets. My stepfather's half-starved hounds were trained to kill prey, not defend."

"The Earl of Craigmore, you mean?"

She shot him a look of fury. "My *grandfather* was the earl. The pig who uses the title now does so without authorization."

"That's not possible," he said in a tone of patience and authority. "Parliament would never give him patent if he could not prove his right to it."

"He married my mother, who by right of patent inherited her father's title. Everyone assumes she petitioned for the scoundrel to have the title as she did for my father. She did not. Since Mortimer hasn't the coin to go to London and vote, no one cares. The locals prefer dealing with a man instead of a woman. No one wants a *countess* giving orders." She didn't even try to hide her bitterness.

She had to leave. She'd never see the earl again. She could spill her anger freely without consequence. Years of holding her tongue, of hiding who she was, boiled to a froth. It felt good to release a little of her pent-up fury and anguish.

"Ah, now I see the problem," he said without surprise at her heat. "The Scots should never have allowed women to assume titles. It confuses too many issues, as evidenced by your predicament. Had the title simply died without issue—"

The moonlight and his closeness were having a dangerous effect. It was a good thing he made her too angry to react. "The Crown would have claimed the land after my grandfather died. My mother's title protected our family trust."

"Things are different now," he said in that same annoying, patronizing tone. "A man can own the land and pass it on to whomever he wishes without the crown's interference."

They were back in the courtyard. As much as she might hope he'd help her, she knew better than to expect a man to go out of his way. And really, there was little he could do. "Different now didn't help my mother *then*. Short of shooting my stepfather, it doesn't help me either. I thank you for your hospitality, my lord. I won't impose on it much longer." She tugged her hand free of his arm and started for the house.

To her alarm, he caught her arm and held her back. "Don't be a stubborn fool. Where can we go to talk privately, without my interfering relations developing the wrong ideas?"

Anxious as she was, it took Iona a moment to grasp his request. When it dawned that he feared being implicated in a romantic entanglement with *her*, she almost smiled at his predicament. She had only to stand on her toes and kiss him, and the nuptials would be practically sealed. The ladies would see to it. No wonder he practiced indifference and avoided Lady Alice.

"You cannot relax and have a conversation with any of your guests, can you? I can see why you don't linger here." She studied the house, uncertain she wanted a conversation with him or anyone else. "I am accustomed to taking care of myself. I don't need your help."

"Pardon my language, but that's a load of bull crap," he retorted crudely. "You may have done everything yourself because you *had* no one else. In Wystan, you have an entire castle full of people eager to assist."

"For ten thousand pounds, I'm sure any number of people are eager," she said dryly. "Even you. But my stepfather is a drunken gambler and bankrupt. There is no reward." There, that should discourage his interest.

"This is not about the reward but your safety." Still holding her arm, he surprised her by starting for a side entrance. "The butler's pantry should be empty by now. We can always pretend we both came down for bread and cheese."

She yanked her arm from his grasp but followed out of curiosity. Could she trust that he didn't want the fake reward? About as much as he might trust her to lie about it being fake—impasse. "I have not followed any man's orders since my mother died when I was sixteen. Do not think to tell me what to do."

"Do I strike you as insane?" He held open the door for her. "I grew up surrounded by Malcolm women. Rainford was being polite by calling them headstrong."

Iona tried to imagine growing up in a family of strong women but she failed even at the concept of *family*. "I wish I had known your family. Mine is isolated. I have no aunts or cousins."

"Lucky you." He led her through the dining room to the baize-covered door the servants used, into a room filled with cabinets of china and crystal. "The servants have learned to leave bread and accompaniments in here so we do not invade the kitchen to feed our late night cravings."

"Thoughtful." She watched as he carved a loaf of bread, realizing she was hungry.

"You barely ate your dinner." He handed her a slice slathered in honey. "Sorry I can't offer tea."

Because everyone had the makings for tea in their bedchambers, Iona realized. In a house as sprawling as this, tea would be cold by the time it came from the kitchen. And he wasn't about to go near a bedchamber with her, she understood.

In the intimacy of the empty pantry, the earl offered a comforting familiarity, as if they might actually be related. He didn't seem particularly fond of family, but she'd like to imagine what it was like to be held and treasured, if only for a few minutes. Foolish, she knew. She'd simply been alone too long.

She stepped nearer the exit. "I am not your concern. I am virtually a stranger."

He leaned his long frame against the wooden counter and finished chewing a bite of the apple he'd chosen. He'd loosened his cravat and collar earlier and unfastened his coat, giving him an unusually rakish air —especially with a beard shadowing his virile jaw.

"You are female, Malcolm, and a guest in my home. Unless you have already murdered your stepfather, it is my duty to shelter you. Is your sister safe? Do we need to send for her?"

Tears sprang to her eyes. She so wanted to see Isobel, to be certain she was safe and happy—"As safe as I am with a reward over our heads." She tried to sound confident, as her mother had taught her. "We thought we were less likely to be noticed if we split up."

"Fine, then let's decide on the level of your danger. Why is your step-father offering a reward he cannot afford?"

"He thinks he can sell my title," Iona said flatly. "I am Iona, the Countess of Craigmore."

EIGHT

GERARD WAS HAVING SOME DIFFICULTY CONCENTRATING ON THE BEEKEEPER'S story while inhaling her lush feminine scent entwined with roses. Did she wear perfume beneath that bulky gown? Had she removed her corset to move so freely?

Grateful her story didn't involve tears so he did not feel compelled to take her in his arms and test his corset theory, he almost didn't register the significance of her declaration.

Even then, he had to take time to process it through his lust-crazed brain. And another moment to reply with his practiced indifference. "Countess? You are heir to your father's estate?"

A countess. He was hiding a runaway *countess* in Wystan. He knew better than to ask questions! Life was far simpler when he addressed only his assigned duties.

"My *mother's* estate," she corrected. "Craigmore is an old title. The writ passes to heirs general. We're Malcolms, after all, and for a hundred years, we bore no sons. It was only sensible to allow the land to pass to offspring of either gender." She nibbled at her last piece of bread. "Of course, even though she's younger by an hour, Isobel could inherit. The title actually goes into abeyance until the Queen decides. We've never had reason to petition her."

Gerard attempted to recall archaic Scots law, but he'd never really thought to need it. "So after your mother died, the title legally went into abeyance, but your stepfather continued using it?"

"Exactly. His only interest is in draining the estate and playing lord of the manor. We're talking about the Highlands. We are accustomed to taking the law into our hands. Those who do not accept an English queen are even less likely to care about the legality of his claim."

He rolled his eyes. "Jacobites, in this day and age."

She ignored his comment. "My real father was a baron, so the locals were accustomed to calling my mother's husband *my lord*. As his daughters, one of us can probably assume his barony. It was another ancient writ." She pinched off a bit more bread. "My mother petitioned Parliament to allow my father to assume the higher title so our area would have better representation, as I understand it, leastways."

"A cynical assessment but probably correct," he agreed, cutting her a piece of cheese. "So your father had every right to be called earl. The locals became accustomed to addressing your mother's husband as lord and didn't worry about the details."

"One assumes. My father died when we were quite young. My mother was already ill. She had no immediate family to rely on. Mortimer was a younger son, a gentleman, and not a bad-looking man according to our nursemaid. After they married, my mother left the burden of tending the land to him, while she took care of us and her bees."

She told the tale as if reading from a storybook. Perhaps that was how she distanced herself from the pain. As heir, Gerard had always felt smothered by his family's constant attention. He couldn't imagine what it would be like without their support, even when he resented it.

"And then your mother died," he said for her, watching warily for tears.

She nodded. "Isobel and I failed miserably at our one London season. We'd attended an English boarding school, but silly us, we'd spent it with books and studies and not developing social connections. Our mother never had our opportunities, so she had only her title to give us presence."

"And no wealth." Gerard fully understood how society worked.

Barren land in the north wasn't much of a dowry. "You and your sister weren't at fault. Society is."

"We simply didn't think it mattered. We wanted to go home. At the time, we didn't know how desperately ill our mother was and what would happen when she died. Once she was no longer there to control the purse strings, we seldom saw Mortimer. That didn't bother us until the merchants closed our accounts for lack of payment."

He could almost hear the sadness behind the finality of her tale. At sixteen, his sisters had delighted in frills, bought books and oil paints and whatever caught their fancy without thought to expense. The beekeeper and her sister probably couldn't even buy food.

"But you managed to scrape by," he finished for her. "What happened to make you flee?"

"Mortimer brought Arthur Winter home," she said, as if the result was obvious.

"Sorry, I don't know the name." But he was already hating it.

"American industrialist, reportedly worth more than half the aristocrats in England."

"Your stepfather gambled against him and lost?" Gerard guessed.

"I have no idea, but that's a likely possibility," she agreed with worldly cynicism. "And Mortimer was probably drunk and bragged of his countess daughters who could magically bestow titles upon marriage. Keep in mind that only the servants ever mentioned the title, usually scolding us for not being proper countesses. It's fairly meaningless under the circumstances."

"But not to an ignorant American willing to spend a fortune to be called Lord Craigmore. Or Lord Arthur, I suppose. It would only be a courtesy title without the patent." Gerard snorted. "Or maybe he'd be called Lord Iona. I'll have to check DeBrett's."

She managed a small smile. "I doubt it works that way. Men are in charge, after all. They'd never allow another man to be demeaned by assuming the wife's name."

"Although it's fine for a woman to be demeaned by taking a man's name. Do not preach at me." Now that there was less danger of tears, Gerard pushed. "For this incompetent duo, you would abandon your queen bee and the safety of Wystan?"

She eyed him with disfavor, which was fine with him. He needed that distance to keep from tugging her into his arms and kissing her until neither of them cared about titles and rewards.

"Try placing yourself in my position, my lord. An entire tribe of eager aristocrats come galloping to your door the instant they hear of a fortune and heiresses. Your host is stewing with avarice at just the mention of a reward. And your sister is even closer to danger. What would you do?"

Danger, the medallion repeated.

IONA WANTED TO WEEP AT THE LOSS OF THIS PERFECT HOME, BUT SHE defiantly waited for Ives to produce magic rabbits from his over-sized hat.

The earl appeared intelligent, strong, and competent, despite his rakish attire and stubbled jaw. She *wanted* him to produce magic rabbits.

Except Rainford and his friends had rode straight here. They would seek other Malcolm strongholds as well. There weren't many. She and Isobel might blend in to some extent, but with that reward—wheat would separate from chaff soon enough.

That anyone would want them enough to pay money for their return had never once occurred to them. They had just been escaping an untenable situation.

"I don't suppose either of you have a suitor or two, do you?" Ives asked pessimistically, jarring her from her thoughts.

Iona almost laughed. "Hardly. Even if we were interested in sheepherders, we terrified them. Isobel once caught the rather handsome son of the local mercantile owner padding our bill, and I verbally shredded him. I could have done far worse. He left town not long after. Why would you ask?"

He shrugged and munched a biscuit. She watched his Adam's apple bob up and down, and experienced a perplexing tightening in her middle. No wonder men hid their throats—they were quite visibly masculine and nothing like a lady's.

His reply jarred her back to reality—"Obvious solution to Mr.

Winter's pursuit is for you to be already married, unless he's as blood-thirsty as you and inclined to shoot your husband."

Iona almost hooted at the notion of marriage. "I'm the one inclined to shoot. I can't imagine Mr. Winter raising a sweat much less a gun. He's naïve. His wealth is the danger. Besides, if I married, they would simply hunt Isobel. Want to find husbands for us both? By all means, keep hunting for a solution we haven't already considered. We thought hiding until he went away would suffice. Canada seems our next best option. Would you care to finance the journey?" she asked in sarcasm.

"If I could afford a journey, I'd send myself to Italy. My family is land rich and blessed with numerous relations, all of whom receive allowances that drain the coffers. My contribution at this point would be to suggest negotiating a huge marriage settlement with Mr. Winter, marry him in name only, let him call himself king or whatever, and take the money and run. Take me with you, if you like." He eyed her with interest.

Iona didn't know whether to laugh or smack him. That the cynical earl might even consider running off with her actually offered tempta-tion. It would never last, of course, but oh, the joy of seeing the world with the freedom to be as she wished. . .

"I am not even certain who I am anymore," she said with a sigh.

"The queen bee, of course," he replied without hesitation. "I've watched you. When you speak, people listen. Hiding is not your nature."

"Neither is taking orders," she admitted with wry amusement. That he'd noticed—tightened her midsection even more. When had been the last time a man had actually talked to her as if she had a brain? Around the twelfth of never would be her guess.

He rummaged in a cabinet and produced a bottle of wine. "So what was your plan that you needed to abandon your queen after—I assume —you hauled her all the way here?"

Iona was grateful he kept his hands occupied. Her desire had not decreased despite the grimness of their discussion. She had to resist leaning closer to him.

"I was hoping she would offer me wisdom. Mostly, I want to know Isobel is safe, but I need to know where I'm going before I can write to her." Iona turned up her nose at the offer of wine. "I don't touch alcohol. I've seen what it does."

"Not in moderation, but suit yourself." He poured his own. "Your sister will write you *here*. There is no reason to leave. Malcolms shelter Malcolms."

She wanted to yank the boyish lock of black hair on his forehead in exasperation. But the earl was large, solidly built, and all male, including the density of his thought processes. She wasn't stupid enough to test his reaction. "Even if *you* trust me when I say the ten thousand pounds isn't real, you have a household of people with dreams who would like to believe they can put the money to good purpose."

He lifted a questioning eyebrow.

She glared at his thickness. "Winifred has a son with a case of consumption so bad that even her healing hasn't helped him. She's kept him alive by paying a sanitarium on the proceeds from the herbal articles she writes from morning to night and from what little her patients pay. She could take the reward and her son and go to the south of France and be with him for the rest of his days."

The earl uttered an expletive and drank his wine.

"Mary Mike is saving to buy a farm of her own," Iona continued relentlessly. "Grace sells her beautiful tartans and blankets in shops to wealthy people so she can provide hundreds of cheap blankets for orphanages and workhouses. She can't forget growing up cold and wishing only for a blanket to call her own. Can you imagine what she might do with the money?"

"Then let's go back to negotiating with your wealthy, naïve nabob for a marriage settlement in exchange for your title," he growled. "Then you can finance every Malcolm here and take sail to anywhere."

Iona was very afraid that might be the only solution.

NINE

PROMISING NO ONE COULD POSSIBLY GUESS NAN—IONA'S—IDENTITY UNTIL
more information was forthcoming, Gerard sent her off to bed for her
own good. Even in that droopy gown, she'd been far too enticing for his
current state of abstinence. Talking to her had been like playing with a
hot firecracker wrapped in pretty golden papers—and just as dangerous.
A *countess*! What more didn't he know about his unusual tenants?

Was it more dangerous knowing or not knowing? Knowing who
might be a danger to Iona seemed essential. He didn't need the medallion whispering warnings in his head to tell him that.

The next morning, he pleaded estate duties and let Rainford and
company ride off without him.

To Gerard's great relief, Lady Alice found a ride in the carriage
hauling Rainford's baggage, so he didn't have to worry about being
waylaid again. Old acquaintance or not, Alice was a pestilence he didn't
need. Let her father take her in.

He spent his morning with the books in the privacy of his keep,
determining everything was in order. The estate still earned enough to
pay his allowance, but if he wanted to make improvements, he'd have to
use his funds, which meant giving up his rooms in London, and any
hope of life outside of Wystan.

The medallion was back in his pocket again, grumbling. Did Lowell think it was a good luck charm and keep transferring it to his fresh clothes?

He swiped at a bee flying too close, scowled at the open window, and decided he was hungry.

Leaving his new valet to fuss over his neglected wardrobe, Gerard warily slipped into the main house for nourishment, entering through the back hall where his Great-Aunt Winifred occupied the official office. She wore her fading blond hair in a high pompadour that he now knew was probably propped up with fake hair, which made her far less intimidating for some reason.

Still, he hesitated. He'd never questioned the ladies over all these years, assuming they functioned fine and didn't need him. He hadn't *wanted* to become involved.

But knowing some of his aunt's story now. . . He ought to hear the rest. He had cousins by the trainload. He tried to place which one was Winifred's invalid son. He conjured up a harmless, scholarly sort he hadn't seen since childhood.

Winifred glanced up and caught him hovering. "Do you realize the price of honey is four times that of sugar? If we can produce clean, unadulterated honey, we can sell it for a fortune. Nan will pay her own way in the first year and make a substantial profit once she has more than one hive in operation."

Pretending disinterest, Gerard leaned his shoulder against the door jamb. The ladies would swamp him with demands if they knew he had started paying attention. "I cannot imagine how you keep books to determine how much each tenant must contribute to the household."

She gestured at her journals. "Pretty much the same way you handle the crops and rents. I know how much it costs to run the household. We have servants sufficient to maintain ten bedchambers. We do not entertain often, so our expenses are steady. Most of the food is grown here, but wax for candles and the like are added to the figures. Although now that Nan is here, we can make our own wax. If we have ten residents, we divide the household costs by ten and consider it rent." She shrugged. "I keep track of our income. Anything we earn over the rent amount is ours."

None of which went to the enormous expense of repairing roofs, plumbing, and rats in the attic, among the other bills accumulating on his desk. But if he closed the castle, where would his relations go? And then there was the enormous Malcolm library. . .

"I trust you pay yourself a sum for bookkeeping duties?" Since attaining his majority, Gerard had left the household books in Winifred's competent hands. If his father had approved of her methods, he'd seen no reason to change them.

She looked at him blankly. "Well, no. We all have our little tasks. Grace provides blankets and weaves shawls for us. Simone makes scented candles to keep the air pleasant and advises us on the resident spirits and what they're telling us. Nan said she would teach the kitchen how to make honeyed candies, and her flower borders keep us in bouquets. We're mostly healthy, so my healing responsibilities are limited. I do the books, for my share."

The bees buzzing lazily in the roses outside the window reminded him of his duty to this estate and the people inhabiting it. Gerard felt as if he were cutting his own throat, but the beekeeper had opened his eyes, and he couldn't go back. "Then essentially, Wystan owes all of you for the cost of your labors. In agricultural terms, you're paying rent from the sale of your crops, but you're also providing essential services above and beyond the income you're recording, right?"

"I'm not sure candies and candles are essential," she said, but it was obvious she was running numbers through her head, trying to puzzle it out.

Unwilling to reveal Iona's secret, he continued the use of the name she'd adopted. "Before Nan arrived, did you buy candies? And if you use her wax, doesn't that save coins? Before you arrived, did we pay a bookkeeper? How would you light and scent the rooms without candles? Would you hire someone to talk to spirits if Simone were not here?" He couldn't believe he was asking these questions, but he never underestimated his family. "How long does it take Grace to make a blanket?"

These women worked all the time. And what did he do? Examine books once a year and make decisions about crops. For that, he earned more than all these women put together. He winced. Cutting his allowance was not why he'd come here.

"To be fair, Grace doesn't have to contribute often. It's not as if her blankets ever wear out. But over the years. . ." Winifred drifted off into a daze—a rarity for her.

"Exactly. Over the years, the estate has benefited even more than I thought from your presence. I assumed everyone paid their own way, but I had not realized you were contributing beyond that. Can you conjure some numbers and let me know what Wystan might owe? I can't say we have the funds, but I'll take a look while I'm here." He lifted his shoulder from the door and trailed off before his aunt emerged from her shock.

Damn and double damn. He'd have to start practicing law just to keep himself in clothes at this rate. An earl practicing law! Society would shake.

He sat down with Avery that afternoon over the estate books. "There hasn't been a raise in tenant rates in years," Gerard pointed out, hoping to bring in more income to cover maintenance, at least. "Most of them have been with us long enough to have improved their plots, and the cost of improvements to the cottages are going up. Isn't it time?"

Avery grimaced. "Their families are growing. We'll lose our best tenants if we ask them to pay more. I wanted to suggest. . ."

He went off into an old argument of removing the orchard and adding sheep that would put Wystan even deeper into a hole before it could pull out. A bee landed on the desk. Avery started to swat it but Gerard waved it away. His medallion grumbled. Restless, he studied the open window. Roses grew outside it as well. He couldn't remember roses there in prior years.

Finally, Gerard couldn't take looking at books any more. He stood up. "I want to have a look at the orchards, visit a few tenants. We'll not survive long if we're spending more than we're earning."

"We're breaking even, my lord," Avery protested. "You've seen the books yourself. There's no need to trouble yourself—"

Buzzing bees and grumbling medallions said there was a need to get out of his head and into the real world. This morning's experience with Winifred gnawed at him. He wouldn't find profits looking at books. He wouldn't find treasure—or danger—sitting on his rump.

He hated the idea of razing the orchards, but if it had to be done. . .

"The beekeeper's honey is already putting the household books in the black," Gerard informed his steward, with only a slight exaggeration.

"Not if you count the cost of new hives and fences and slowing down the apple harvest with those ridiculous borders." Avery stomped out after him. "Mark my word, my lord, those hives will be more trouble than they're worth. They should be removed with the orchard."

"Why do the sales of our cider continue to decline?" Gerard strode for the stable. "I thought the improvements we budgeted should have turned sales around."

He should have spoken with the old man in charge of the orchards yesterday, but he'd done his usual cursory ride in his hurry to leave. The whole point of paying an estate agent was for the *agent* to talk to the labor.

But then, he'd thought he had Winifred to do the same for the household. He was the friggin' earl. He was *supposed* to know more than Avery and Winifred. He *did* know, but he could only use what he'd been told, and they hadn't known what to tell him.

And he hadn't *asked*. He'd simply skimmed the surface, let everyone continue as they'd always done, and never once questioned.

Riding in front to avoid replying, Avery cursed at a sight Gerard couldn't see yet, and spurred his mount ahead.

His educated land agent seldom behaved as less than a gentleman. Gerard scanned the orchard for what had Avery agitated. A fox? A poacher?

All he could find was Iona talking to the wizened old orchardist.

Iona had known they were coming—the bees had warned her.

But after last night, she had to learn how far she could trust the Earl of Ives and Wystan. A landowner who only visited once a year didn't rate high on her trustworthy scale, but for now, she gave him benefit of the doubt. She'd deliberately detained the orchardist until the earl arrived.

"What are you doing here?" Avery snarled as he rode up in a flurry of dust. "We don't need you slowing down the harvest."

"I don't think Nan and Barkley are interfering with the pickers," Gerard said with unconcern, riding up behind his agent. "How do you do, Barkley? And how do our apples fare this year?"

Iona had learned the old orchardist had given charge of the picking to his eldest son years ago, but he still knew his trees. She waited for Barkley to speak what he'd told her.

Instead, the old man gave Avery a wary look and merely said, "I'm right fine, my lord."

Angered by his need for reticence, Iona defiantly answered the rest of the earl's question. "The orchard is *aging*, my lord. The oldest part should have been replaced a decade ago. One bad winter is likely to take half your ancient trees."

The earl frowned. "I thought we had a rotation plan in place, Avery?"

"The trees are fine," the steward growled. "Females don't know anything."

Avery reeked of a liar's rancid sweat. He knew what was wrong.

"Barkley knows trees better than anyone," Iona retorted, glaring at earl and steward. "Tell him he'll keep his position if he answers truthfully."

"Of course you'll keep your position, Barkley," the earl responded with unusual snappishness. "You've worked for us long enough to retire with pension and cottage, if you wish."

"He's an old fart, set in his ways," Avery protested. "He should have been put out to pasture long ago. As you saw yourself, the profits from the orchards have been in decline for years."

"Because you won't let me improve them!" Summoning up his courage, Barkley finally spoke up. "I been telling you that you can't make money without spending it. The trees need replacing regular like."

"The orchard is a significant part of our income. I know the budget isn't large, but we had a *plan*." The earl waited for his agent to explain.

Iona was still furious at his carelessness, but she tamped down her temper at this evidence that the earl was guilty only of expecting loyalty from his employees.

"Tell Lord Ives what this year's budget was spent on," Iona suggested, using the pleasant voice she'd learned from her mother—just before she swatted someone, literally or metaphorically.

"A prettier cottage for Bess," Blakely spit out.

He'd been a little cruder when telling Iona where the money had gone. Beekeepers didn't rank with earls. It was amazing what one could learn from this side of the class divide.

"Bess? In the village?" The earl didn't raise his voice, but the question demanded answer. "Have we purchased her lot?"

"It's a good property, my lord," Avery replied defensively. "Brings in a decent rent."

"For whom?" Ives demanded. "I'm fairly certain I didn't notice the rents on the books. Perhaps we should go back so you can show them to me. I trust the income is more than the lost cider profits?"

"Perhaps you should speak with your tenants more often, my lord," Iona said evenly, unable to resist digging in the knife just a little. "People can tell you more than books."

She walked away. What the earl did next would tell her if she could trust him with her future and that of her sister.

She didn't need the bees rising protectively around her to tell her he was furious. She could smell it. She reassured her workers and sent them back to the hive.

When she returned to the house to wash hours later, the ladies were all abuzz.

"He threatened to horsewhip him!" Grace said, scandalized.

"I heard he flung him out on his ear," Simone murmured in wonder. "I've never seen the earl angry. He's always been such an even-tempered, polite boy."

Iona hesitated on the bottom stair. "What happened?"

"Avery!" Winifred said, obviously disgruntled. "My nephew has gone mad and thrown out his estate agent. I know Avery is an arrogant toady, but he's all we have. Who will be in charge of the harvest now? I certainly don't have time or knowledge."

"The earl let Avery go?" Iona asked in astonishment. She hadn't thought he'd go that far in dealing with a gentleman who had evidently worked here for years.

"He was *stealing*," Grace whispered. "He had such a good position too. It doesn't make sense."

"Of course, it makes sense," Mary Mike said callously. "The earl took charge of the estate when he was barely out of school. Avery thought he knew better than an Oxford scholar. I daresay he's been fudging the books all along, but he got greedy."

Avery had done more than pad his mistress's cottage?

Lord Ives had given Avery the boot. What would he do now?

But mostly, he'd proved he could be trusted. Holding hope in her heart, Iona hurried up the stairs to wash for dinner. If she could trust him. . .

She could leave her hive and head for Edinburgh. Maybe she could borrow a pistol.

Unlike Mr. Winter, she'd learned to shoot to protect what little was hers.

TEN

Lowell snipped at a loose thread, straightened Gerard's cravat, and stepped back to eye him critically. "You'll be needing a trim shortly, but you'll pass for these parts. Your wardrobe, however, is in severe need of replenishing."

Gerard resisted rubbing his newly-shaved jaw and gritted his teeth. It had been a long rotten day, and he was in no temper for debating the cost of a new wardrobe for riding herd on sheep.

Booting Avery had been necessary. He couldn't have thieves working for him. But it left him seriously in the lurch.

"Clothes are my least concern. My bank account needs *severe replenishing* first," he admonished. "And if I'm surrounded by scoundrels, I may have to examine the damned bank as well."

Worse yet, he had to go down to dinner and reassure a roomful of rattled ladies worrying about their future. An estate with no steward or land agent would slide into penury soon enough.

This is what he got for listening to a damned beekeeper—correction, a countess! Avery had been right about one thing. Iona was a troublemaker.

The medieval paneled hall grew silent the instant he walked in.

Gerard amused himself imagining a roomful of lords falling silent in awe as they awaited his majestic oratory.

Little old ladies with fake hair propping up their white curls simply didn't convey the desired reverence and respect.

His great-aunt waited expectantly on her throne, however. The women were actually *waiting* for him to speak first. He'd savor the moment while he could. Gerard poured himself a glass of good Scots malt and donned his practiced nonchalance.

"I will begin a search for a new agent immediately," he reassured them. "If you wish to write your relations and make inquiries as well, I would appreciate that."

There, that sounded practical and not like he wasn't mentally lambasting himself for dismissing one of his father's hires. What in hell did he know about finding agents? Nothing. Blithering nothing. But he'd spent his life learning diplomacy. He knew how to communicate for the desired result.

"*Why* did you dismiss Avery?" Winifred asked, unable to hold her tongue longer. "He was a good agent and has worked here as long as I can remember."

Gerard swirled his whisky in his glass, weighing his words. "I promised him a decent reference if he returned what didn't belong to him. Let us not malign his reputation further with gossip. I'd rather the subject not go any further than this room."

Personally, he'd have wrung Avery's neck and thrown him to the wolves. But letting his temper rule wasn't necessarily what was best for all—a hard lesson learned over his father's knee.

Instead, he'd had Avery sign over the property that he'd bought for his mistress and improved with estate funds. In return, Gerard had given him a reference stating that Avery knew his profession but couldn't be trusted as an agent who handled contracts and funds. Still, he was educated and experienced and could easily fulfill the management duties of a steward. It would be a waste to throw him into the street because he let his cock rule his brain. Avery's next position might entail dealing only with the laborers, but he wouldn't starve.

The ladies peppered him with more questions he was either reluctant to answer or couldn't. Over his glass, Gerard searched the shadows for the little countess. She had a bad habit of hiding, but he found her in a wing chair that nearly engulfed her. She was pensively studying the fire.

Tonight, she wore a lacy adornment on her cropped hair and not the false chignon. The only difference between her dumpy morning gown and the dinner gown she wore tonight was the fabric and color—a light gold crepe versus her usual drab gray wool. She'd draped a blue-and-gold shawl over her shoulders so he couldn't see the neckline, but he ventured it wasn't as daring as last night's. She had a dreadful seamstress.

As if making a decision, she set aside her untouched glass of sherry and interrupted the pestering questions. "Ladies, the earl is a gentleman. You'll not pry gossip from him. The question becomes, what can we do to help until he is able to locate a new agent or steward. The apple harvest is under way, the fields need plowing, and the wheat needs threshing. It's an important time of year. Does anyone know anyone who can help?"

That nicely summed up the situation and diverted the conversation. Did she really think his eccentric tenants would thresh wheat? Or even know how?

"Will you be staying until someone is found?" the countess asked, making him pay for the diversion. She rose from her hiding place and fixed her long-lashed, golden-brown eyes on him.

Well-practiced in detachment, Gerard resisted tugging his cravat. "I need to find a buyer for some property in the village. Once I start receiving replies to my inquiries on both the property and the position, I may have to consult with solicitors and interview references. I'll be away a good deal."

He'd wanted to be in London this week. He wanted to *find* funds, not spend them. He didn't want these women to start relying on his presence. But he knew his duty. Orchards had to be improved, and at minimum, a steward must be hired. He had to stay—for now.

"Your workers aren't likely to listen to women." Iona added one more concern, while overriding all the other ladies without raising her voice.

Or maybe he was more attuned to her than the others. She was completely correct in her assessment. His workers weren't bees. They wouldn't work for women, not even a queen bee. Of course, from her tale, he gathered she knew the difficulty from experience.

"I have a few trusted tenants who can take charge of their particular endeavors." He wished the interfering countess to the devil even while understanding the ladies needed to hear this. "Barkley and his son can handle the orchard. I'll let the shepherds know Wilson is in charge of the herd until I say otherwise, and so forth."

"If a situation rises requiring a decision only you can make, would these men listen to a woman?" Iona asked, drifting closer, the light of interest in her eyes.

Where the hell was she going with this? Gerard gritted his teeth. He didn't care who she was or what title she wore. He wasn't putting a delicate young lady in charge of large, crude men. His workers weren't that enlightened.

"It's doubtful," he said flatly, hoping that would discourage her.

"What about Mary Mike?" she asked.

That knocked him for a loop. He was pretty certain the entire room fell silent, except for the ringing of doom in his ears.

He didn't want to embarrass his cousin, but he couldn't help studying her. Mary Mike was tall, just under six feet, broad at the shoulders but neither stout or slender. If she had a chest, she hid it under double-breasted coats similar to a riding habit. For dinner, she usually wore a straight skirt, but he knew she preferred split ones so she could ride astride. She was a formidable horsewoman—and had a way with animals.

"I can do it, my lord," Mary Mike stated without equivocation. "I've been working with your sheep and stable foremen for years. They just call me Mike or Malcolm. To put it bluntly, we've developed an excellent breeding program. They trust me."

Gerard considered pounding his skull against a wall. Breeding program. The woman had said *breeding program*. And no one gasped. He had to remember Wystan was another planet, one run by abnormal women.

"But it's the apples and wheat that need attention now," he reminded her. "We bring in men who don't know you."

"If you'll allow, they won't know I'm a woman," she said in satisfaction. "I can ride those fields better than Avery ever did."

Gerard remembered why he avoided his estate three-hundred-sixty days of the year. The women were insane and did their best to drive him down the same path.

"She can do it, my lord," Winifred said firmly. "You won't know it's her when she rides out."

They were effectively telling him that a woman—a *lady*—could be as good as a man in an all-male terrain. He couldn't see it. The men were crude and frequently aggressive. They needed someone who spoke their language. Even he was at a disadvantage. It required a man in the middle who could speak to both classes—like Avery, dammit.

"Women are very adaptable," Iona said with confidence. "We have to be. You'll be here part of the time. Watch and see."

He could imagine the little countess now, walking the fields of the north country after her mother's death, beating sheep into submission through sheer strength of will. He threw back his whisky, swallowed his doubts, and nodded. "Let's test it then. I make no promises. If the men get drunk at noon or drive sheep over a cliff, that will be the end of the experiment, understood?"

Mary Mike held out her hand like a man. "I'm honored. Thank you, my lord."

He shook, as if she were a man. He could almost sense a collective sigh of relief.

"Ceridwen says you're one of us," Simone said with satisfaction. "Is dinner ready yet? After all this tension, I'm quite famished."

The bell rang as if her words had yanked the ropes. Or maybe the ghostly Ceridwen.

Before the beekeeper could vanish, Gerard caught her arm and all but dragged her into dinner.

If he wasn't careful, he'd make her *his* countess, just to handle the residents of his castle. But she was an impoverished, managing Malcolm, and the very last kind of wife he needed. He would try not to want her too much.

～

AS THE SOUP WAS SERVED, IONA WAITED FOR THE EARL TO SCOLD HER FOR her interfering ways. When she had corrected her stepfather, he'd usually shouted and stomped off, leaving her or Isobel to manage what needed to be done. The earl retained his diplomatic façade, as always, but he was steaming. Even over the heady scent of the chicken broth, she could sense his fury and confusion.

And integrity. She hadn't smelled integrity often, so she'd been unable to identify the scent at first. It was much like being unable to judge the taste of a spice by its smell. But now she recognized that it complemented the clean fresh odor of honesty well.

She savored the soup but still the earl didn't speak except when spoken to. He could hold his raging temper—nice.

Hers wasn't a retiring nature. She'd simply learned to disappear in self-defense. But the earl knew her story, most of it, anyway. If she didn't mean to hide while she was here, she might as well shake off the rest of her invisibility and try to remember who she was.

"You are perfectly free to scold for my managing ways," she offered. "I've been locked in my room, threatened with a whip, and had feces flung at me. I will assume you'll be more polite. And since I have to leave anyway, you can even throw me out, if it will make you feel better. But I must say, you dealt with the ladies beautifully this evening."

The earl's jaw muscles tightened over aristocratically high cheekbones and his midnight eyes glared. "You are not at fault for Avery's theft."

"But you were perfectly content to let him go his own way until I interfered." She needled him just a little to deflate the steam.

"I would have been perfectly content on the way to bankruptcy," he retorted in a low voice so Grace on his other side could not hear. Politely, he turned to Grace and asked a question about her loom.

"Mary Mike will make an excellent steward," Iona suggested when he turned back to her. "She is better educated than Avery and already knows your property."

"She can wear what she likes, but she is not a man," he said through clenched teeth. "I cannot single-handedly change the world. The men need to respect the person giving orders."

"Thank you for letting her try," Iona said demurely, now that he seemed to be calming down. "I've seen her work with your grooms. I'm not sure they realize she's a woman any longer."

The earl rubbed a tic in his cheek. "This is not suitable dinner conversation. I cannot even imagine the scandal if word goes out that I have a woman masquerading as a man running my estate, and it will. She won't be able to negotiate or sign contracts with banks or others."

Iona winced. She had no answer for that. She was relieved when he turned his attention elsewhere.

He glanced down the table. "Mrs. Merriweather, do you know if there has ever been a discovery of Roman ruins or artifacts hereabouts?"

As the Malcolm Librarian, the slight, older lady held a paying position even higher than Avery's had been. She was the only woman currently on the premises addressed with formality. She wrinkled up her eyes in thought, then shook her gray curls. "Not that I recollect, but I'll ask the books this evening, shall I?"

"I would appreciate that, thank you." He turned to Mary Mike. "In your wandering, have you noticed anything that might be the remains of an old keep?"

Iona cut into her fish and wondered what was on his mind. And why he'd set her at his right if he didn't want to shout at her. Smelling integrity didn't answer her curiosity.

"There are outcroppings of rocks all over the fells but none that appear to be more than a shepherd's hut," Mary Mike acknowledged. "The plowmen occasionally turn up a coin or two but nothing of significance."

Iona eyed the earl with interest but didn't speak up again. If she wanted him to help her, she shouldn't push him too far. He didn't need to remind her that she was small and weak. Sitting next to a muscular man like the earl reminded her of all she was not. Her wits were her best defense.

As the last of the dessert plates were carried away, the earl bent toward Iona again. "May I have a word with you without everyone watching?"

A tingle ran up her spine, and she was pretty certain it wasn't of fear. Ives was extremely handsome, after all, and she wasn't immune to masculine interest.

"You should probably ask *Mike* to linger over port," she said, lips twitching as his steam level rose again. "I usually check on my queen at this hour. While you talk to your new steward, I'll sit with the ladies a little before going out."

"You go out in the orchard at night *alone*?" His voice rose.

"Talk to Mike." Iona stood up with the other ladies and left him simmering.

Yes, she was a managing, interfering female, but the earl wouldn't have to put up with her for much longer.

And a good thing, too. She was enjoying her brief freedom entirely too much. Not having to watch her tongue or mind her back gave her time to think about what she actually wanted.

She wasn't certain what she wanted in the long term, but right now, she wanted her sister and her hive safe, and she'd like to kiss the Earl of Ives and Wystan, at least once. Before she could have anything, she had to pry Mortimer out of her life.

Once her stepfather held no threat over her, she'd be able to think clearly again—because wanting an English earl with little more money than she had made no sense at all.

ELEVEN

LEAVING THE CASTLE AND STRIDING FOR THE ORCHARD, GERARD LONGED TO be anywhere but Wystan. He'd not been able to concentrate on his conversation with Mary Mike while he worried over the damnable countess out here alone. This might not be the city, but foxes, poachers, and other rogues all roamed the night. Did she plan to hex them?

He found Iona just where she'd said—communicating with her *queen*. She'd wrapped a cloak around her against the cool night wind. With the hood up, she looked the part of witch. But when she heard him coming, she dropped the hood, and moonlight caught her corona of golden hair, and it was like watching the sun rise. He could almost believe in magic.

Treasure comes with danger, the medallion said grumpily.

"You wished a word with me, my lord?" she asked politely as he approached.

Why did he have the impression that he could have been a monster, and she would have faced him equally coolly?

"I simply wanted to assure myself that you weren't planning on doing anything hare-brained like running away." Now that he'd said it, he felt a right fool, but he'd needed this moment with her alone, just to settle his temper.

No one ever stripped away his polished veneer the way this diminutive female could. That was a problem. Next, he'd be telling her about the voice in his head crying *Danger*, and he'd be a laughingstock within weeks.

Although once his friends learned about Mary Mike, that would happen anyway.

The countess shrugged. "First, I need to determine if the Queen is at Balmoral yet or still at Holyrood. I assume she might have left staff at Holyrood, so Edinburgh would be simpler. *Then* I'll run."

She dimpled up at him, apparently recognizing that she was only raking the coals of his ire. The damned female was a manipulator par none. How did she do that?

Then remembering his mother's dangerously sensitive abilities and Iona's mention of *smelling* his lust, Gerard wished he'd never requested this meeting. He should be riding the hell out of here before the beekeeper had him turned inside out so she could examine his innards. Wrapping himself in a cloak of ennui wouldn't deceive her perceptivity. He already felt raw and exposed.

"You cannot directly petition the queen for your title," he told her, hoping to nip this inanity in the bud. "It has to go through proper channels, and that will most likely include a parliamentary committee and more red tape. It is not a simple matter."

"The queen can make it simple, if she wishes. Is your father on her right or wrong side these days?"

She may as well have smacked him, inquiring about the marquess's aid as if Gerard were naught more than a stepping stone. He understood why men might threaten to horsewhip her. "Politically, they're at odds. Personally, Vicki likes looking at him. He occasionally gets away with metaphorical murder. And I am not applying to my father on a matter of no concern to him. He has enough to do."

She nodded. "Fair enough. I'll ask the ladies at the School of Malcolms. I need to go to Edinburgh. Would you be interested in helping me to do that?"

"Why?" he demanded. "So you can sell yourself to the American, then run away again?"

It would be just like the damned noble countess to sacrifice herself for her sister.

"I have given our discussion some thought. I have never been particularly interested in marriage or children. I want a freedom that women aren't permitted. I'm not like Mary Mike. I have no desire to be a man. But I would like to have the ability to improve my estate, experiment with my bees, travel to London. . . all things I cannot do now. As a married woman with wealth, I could do a great deal more."

She gave him one of her enigmatic molten-honey looks. "What I need is a good negotiator. I thought your father might be a possibility. Mr. Winter would probably genuflect to a marquess. But the ladies will know someone."

Gerard clenched fists, molars, and lips to prevent steam from escaping. Inhaling carefully, he managed not to shout. "You are doing this on purpose, aren't you? Couldn't you simply ask me to take you to Edinburgh and negotiate with Winter? Why torture me?"

Her eyes widened just a little. "I don't know why my choosing my future would be torture for you. And I have no idea if you're a good negotiator."

No one had any idea what he could do, including himself. He'd never really been given the opportunity. But his cranium held encyclopedias of knowledge—and apparently the voice of a Roman soldier who chuckled.

"You don't need a good negotiator, you need a magician," Gerard told her callously. "There is no way on heaven, earth, or hell that Parliament will allow an American to be an earl. You can petition for *your* letters patent, if you like, so you can claim the title, lands, and vote. But he will never be allowed to be anything more than Lord Arthur, your consort."

"He doesn't know that, though, does he?" she asked, looking thoughtful. "If I'm given letters patent, then I can vote? That would be singularly amusing. I think Isobel would enjoy it more than I would though."

"You mean your sister is even more of a managing female than you?" he asked, unable to quell the horror in his voice.

The lady laughed. "My sister is much quieter and more devious. She likes managing books and leaves people to me. I've often thought that together, we might make one whole person. I'm not certain either of us has what it takes to be a parliamentarian, but she'd listen to speeches more patiently."

Treasure, claim her! shouted the insane voice in his head.

Gerard was quite clear that *he* wasn't insane. He knew he only had to take the medallion out of his pocket to have peace and quiet again. He had a table full of artifacts to prove that. He might be stupid for listening to the voice though.

But honestly, the soldier wasn't saying anything that Gerard wasn't thinking. Except he couldn't *claim* a lady without marriage. One did not lure virgins to bed without expectations.

"You have the determination to make a most excellent countess," he told her, before he knew what he meant to say.

She gazed up at him in astonishment, her long lashes trapping him like a bee in a flower. If this might be his only chance to simply hold her. . .

Gerard circled Iona's slender waist, bent down, and kissed her luscious lips, just to see if they tasted like honey. They did.

For moments out of time, she clung to him, allowing him to savor her sweetness, giving him access when he pressed for more. The instant his hand roamed below her waist, she shoved away, panting hard and keeping her distance, glaring warily.

Had the beekeeper not been an impoverished Malcolm, he'd be proposing marriage right now. He *wanted* her, any way he could have her.

All right, that might be insane.

Without apology, Gerard dropped the medallion in the grass and ground it into the earth with his boot. "So it's agreed—you'll stay here while I ride out to do interviews and sell property and learn what I can of this reward being offered?"

She brushed herself off as if they hadn't just shared the deepest, most soul-wrenching kiss he'd ever experienced. She was giving him a taste of what other people might feel when confronted with his indifference. It twisted his gut.

"I have no say in what you do, my lord, any more than you can dictate what I do. Cast me out if that bothers you. I need to write Isobel to let her know I'm safe for now. Good evening." She bobbed a very small curtsy and strode off, revealing dainty shoes instead of boots.

He had the brains, wealth, and power of two men. She admitted she was a halfwit without her sister and lacked so much as a farthing to her name. And after she'd kissed him as if she meant it, she'd cut him off at the knees.

There was a lesson to be learned from this, but he'd be damned if he knew what it was.

Grabbing the medallion from the earth, he shoved it in his pocket. The soldier grumbled and muttered all the way back to the castle.

"I ANSWERED A FEW QUESTIONS ABOUT BEES," IONA SAID, HANDING HER missive over to Mrs. Merriweather the next morning. "Would you be so kind as to post this to Calder Castle?"

"Of course, dear." The librarian slid the folded sheet into an envelope. "Should we have told the earl that Calder's steward is female? Would that make him feel better?"

Knowing that the librarian had recognized her relationship to said steward, Iona fought her concern and allowed herself a small smile. "No, let the earl think he's being persecuted. It's good for his soul."

She'd been a fool to let him kiss her last night, but she'd wanted it so very badly... She was still a little giddy at being held and desired, if only for just a few minutes. But now she had to adjust her thinking back to normal. "The earl has had everything his way all his life, hasn't he?"

Mrs. Merriweather considered that for a moment. "In a way, I suppose. But Gerard has had to prove himself to much older half-brothers who didn't inherit the title or estate. Worse yet, the marquess has lived with tragedy all his life, including the loss of his first legitimate son and heir. Gerard was a late arrival, after the family had despaired of having another son. The marquess places rather large expectations on him in consequence. He's never really been allowed to sow wild oats."

Iona wagered he'd sowed a few. A man didn't kiss like that without knowing what he was doing. Then she remembered Lady Alice and grimaced. She wouldn't be another notch on his bedpost.

"Why didn't his half-brothers inherit?" Iona knew better than to express interest, but now that she'd quit hiding, she was trying to find herself again. Her real self was dangerously inquisitive.

"The marquess wasn't married to their mother, dear," Miss Merriweather said with a twinkle in her eye. "She was an actress, I believe, and her sons are twins. Twins tend to run in the Ives family."

"As do bastards," Iona said pertly, recalling what she'd heard from Isobel about Max Ives, her employer. "Handling resentment from a position of power is scarcely a hardship."

"A position of power tends to be lonely," the librarian admonished. "And the earl has more or less been wrapped in cotton batting all his life for fear anything might happen to him too."

"The exact opposite of me!" Iona tried to laugh it off, but inside, she understood what the librarian was saying. As a man of integrity, the earl would never unleash his passion or do anything that would bring shame on his aging, worried parents.

So, she was on her own. It wouldn't be the first time. She'd make inquiries about a good negotiator with the ladies at the School of Malcolms, and with Lydia, the librarian at Calder Castle. She had options, of a sort. She simply needed to time her departure to suit the best possible conditions.

The earl rode out and didn't return for dinner that evening. Iona didn't know whether to be relieved or concerned. Deciding it was easier not to think of the earl at all, she went about the important business of securing her hives for the winter.

It broke her heart and frightened her more than a little to leave her favorite queen behind, but if she had to put an end to Mortimer's depredations in order to reclaim her life, then sacrifices had to be made.

Over the next week, Iona prepared her honey and the candies she'd promised, and rebuilt the hackles to protect the old-fashioned hives. The Langstroth book arrived, and she poured over it from beginning to end, taking notes, drawing sketches, dreaming, and wishing she could take the precious volume with her. Instead, she showed it to the estate carpenter so he could better understand what the bees needed. Her notes and sketches she packed in her bags, in case she never returned.

She hoped desperately that she could return here in the spring to introduce her queen to her newly-constructed palace.

On the days the earl stayed at Wystan, he spent his time riding the fields, overseeing his new steward's work, and his nights in his tower. He didn't seek out Iona, as was perfectly proper. He was a busy man. She was nothing but a tenant to him.

That didn't mean she couldn't wish otherwise, but she didn't have time to waste on wishes. Remembering the earl's questions about Roman ruins, she had consulted her queen before tucking in the hives for the winter. When she had time, Iona roamed the fells and dales, looking for the ancient mulberry the worker bees had noticed. Bee minds recalled pollen fields better than old buildings, but the memory of warm stones and what might have been an old garden came through.

Mary Mike knew nothing about mulberries, but Iona had studied mythology and herbals and knew the tree had ancient history. An old garden and old stones might yield whatever the earl was looking for. She would like to thank him for his generosity and maybe inspire him not to neglect her hives once she was gone.

As it happened, the earl had been away for several days, and Iona was growing restless, when she stumbled upon the stone foundation near an almost dead tree. The frost had killed back much of the vine and weed, leaving only a bit of green boxwood clinging to the heat of old, squared-off stones.

During the summer, the spot would be lush with weeds and herbs, if she identified the leaves and stalks correctly. The stones would have been invisible unless one was directly on top of them. The shepherds might have eaten their lunches here, but no one else had reason to traverse this distant hill.

She tidied the stalks a little, disturbing the earth by pulling weeds, clearing space for the wild garlic, celandine, and watercress. She'd never had a great deal of time for gardening, but she'd learned herbs and foraging from her mother. Iona preferred working with flowers, simply because of her bees and the scents. But all plants interested her.

She sketched a hasty map and image of the location, but she found no artifacts that might interest the earl. Plants probably didn't matter to him if he was asking about Roman coins.

When she returned to the castle with her sketchbook, Mrs. Merri-weather called to her.

"You must have intrigued Calder Castle with your bees. You have another letter." The librarian waved an envelope.

Iona's stomach plummeted to her feet. Isobel was endangering both of them to write directly again. Managing a smile, indicating her dirty gown, she took the letter and hurried off with it.

Once in her room, she hastily unsealed the missive, lit a candle, and copied the secret code that appeared.

Too many suspicious inquiries. Must leave soon. Where?

Iona began packing her valise.

TWELVE

GERARD SPRAWLED HIS BOOTS OVER THE CARPET OF THE INN ROOM HE AND the banker had hired for this meeting. He yawned as Avery's mistress wept and employed her charms for the sake of the bespectacled businessman. The Berwick banker merely polished his spectacles and glanced to Gerard for aid.

"Bess, the house does not and never did belong to you, no matter what Avery told you," Gerard reminded her with his best aristocratically bored drawl. He had learned from an early age that people expected things of him that he could not give. It got old. "We are doing our best to be fair. If you paid rent, Avery did not record it on the estate books. I will not question the past two years that you have apparently lived at my expense. But going forward, you must make choices."

Still young and beautiful in a round-faced, cherubic way, Bess blinked her long fair lashes at him. "But I have nowhere to go," she pleaded. "It is my home! What shall I do?"

Gerard had a multitude of sisters, female cousins, and aunts, along with all the ladies at Wystan, and was not swayed by feminine attempts to garner his pity. He knew perfectly well that Bess was as much of a businesswoman as the banker or she would not have landed herself a substantial cottage in the village where she entertained men and dressed herself in fine gowns.

"You may follow Avery, I suppose, if he wants you. Otherwise, we have offered you two respectable choices. Mr. Pettigrew here will buy the property from me, and you may pay him rent, with the understanding that the house is his to do with as he wishes. Or he will arrange a loan so that you may buy the house and make payments at a very fair rate of interest, with the understanding that if you miss payments, he can take the house away. I cannot make it any more clear than that." Gerard impatiently jingled the coins in his pocket.

"How will I ever make payments of any sort?" she asked with a quivering lip, dabbing at her eyes with a lacy handkerchief. "Avery managed all that sort of thing for me."

Gerard wanted to return to the castle before nightfall. Once he concluded this transaction, he'd have funds to begin repairing the orchards. He wouldn't be any wealthier, and the castle maintenance still had to be paid, but his duty in Wystan would be done. He supposed he should linger longer to oversee Mary Mike, but she was doing a better job than he ever would. He'd simply have to come back more often until he was sure the men continued to respect her.

For the sake of expedience, he leaned forward and glared at the weeping, calculating wench. "You make the payments the same way you paid Avery, bought your pretty gowns and jewels, and pay your servants. You may have to cut expenses, but I'm sure you will figure it out as most people must. If you feel you are not capable, I'll let you know where Avery has gone and help you sell your household goods so you may follow him, and Mr. Pettigrew may sell the property. Now choose, so we may all move on with our lives."

She shot him a baleful glare. "You have no understanding of what—"

"On the contrary, madam, I have a complete understanding of what you require. I'm not unfamiliar with the needs of courtesans. I'm simply not interested. This is business. If you wish to run a business, then you must learn to be practical and not weep like a child. That only works on feeble-minded fools who think with their lower parts, and that is decidedly not me."

Every once in a while, it paid to show how he felt. Bess pressed back in her chair as if he'd shouted at her. He hated being a bully, but sometimes, it was necessary.

Gerard stood. He could not help that his height was an additional intimidation. "I need to ride on. Pettigrew, I rely on you to see the funds are transferred to my account. You have the deed, and she's your problem now."

Despite his milquetoast looks, the banker had a heart of solid granite. Gerard had offered him a good price just to be rid of the property and have the funds for his orchards. He could rely on Pettigrew.

He needed to be in Edinburgh, determining what was happening with the louts attempting to locate Iona and her sister. Leaving the inn, heading for the stable, Gerard was striding down the market street when the mercantile owner ran out, waving a paper.

"My lord, a telegram just arrived. I was about to send my boy out with it."

Gerard's innards ground. Telegrams were seldom good news. Murmuring a few pleasantries, he handed the shopkeeper a coin and continued on. Not until he was alone did he tear open the envelope. From Rainford.

Twins Age 23 Runaways Any newcomers?

The marquess had evidently reached Edinburgh and was searching for the missing heiresses—rather than court his own, of course. Gerard wasn't too worried about Rainford. The marquess didn't need the reward and was simply escaping his family for a last fling at freedom.

It was the less-wealthy men following Rainford who worried him.

Gerard rode home in the dark, trying to work out how to handle his beekeeper's ardent suitor. He had promised she'd be safe at Wystan, and she would be. She was of age. Her father couldn't force her to leave. But fortune-hunting mongrels might be desperate enough to stage an abduction in return for a reward or for the *heiress* herself.

And Gerard couldn't protect both Iona at Wystan, and her sister, wherever she might be. Putting them in one place might be doubly dangerous, as they'd already assumed. Apart, they could blend in. As twins, they'd stand out.

Perhaps he could explain the dilemma to Rainford. The marquess had the wealth to send the women to China, if need be. But Gerard would need Iona's permission to spill her secrets. She didn't trust easily, for good reason, it seemed.

He rode in, sweaty and stinking of horse. Throwing the reins to the stableboy, he hurried to his tower to bathe. He might have time to catch some of the women still in the withdrawing room. He didn't dare hope he'd find Iona. And he couldn't arouse suspicion by sending for her. Damn.

Lowell greeted him without fuss, filling his bath and fetching clean clothes. The old batman made an excellent valet, Gerard admitted. He just didn't need the extra baggage or expense of a personal servant. He never stayed at Wystan for long. He didn't need a valet at Iveston Hall, where the family estate swarmed with servants. His flat in London was small. He'd be forced to find a larger one—more expense—or settle in the family townhouse. He shuddered at the idea since the ancient edifice spilled over with his relations and any of their friends who needed a temporary home.

Could he send Iona to his family? What explanation would he give? His mother could sense a lie from a mile away.

Since dinner was over, the kitchen sent up a hot meal to his room. After bathing and dressing, Gerard took the tray to his desk, where he flipped through various papers the women had left for him. Mary Mike was more efficient at communicating than Avery, he noted. She'd already acquired estimates on replacing the older trees, along with the cost of the new hives and the hedge to protect them.

He uncovered a sketch of a hillside with a dead tree and a list of herbs to be found there. Puzzled, he almost set it aside in his haste to hunt for Iona. But as he finished off his wine, he studied the sketch, trying to figure out why it had been left on his desk. The writing was not Mary Mike's.

The sketcher was no artist, but something about the drawing compelled him to study it. He could determine what appeared to be square stones among the penciled weeds. In the distance, he thought he could see the top of Wystan's tower. *Village* was penciled in to the west of the tower and *Orchards* to the east. So it was a map of sorts, to a patch of weeds and stones.

He picked it up and received a shock that shot up his arm as if he'd been electrified. He occasionally picked up on vibrations from old artifacts that called to him, but this. . . This was abnormal.

He hastily strode downstairs in search of anyone who might still be around in the main house. He met Mrs. Merriweather on her way to her room, and she greeted him cheerfully.

"There you are, my lord! We've missed you. I've not found anything in the library yet about ancient ruins, but I see you found Nan's sketch. She said the bees showed her that spot. She didn't find any artifacts, but she thought the stones and garden looked very old."

Iona had done this? Gerard had to work at displaying his usual nonchalance. "I should thank her," he said politely. "I'll ride out and look for this in the morning. Is she still about?"

"Oh, no, she left this morning." Mrs. Merriweather's smile faded a trifle. "We tried to persuade her to stay, but she received a letter and said her family needed her. I do worry about her, but there was no persuading her to wait."

She'd left! She'd run away even after he'd promised her safety. He would kill her if he ever found her. She couldn't leave him. . . She had.

It tested all his diplomatic skills to refrain from punching a wall and roaring his rage. "Did she say which direction? I have to leave soon. I might catch up with her and see that she travels safely."

Mrs. Merriweather frowned. "The only letter she received was from Edinburgh, my lord, but she didn't say where she was going. Does it matter? I can write—"

If she had a letter from *family*—he could guess who wrote from Edinburgh. Biting down on his fear and fury, he waved off that suggestion. "I hope she had sufficient funds to take the train and not a coach."

"We paid her in advance for the honey sales. It seemed the right thing to do. She was worried about her bees, but we assured her we'd take the best care of them. I suppose it's better that she travel before the weather worsens. Is there anything else I can do for you, my lord? My kitten and my rocking chair are waiting."

"No, I thank you for explaining. Perhaps I'll look for Mary Mike to see if she can provide better directions to this hill." He continued down the corridor, his stomach grinding as if he'd eaten glass.

If he asked questions, the women would want explanation of his interest. He didn't have a good explanation, except for the fears Iona had confided and weren't his to reveal. The sketch was all he had.

He carried the paper into the withdrawing room where Winifred and Simone cut up map pieces they'd glued to sturdy fabric. He'd seen them creating puzzles before, although he had no idea what they did with them.

"I was hoping to find Nan to explain this sketch to me, but I understand she's left?" he asked idly, studying their puzzle pieces.

He knew from experience that the women only told him what they thought he needed to know. And most of the time, they concluded he didn't need to know anything. Shouting at them wouldn't change their minds.

Winifred took the sketch and examined it in the oil light. "Very pretty. That looks like a mulberry tree. Oh, yes, she notes that in the corner. Interesting. No, she didn't mention this to us, but she left in a bit of a hurry."

"The market cart couldn't wait for her to say her farewells." Simone snapped two puzzle pieces together to see if they fit. "The driver had to be back in the village before dark. I only saw her go because I was in the kitchen. She left us a lovely thank-you note and apologized for her haste."

Gerard didn't think pounding them over their pompadours with a piece of paper would help. "She didn't say why she left? Or where she was going?"

"Of course not, dear," Winifred said soothingly. "We don't ask questions. If she wanted us to know, she would have told us. The bees are apparently settled in for the winter, so she may have decided she wasn't needed here for now."

Gerard didn't believe for a moment that one of the witches hadn't questioned the girl, but he couldn't accuse his great-aunt of lying. "Very well. Then perhaps I'll leave hunting for this hill for another time. Tell Mary-Mike that I will be back in a few months to see how she's getting on. And if she has need of me, to address my man of business in London, as always. He'll know how to find me."

He walked off on the non-informative ladies. Two could play this game.

She'd left with the market cart. There was a coaching inn in the village. He may have just missed her. He'd ride out first thing in the morning.

But Gerard had the strong suspicion that she'd gone to her sister—who would be the only person who knew how to reach Iona. And if the letter came from Edinburgh, then that must be where the sister resided—in a nest of Malcolms.

It was also where Rainford and his pack of hounds were sniffing and where the unwanted suitor apparently stayed.

Damn the woman, did she want to get caught?

Of course she did. She wanted to marry wealth and be free to do as she pleased. He ought to leave her to her own devices.

Unfortunately, the piece of paper in his hand was vibrating with a woman's panic and terror, and Iona had been the last woman to handle it.

THIRTEEN

COLD, GRIMY, AND EXHAUSTED, IONA ARRIVED AT THE TRAIN STATION IN Edinburgh wishing she were wealthy enough to own a private traveling carriage. The journey from Northumberland's wilderness had involved a series of transfers from coach to train and from one line to another. She'd thought that an advantage when she'd gone to Wystan, believing no one would ever look so far from civilization.

She hadn't considered the disadvantage of *leaving* Wystan.

At the station, she made inquiries and set out in the direction indicated. She had coin enough for a room on the outskirts of the city—a long way from the castle she'd been living in. Six months of luxury and security had given her a burning desire to have that forever for Isobel as well as herself.

If marrying Awful Arthur would give her wealth, she could do it.

A neat row of townhouses revealed several Rooms For Let signs. Calling herself Nan Jones, claiming to be a teacher, she found a garret that would suffice.

Miserable, missing her bees, terrified for her twin, Iona wanted to go to Isobel immediately, but it was much too late in the day. She washed, changed her attire, and set out to find food.

While she was wandering unfamiliar streets, she spent a few precious coins on stationery. One did not address a queen or her cabinet with cheap note paper.

Along with bread and cheese, she bought cheap wine, walnuts, and salt. Back in her room, she began the laborious process of dying her distinctive golden-brown tresses to the deepest brown she could achieve. She would almost match Isobel, unless her sister had let hers wash out. If Isobel cut hers, there might be an advantage in playing each other as they had as children.

Accustomed to lonely nights, Iona still missed the company of Wystan's ladies. She ate her solitary meal, washed, dyed her hair, and let it dry while she drafted letters in her notebook. She would save her precious stationery for the final product. Writing a queen couldn't be done in a slapdash manner.

She hesitated even more over how to write Isobel. She didn't want her sister vanishing out of fear, but it had been nearly a week since that last letter had been posted.

Deciding final drafts would wait until morning, when she was less tired, Iona retired to her lumpy bed. Train whistles woke her through the night, and she nearly wept in frustration and fear. It had almost physically hurt to run away from the earl and his promises. She was no doubt better off leaving him behind before she came to rely on him too much.

In the morning, she boiled water for tea, toasted the last of her bread, and copied off the final letter to Queen Victoria. Then deciding she needed to see Isobel before making any further decisions, she wrote a reference letter for Nan Jones, master gardener, and signed it with the name of the Craigmore minister so Isobel would recognize her. Since she only intended Isobel to see the letter, Iona didn't worry about impressing anyone with proper paper.

In the wee dark hours, she'd dreamed of noble knights—in the form of the earl—riding to her rescue. But despite his kisses and lust, Ives was a busy man. Now that she was out of his demesne, he had no reason to care what she did.

She might long for a shining knight, but she and her sister were all they could count on. She posted the letter to the queen.

With regret, she cut off another pearl from her mother's wedding necklace. The countess had been justifiably proud of the exquisitely matched pearls, but she'd had the long chain cut in two to provide chokers for both her daughters for their one season.

And now they were using the heirloom to sustain their freedom. Iona had become inured to cutting up her mother's legacy, but a tear still crept down her cheek as she took money in exchange for precious memories.

Then she bought a train ticket to the Calder station. In Calder, she found a carter waiting to see if there were any guests for the castle. She climbed in with a load of building supplies heading that way.

Calder Castle wasn't as impressive as Wystan. It was an ancient stone fortress with crenellations, a Gothic exterior, and an incredibly large tower keep. The courtyard teemed with men carrying tools and building materials.

Hoping to avoid being seen by Lydia, the Malcolm Librarian, or Mr. Ives, her husband, Iona pulled her old-fashioned bonnet closer and aimed for the kitchen door in the rear. It helped that she and Isobel knew more about kitchens than ballrooms. Going in through the kitchen also meant her sudden appearance wouldn't startle Isobel—always a bad thing.

She handed the reference letter to the elderly butler to whom the scullery maid presented her. He carried it off into the depths of the house, leaving Iona twiddling her thumbs and wondering if she could afford a night in the village inn if Isobel were not here.

To her relief, her sister rushed in with no sign that her arrival had caught her by surprise. "Iona, thank the stars! I was so worried. Let us go to my room. The castle doesn't have a steward's cottage, but I have my very own lovely room."

"Don't you have an office?" Iona asked worriedly. "Won't people think it odd if you interview me in your chamber?"

Isobel huffed a sigh. "I hate this. Of course, you're right. My office is a cubbyhole full of moldering old bookkeeping journals. Let me take you out to the kitchen garden."

She pulled on a cloak and they walked into the cloudy, windy afternoon.

"I've written the queen," Iona said without preamble. "Mother always said we should if we needed help. I have asked her to grant one of us a letter patent."

"What good will a useless title do?" Isobel asked bitterly. "We can't go to London and vote that Mortimer be hanged."

"Aye right, the country has gone to the verra dogs since the Brits took over," Iona said in amusement. "All good Scotsmen should be allowed to hang thieves."

"Yes, quite. So I repeat, what will we accomplish?"

Iona took a deep breath. "If I can find someone to negotiate for us, I could marry the American swine and take a large settlement in return for his calling himself Lord Arthur. We could use the money to return to Craigmore. We'd put new locks on the doors and hire guards to heave Mortimer out. Or we could go to Canada. You could dress in silks and pearls and find a real husband. With money, we have choices."

"I'd rather muck pigs than wear silk," Isobel said. "You're the eldest. I suppose it's only proper for you to take the title. But oh, Iona—it would be such a lonely life! Can you lock out a husband as well?"

"That would be part of the settlement," Iona said grimly. "He could take his title and return to the Americas. Or parade about London, I don't care, as long as he stays away from us. We wouldn't be part of the agreement. I know you would make a better countess. You've always wanted to return Craigmore to our grandfather's glory, but you want a husband and children as well. I'd rather see the world. I don't think I'd mind living in sin should I ever find a man worth having."

Isobel grimaced. "Let's go back to that point about negotiating a settlement. How in all the world would we do that?"

"Therein lies the difficulty—we must choose whom to trust with our identities. At the moment, the only people who know both of us are the Librarians. The Earl of Ives and Wystan knows only mine."

As the train pulled into the Edinburgh station, Gerard set aside his newspaper and gathered up his hat and coat. Lowell had already gone in search of the baggage, proving his usefulness again. At least a valet didn't cost as much as a new roof.

"The Royal, sir?" Lowell asked, juggling both their valises.

"It's a place a wealthy American might stay if he wished to hobnob with princes, isn't it?" Gerard said in resignation. It would also put a pretty hole in his pocket.

"Indeed, sir, if they are not actually staying with princes," Lowell said in the dry manner Gerard was learning to appreciate.

In comparison to London's older, more grandiose hotels, this pragmatic Scots one lacked opulence, but the staff responded to aristocratic titles with the same alacrity. Gerard asked if Rainford happened to be staying there and was assured the clerk would let the marquess know of his arrival. He asked for a copy of DeBrett's to be sent up with his tea.

A plan ground in the back of his brain, but he needed to find the damned countess for her approval. The Roman soldier in his head grunted. Was the spirit psychic or simply disagreeable?

After he reached the suite he'd been assigned, Gerard sent off several notes to family and acquaintances. The DeBrett's list of the aristocracy merely confirmed what he already knew. He didn't want to reveal anything that wasn't available to all.

He paced the chamber impatiently until a servant knocked with a reply from Rainford. Lowell made an attempt to protest that he hadn't dusted off his travel dirt, but Gerard didn't have time for niceties. He had to find Iona, and he needed to set his half-baked plan in motion before he set out.

Dressed in impeccable gray evening attire, Rainford raised a quizzical brow at Gerard's travel clothes but unquestioningly followed him to the hotel's spacious tavern. Dark-panels, dim lights, linen tablecloths all spoke of a sophistication not to be found in a normal pub. It looked like just the place to find a wealthy American and bad food.

Gerard studied the company as they entered and chose a table visible to the other occupants but far enough away not to be overheard.

"You have news about the missing heiresses?" Rainford asked.

"Have you even checked your DeBrett?" Gerard asked. "Craigmore isn't the earl, and he isn't their father. I am not catching those women for his sake."

"Not even for the reward?" the marquess asked cynically.

"My family would hunt me to ground and torment me until death if I turned those women over to a man they've had reason to run away from. The question becomes, why did they run away and how can we assure their safety?" Gerard surreptitiously studied the tavern's patrons as he sipped the whisky they'd ordered.

"I've made my own inquiries," Rainford admitted. "Craigmore, or whoever he is, is in debt well over his head. He doesn't have money for a reward. Half the fellows who followed me up here have gone home after we discovered that."

While pretending intense interest in this conversation, Gerard spotted the surreptitious glances sent their way. Aristocracy was easily recognized when they set out to do it, as he had. People were predictable. He watched with cynicism as word spread around the tavern and heads swiveled in their direction.

"Dullards. Two marriageable aristocrats with the potential of titles and probably access to the queen. . . who would want women like that?" Except like Gerard, Rainford's friends needed *heiresses*.

The marquess glanced in the direction of Gerard's interest. "Any of those crass fellows might want a penniless aristocrat, I would guess? We're rare breeds, and the uninitiated think peers have access to wealth and power untold. So my answer is—a wealthy Cit."

"No one uses that term anymore," Gerard said with a laugh. "Everyone is a merchant, but I'd add a *wealthy American*. Any of those around that you've noticed?"

"You know something, don't you?" Rainford narrowed his eyes and waited.

"I do, but it's not my information to impart. You can work it out without me saying more. So our problem is two-fold—finding the women and cutting off their stepfather's access to them. Can you find out more about Mortimer? He's the man posing as the Earl of Craigmore."

"I've already located him. He's living above a gambling house over in Old Town." Rainford nodded his blond head toward a table of well-dressed gentlemen. "Coincidentally, the stout American over there in the plum waistcoat has been seen regularly at the tables in the same house."

Gerard sat back and smiled in satisfaction. "I'll set Lowell on the trail. The servants are far better at this than we are."

"I suspect the Cits are working up their courage to approach." Rainford threw back his whisky and rose from his chair. "Don't find the girls too soon. I'm enjoying this."

Before any of the gentlemen at the other table could reach him, Gerard rose, put on his hat, and walked out—giving them the cut direct as his father would have said. Some days, it almost paid to be a titled lord—if only it paid in cash.

Back in his suite, he had telegrams and messages waiting. Sorting through them in satisfaction, Gerard realized Rainford was right. This was almost fun—if he weren't so stupidly worried about an independent female who couldn't wait for his help.

If it weren't for the fear and panic he'd sensed on her map, he'd say to hell with her and head back to London to see if he could raise funds there.

Now was a bad time to develop new eccentricities.

Satisfied that his local relations were apprised of his arrival and working on the situation, Gerard grudgingly took a bath using the hotel's inadequate resources, ate his supper, and ordered Lowell not to unpack.

The train to Calder left in the morning.

Lowell gazed upon the stone edifice Gerard's cousin Max euphemistically called Calder Castle. "You left a luxury hotel to stay in a medieval fortress? Will we have to boil our water?"

Gerard chuckled. "You have much to learn about my family. I can assure you these accommodations are vastly preferential. The only downside is that they contain family."

Lowell snorted in appreciation and shut up.

"I need to do some reconnaissance. Tell anyone who asks that I'm stretching my legs and will be in shortly." Leaving Lowell and their mounts at the stable, Gerard strolled through the busy courtyard toward the back of the castle.

Max had showed him all around the last time he'd been here. The castle sat at the top of a high hill. The front overlooked a steep bluff. The back was where the fields started. They had no orchard, but there were stone fences that might protect hives.

Of course, his chance of finding Iona was slim and catching her by surprise almost none. He simply followed the idiot voice chanting *Treasure* in his head that drew him down an uncultivated lane behind the wall. Far down the hill, a stand of head-high bushes provided a nice windbreak—

And there she was, murmuring to the hives as she wound binding around the straw hackles to protect the bees through the winter. She wore the familiar short gown over trousers and boots, but she'd let her bonnet and veil down in the noon sun.

He winced at the dark brown she'd dyed her hair, but he was too exultant at finding her to complain.

Before he could come within shouting distance, she slipped into the bushes and vanished—as if the bees had warned her of a stranger. Cursing, Gerard shouted anyway, but the wind carried off his calls. Even if she heard him, she'd probably run. She had no reason to know who approached.

At least he knew she was here and safe, he grumbled as he trudged back to the castle. That should be enough.

It wasn't. Memories of a heated kiss, tears of despair, and courageous vows—and fear—rubbed at his formerly distant soul.

Max Ives met him as he reached the courtyard. A giant of a man, Max swatted Gerard on the back in an attempt to make him stumble. Familiar with his cousin's tactics, Gerard side-stepped and punched a massive bicep.

"Good to see you, too," he said dryly. "How is family life treating you?"

"Better than my vagabond days," Max crowed, gesturing at the yard full of workmen. "Who knew I could stay home and still engineer?"

"Wealth has some privileges," Gerard said, following his host inside. "Has your bride located the missing heiresses yet?"

"And do you think Lydia would tell me if she had? Until the runaways are ready to make themselves known, we can only hope they're safe." Max led the way to a dark room of heavy furniture that he'd claimed for entertaining his male guests.

Currently assured that Iona was safe, Gerard examined his surroundings. "I like what you've done with the place. The building blocks on the billiard table are particularly unique."

He strolled over to the table of artifacts Max had dug out of the sewers and dungeons beneath the tower. Poking around in pot shards, coins, and utensils he couldn't identify, Gerard didn't find one that called to him as the medallion had.

Max grinned and circled his handiwork on the table. "It's a model of the keep. I want to shore it up so it won't lean again. Lydia can't picture what I mean to do unless I show her."

And since Max could barely read, he liked working with his hands. Gerard didn't feel quite so uncomfortable with his own peculiarities when he was with someone who understood. That didn't mean he had any intention of mentioning voices in his head.

One of these days he might explode with all the secrets he hid. "When you run out of projects here, you can probably hire yourself out to repair all our crumbling edifices. You'll never need to leave for foreign shores again. Will you miss the travel?"

Max poured a finger of Scotch and handed it over. "Ask me again after the babe arrives. So what mysterious errand brings you up here? Do you think we hide heiresses in our cavernous and empty rooms?"

Gerard disliked lying, but until he had Iona's permission to tell her tale, he had to fudge the truth. "I sacked my estate agent. The women want me to hire a female steward like yours. I'd like your opinion of how she handles the workers, and I'd like to talk with her."

"Nope, you can't have Bell. Lydia swears by her." Max circled his building blocks, poking at them here and there.

"I already have someone in mind, so no, I'm not stealing her. I just need some idea of how she manages the laborers. Did I meet her when I was up here for the wedding?" Now that he thought about it, he had some recollection of a small, dark female being introduced as the new steward. He hadn't thought anything of it at the time. Calder Castle wasn't a working estate. It had a few tenant farmers, and the steward mostly handled rents and maintenance. An accountant could do it.

"Most likely. Bell came to us just before the wedding." Max stopped sipping and narrowed his eyes. "The ladies at the school sent her. You think she's one of the heiresses? I'm not letting you have her for the reward."

"The so-called earl can't afford a reward. They're being hunted. Keep your steward safe, and she's all yours—or Lydia's. I would simply like to speak with her." Gerard knew his family was quick. He hadn't had to reveal a thing.

Max raised his eyebrows, pulled a bell rope, and sent a servant in search of his new steward.

A short while later, a drab female in vaguely fashionable dark skirt and white bodice appeared in the doorway. "You have a question, sir?"

Gerard's pulse escalated, and he bit back a grin of satisfaction.

"Bell, Lord Ives would like to ask you how a female steward handles obstinate laborers."

At this idiocy, Gerard threw his host an incredulous look. "You don't even know your own steward? That's not Bell, that's her sister."

FOURTEEN

Iona bit back a laugh at the earl's reaction and curtsied. "Most people can't tell us apart, my lord. I daresay only our mother knew. What gave me away?"

"Your imperious air," Lord Ives said grumpily, leaning against the mantel and swinging his whisky glass. "I've only met your sister once. She's either a very good actress or she's a much mousier version of you."

Iona was almost giddy with relief that he had actually come looking for her. She'd never had anyone other than Bell and her mother who she might hope to depend on. Despite the earl's unhappy demeanor, she could smell his relief. "I told you Bell is the quiet one. That doesn't mean she's mousy, by any means."

She turned to Bell's employer, who leaned against the billiard table and didn't seem particularly happy to discover a cuckoo in his nest. "I apologize, sir. I have not tried to play Bell since we were children. I merely wanted to protect her from strangers."

Mollified, Mr. Ives nodded. "Lydia knows you're here?"

"She doesn't, actually. There didn't seem to be any reason to disturb the Librarian."

Looking particularly striking in his tweed country clothes, the earl narrowed his midnight eyes. "Do the pair of you trust no one?"

Iona glared back. "Not if there's any chance others will be harmed. My stepfather is a desperate man."

"And you think it's safer here than Wystan?" he demanded, as if insulted—as if it mattered to him.

She desperately wanted her safety to matter to him, but his pride was probably more affected. She responded with tartness, enforcing her distance. "No. We needed time together to plan our next move. If you're truly interested in helping, we can proceed with our plans. Is there any way to determine if Mr. Winter has the funds to pay the reward? I dislike relying on rumor and braggadocio."

Surprisingly, Maxwell Ives replied. "My man of business is on his honeymoon, but I've had one of his associates look into the reward situation. With a little persuasion, Craigmore has placed the ten thousand pounds into a bank account, with an Arthur Winter as the signee. If the gentleman really is Winter, he's worth several fortunes."

As if she'd been summoned, Lydia strolled into the room, looking stern. "No one interrogates my staff except me." She turned to Iona. "Are you Isobel or Iona?"

"Iona." She curtsied. The Librarian was an extremely perceptive soul.

"And she's interrogating *us*," the earl said in disgust. "May we all sit now? I have a feeling I'll not like anything she says."

"I've sent for tea. I needed a break anyway. Iona, have a seat. I'm glad to see you've finally come to your senses and are ready to ask for help."

Lydia took a seat on one of the leather chairs and put her feet up on an ottoman. "I'm not inclined to ladylike grace," she told Gerard, unapologetically.

"You are far more gracious than most of the females in my family," he replied, still sounding irritable.

Iona gathered from his glare that she was included in that company, although if she were part of his family, the relationship dated back to the medieval era.

"I've never seen our lordly Ives express anything except cool composure," Max said with a laugh. "I think you're crawling under his skin, my lady."

Iona hoped she disturbed Ives as much as he disturbed her, but irritableness was not the reaction she preferred. She took a chair some

distance from where the earl leaned against the mantel with unconscious, virile, grace, even in his country attire.

"Bell and I did not think we needed help when we set out," she said
primly. "We meant only to wait until Mr. Winter went away. We did not
count on his determination to buy what he can't have."

She gritted her teeth when the earl unfolded himself from the mantel
to pull up a chair beside her. His masculine scent drew her like a bee to
lavender. She sensibly looked toward Lydia and not the man at her side.

"You are of age," the Librarian insisted. "Your stepfather cannot force
you to marry against your will."

"But he can make our lives even more miserable than they already
are. We thought it might be more agreeable to make our own way for a
while. I do not miss Craigmore in the least. If I didn't fear for Bell's
safety, I would have stayed in Wystan."

"So now that you know we won't turn you in for the reward, you'll
go back?" Ives asked, not sounding in the least hopeful.

"No, now that I've had a taste of freedom, I mean to keep it." And
she meant it. She was tired of dodging and hiding. "Short of killing
Mortimer, freedom means I need money—enough to dower Bell and to
pay Mortimer to stay away. To that end, I've written the queen for my
letters patent. I shall sell my title to the highest bidder, with the understanding that the marriage is in name only."

Bell had been the one to come up with the *highest bidder* notion. She
was quite good with money. Iona sat back and waited for the explosion.

Instead, the men sat there and glowered, and Lydia pursed her lips in
thought.

"An interesting solution, certainly," the Librarian said as a tea tray
was carried in. "Are annulments still allowed?"

Iona's lips quirked. "I like the way you think, but any man stupid
enough not to include a clause to that effect deserves to be robbed. No, I
mean to do this honestly. I'm not a love and marriage sort."

Although she was most definitely interested in certain aspects of the
wedded state—just not with a boring toad like Arthur Winter.

"Honest but mercenary," Maxwell Ives muttered. "What if I just give
you ten thousand pounds?"

That shocked her, and it took a moment before she could recover and shake her head. "That's very generous, but I recommend loaning Lord Ives the sum he needs to repair his roof. I intend to demand a larger settlement than that, plus a monthly stipend. I will not sell myself cheaply."

"That almost guarantees Winter will win," the earl pointed out. "No one else is insane enough to want a worthless title or stupid enough to believe he'll buy an earldom."

"Unfortunately true," Iona agreed with a shrug. "But if I say we must advertise in America and Europe before deciding, I can hope he'll agree to almost anything for a pre-emptive bid."

Silently, the earl reached for his whisky instead of the tea.

AFTER A DINNER IN WHICH GERARD COULD EASILY DISCERN IONA AS THE leader of the sisters, he was forced to admit that claiming her title was a good move. It was the rest of the plan that irked him beyond measure.

But after he and Max shared a drink, made a few plans, and returned to join the ladies, they discovered the twins had vanished again. Lydia swore the queen bee hadn't flown the hive, but Gerard didn't trust the deceptive little witch. Fingering the chuckling medallion in his pocket, he climbed to the parapets, following the soldier's instincts for locating treasure.

Treasure, indeed. If Iona Ross was the soldier's idea of treasure, he'd fling the medallion into the ocean on his way to Italy.

He found her communing with the clouds and wind, leaning into the parapet with her cloak flying around her. "You'll need a broom to fly," he said, trying not to startle her as he approached.

She huffed a laugh. "Only another Malcolm is allowed to say that to me. Do you have a gift?"

He wasn't about to open his veins and bleed. "The family is eccentric enough without the heir claiming psychic ability. If you're not planning on flying, what the devil are you doing out here in the cold?"

"Psychic? From the Greek?" She turned, leaning on the wall—which might give way at any minute—and let the wind blow the hood back from her pixie curls.

"My cousin Phoebe came up with the word. Don't blame me. Could you stand over here where I won't fear you'll fly into the night or turn into an icicle?" Gerard indicated the more solid wall enclosing the stairs, where he stood.

"This isn't cold," she scoffed, but she obligingly stepped into the lee of the wall. "It's just a brisk breeze reminding me of home. Craigmore's bluffs overlook the Moray Firth. You Southerners are thin-skinned."

"In more ways than one. We're more inclined to shelter our ladies and children than turn them into Highland warriors. You almost gave me heart failure when I returned to find you gone." He hadn't meant to admit that, but the damned female was so slight and fragile that he honestly feared she'd blow away.

Which was sheer idiocy, he admitted. He'd seen her right the hive and manage the hackles and haul buckets of honey. He had no doubt that she'd sheared sheep and dragged them out of sinkholes as well. She was supposed to be a damned *countess* and sit on tuffets!

She turned her heart-shaped face up so he could almost see the curve of her lips in the dark. "No one has ever cared if I came or went. I seldom give it any thought. I do what needs to be done, knowing Isobel understands and can find me right enough. I'm a little in awe that you bothered."

"Bothered?" Gerard thought his blood might boil. He blocked the wind with his back and placed a hand on either side of her head. She merely tilted her head up expectantly. "I'd like to show you *bothered*."

Surrendering his practiced indifference, he placed his mouth firmly over hers. She didn't even jerk with surprise but encircled his neck with one slender hand and pulled him closer. *Bothered* didn't even come close to his reaction.

He swore she smelled of heather and roses and tasted sweeter than her honey. He consumed her mouth as if she were the honey cakes he loved. Her tongue entwined with his. He didn't know if she understood the tantalizing offer she extended. Her hand ran up into his hair, and he couldn't resist touching her in return. He tried just smoothing her hair, twisting the curls in his fingers while his lips sampled and slaked his thirst. But it wasn't enough. When she raised herself closer, he cupped her breast.

The brazen woman wore no corset under the dowdy gown she'd worn to dinner. She moaned when he caressed her through layers of fabric, and his cock came to instant attention.

She was a Malcolm, he told himself, trying to force himself away.

But a Malcolm beekeeper was of no danger to him, his other half argued.

She was a virgin countess— That kicked some sense into his brain. Virgins meant marriage.

But Iona ran her slender hand beneath his coat, and Gerard couldn't release her if his life depended on it. It *might* depend on it. Her touch raced his blood and kept his cold heart beating.

He cupped her bottom and lifted her into his arousal while their tongues battled. She moaned again and wrinkled his waistcoat by clutching it with both fists. When she balanced her precarious position by raising a leg to wrap around him, he almost spent his seed right there.

It had been far too long since he'd sent away his mistress.

He pushed his hips into her so she couldn't fail to notice his arousal, then regretfully pulled away, setting her back on the solid roof again.

"I want you," he said with certainty. "But there is no future for you in what I want."

"And none for you," she retorted, pushing further away and running her hand into the hair he'd so thoroughly mussed. "But I wanted a taste of what I'll be denying myself. I understand now why wives might entertain lovers."

"Especially if their husbands are obnoxious mushrooms." Gerard straightened his waistcoat as best as he could, but there was no reducing his arousal despite her crude assessment. "That's what comes of marrying for titles and wealth."

She shrugged and drew her cloak closer, gazing past his shoulders to the scuttling clouds. "My mother married for love. He died and left her in poor health, with two young children, and an estate she couldn't manage on her own. Wealth and freedom seem eminently more practical to me."

That removed some of his starch. Working to regain his normal veneer, he leaned his shoulders against the wall beside her and let the cold wind take care of the rest. "My parents married for love. My father is an irascible curmudgeon, but my mother mysteriously adores him. And he worships her, even after all these years. I'd like to have that someday."

"Well, you will someday have wealth, title, and freedom, so maybe you can. It's different for a woman. We're tied to the man we marry, for better or worse. I'm not impractical enough to throw away what little I possess in return for something as fleeting as love—or even lust."

Gerard snorted. "What little wealth I may ever have goes to support a large and demanding family and a plethora of servants and estates. The title encompasses so many responsibilities that once I inherit, I doubt I'll ever have the opportunity to travel again. So I'm not seeing freedom in my future. I'm not entirely certain *freedom* in your sense of the word is even possible, unless you own nothing and care for nothing."

Which was what she'd gain if she married Arthur Winter, he realized.

"You will someday be able to travel, even if it is for only a few months at a time. I will be tied to the cold shores of a barren estate for the rest of my life unless I marry wealth. Freedom comes in different sizes and shapes. I'll trade the prison of my life for caring for nothing, thank you," she said, confirming his thoughts. "Will you help me gain my freedom?" she asked, turning her head as if she could study him in the darkness.

"Will you let me try it my way first?" he retorted, glaring down at her, unable to remain dispassionate with this wretched female. "Can you admit that I may have a little more experience in the ways of society than you do?"

He could only see the white outline of her face beneath the dark cap of hair, so he couldn't read her expression. She stood still for a moment— and he realized that stillness was an unnatural state for her. She should be humming and flitting about like one of her subjects.

"Only if you take me with you and explain to me what you plan as you go."

"Take you into gambling hells or worse? You don't know what you ask."

"I do and I will," she vowed, as if they were in a church. "And if you don't take me, then I'll find someone who can."

He was damned if he did and damned if he didn't.

FIFTEEN

"His lordship is furious with you," Bell whispered the next morning as she tidied the bow on Iona's small straw cap. "Are you sure you wish to go with him?"

"Nonsense. Lord Ives doesn't care what I do one way or another. He is simply unhappy at being thwarted. Men are frequently like that. He'll come around." Iona straightened the frock Bell had loaned her. Had she Bell's salary, she'd have purchased bright red to go with her ugly chestnut hair dye. But Bell was trying to blend in with the woodwork by wearing browns and tans. Even the bustle was small and unassuming. Still, it was more fashionable than any Iona owned.

Deciding whether she wished to be Nan or Iona matched her confusion over wanting to both strip off the folds of coffee-colored lace to uncover the revealing neckline and wishing to don a heavy shawl to conceal the form-fitting bodice. She still didn't really know who she was.

Kissing Lord Ives last night had not helped her confusion. May the good Lord in heaven help her, but she had *wanted* the man last night. She'd wanted all the sensations his experienced lips had promised. She'd wanted to know the meaning of the pressure between her legs. By all that was holy, she'd wanted to lift skirts and petticoats and learn the animal act they'd simulated.

And she wasn't entirely certain she wouldn't encourage him to show her.

She hadn't felt this heady with excitement when she and Bell had plotted their escape.

"Lord Ives doesn't strike me as a man who can be wrapped around your little finger," Bell warned. "You may make country lads dance to your tune, but he is no green lad."

Iona beamed at her reflection in her sister's mirror. "I am in no danger wrapped to the ears in your bland flounces and frills. I look like a dowdy spinster in this. Really, Bell, you need to add a little color to your life. You should have seen the gowns in Rainford's ballroom! It was like watching a dancing rose garden with bare shoulders. The earl is accustomed to ladies who flirt their wares. He'll not know I exist."

Bell smacked Iona's hand without anger. "That is my very best Sunday dress you disparage. I should send you off in my official uniform. If you are to entice Mr. Winter into marriage, you'll need to look more like a countess. You'll have to sell more pearls."

Iona hugged her sister. "I'm sorry. I know you're worried. But don't you see? Nothing I do can be much worse than returning to Mortimer's destruction. Look at this as an adventure. If I fail, we know we can find shelter with the Malcolm ladies. If I succeed, you can have the estate, and I can have my freedom. It's worth the gamble."

Bell hugged her back. "I know. But I so much wanted us to be like normal ladies, with friends and family and someone to love and children romping about our feet. That's silly, I know."

It was especially silly for Bell, who had been known to fall senseless when anything from sheep to men caught her by surprise. There was a reason she was the quiet twin. She would never know *normal*.

"It's not silly. We will arrange it," Iona insisted. "Keep studying Lydia's library, learn more about your condition, and I'll be back before you know it." Iona kissed her twin's cheek and hurried down the stairs. The train left Calder station early.

Lord Ives impatiently stalked the foyer while his man ordered his bags carried out to the cart. The earl was wearing a tailored, shoulder-hugging, collarless coat of a dark blue that matched his eyes. He slapped on his top hat and glared at her as if it were all her fault that he wasn't on the train yet.

Since he was always diplomatically polite to everyone else, she was apparently the only one gifted with his glares and impatience. She smiled pertly up at him, then adjusted her straw hat, using the mirror for that purpose. "You can pretend not to know me, you know. No one will notice one more stray Malcolm leaving her family's journals at the library."

"And I'm to have you riding in the cattle car with the servants, right." He strode out, not offering his arm, as if she were, indeed, a servant.

She had fully expected to ride in the cheap seats, as she had on the way up. "I can buy my own ticket," she reminded him, following him out to the cart the castle provided for transportation until a better road was built.

"With what, your honey? And I wouldn't put it past you to vanish again." He assisted her into the cart seat, then climbed in beside her. "Keep in mind that I'm only in this for the reward. If you want to do this, then you had best work with me."

Iona pondered that ultimatum until they'd reached the village and disembarked where the driver couldn't hear them. "I think you may have turned that around a little. If you wish to claim your reward, you must work for *me*."

As his valet arranged their tickets and baggage, the earl lifted a rather pointed eyebrow with incredulity. "And precisely how were you planning on arranging negotiations without me?"

She shrugged. "Apply to the School of Malcolm ladies and ask for a solicitor who might be trusted. And I *can* tell if he's trustworthy, you realize."

She could tell he wasn't pleased, but he couldn't argue with her ability. That was a new experience—a man who didn't think she was helpless or crazy. *And* he was a good kisser. A pity he would run away as soon as he had the money to repair Wystan.

He assisted her into the first-class train car. "Fine," he grumbled once they were settled in a private compartment. "Let us compare plans. Yours seems to still involve marrying the purple-vested mushroom, correct?"

"Purple-vested mushroom?" she asked in amusement, basking in this private, luxurious environment, bouncing a little on the cushioned seat. "I see you have met Arthur."

"I have avoided meeting him. I had to be assured I could find you before proceeding. You are avoiding my question." He sat across from her and set his tall hat on the seat.

"I told you, I am an honest person. If I negotiate a marriage settlement, of course I will marry him," she said primly, although everything in her soul rebelled at the notion. "What did you have in mind?"

"Verifying he actually has the funds. Testing his integrity in carrying out any settlement. Writing a contract that includes a forfeiture leaving you a generous sum if he defaults on any morals clause I include. Then seeing that he defaults."

Seeing that Winter defaulted on a morals clause? She'd never heard of such a thing. "I'm impressed," she admitted. "You think Mr. Winter is that desperate for a title?"

"I have no idea if he beats women or drinks like a fish. I've not had time to learn, have I? My first duty, of course, will be to impress on him that Mortimer has utterly no power over you, that you are entirely independent, and the choice is all yours."

"Good luck with that," she said scornfully. "In what world do men accept that women are not chattel?"

"Scotland is a little more forward-thinking than most places. Mortimer is simply a feudal throwback. I've arranged for you to stay with some of my family, Viscount Dare and his wife. They're both Malcolms, so you'll like them." He slumped in the seat, crossed his arms, and closed his eyes as if to sleep.

"Mortimer is slime with spies over half the country. They will report my presence the instant I move in. So quit looking smug. You don't know my stepfather the way I do. You'll need my help."

He scowled but didn't open his eyes. "I'll shove you in a trunk and ship you."

She grinned. "You want to kiss me again and don't dare."

"Perfectly correct. Now shut up and let me plot."

That thrilled her more than she'd admit. She settled back and continued building the barrier she needed to continue dealing with this man. "You can't plot without me. I shall get off the train where I got on. I will check for mail at my rooming house, although I don't expect any yet. I will pack a valise. If your servant stops off with me, he may carry the valise to whatever destination pleases you. I will then make my way there on my own, when I am ready."

"This is not the north country," he protested, sitting up and glaring. "A young lady does not traipse about the city alone."

"Then I shall arrange to be a man."

GRITTING HIS TEETH, GERARD WATCHED AS LOWELL AND THE COUNTESS climbed off the train in a particularly non-descript area outside Edinburgh. He didn't know the city well enough to hope she'd found a decent residence in these dismal environs.

Arrange to be a man, indeed! Remembering last night's kisses, the way she'd felt like heaven in his arms, and her wayward response when he'd pressed his attentions—

Made him hard all over again. Dammit it all to hell and back—she was a *virgin*. He didn't touch virgins, though he might risk it for one who was wealthy. He should find a wealthy, non-Malcolm virgin and see if she kissed like the countess.

She wouldn't, of course. He'd had far more experienced women at his beck and call and none had tasted like Iona. He could almost understand why animals would risk the wrath of a thousand bees to sip honey like that.

He wasn't in any humor for pacifying his cousins when he arrived at the station without their guest.

"Did you lose her, Ives?" Lady Phoebe demanded. Tall, with masses of unruly chestnut hair, she'd actually dressed like a lady instead of a hooligan for the occasion.

"I'm sure there's a good explanation." Azmin, Lady Dare, reassuringly patted Phoebe's arm. Half Hindu, she preferred the loose, colorful silks of her home, but today, she too had dressed as an English lady to meet their unknown cousin.

"The explanation is that the lady trusts no one and has chosen to arrive on her own." Gerard picked up his own bags since Lowell wasn't there. "I have left my valet to guide her but cannot tell you more."

He stomped down the platform with the women trailing after him.

"Zane says you are welcome to stay with us as well as the countess," Azmin said cheerfully. "Phoebe's house is smaller and filled with animals and guests. Our enormous house is positively empty with everyone scattered. It should be more private than a hotel."

His prey could be found at the hotel. Privacy with a countess who kissed like a courtesan probably wasn't the wisest idea. But a private residence would save him coins.

What were the chances he'd win the reward and have enough to pay a hotel bill?

About equal to the chances that he could resist temptation.

"I'll be along later," he agreed, against his better judgment. "I'm grateful for the hospitality but have a few people I need to see first."

"We're not interested in *you* anyway," Phoebe said cheerfully. "We're here to meet our new cousin."

The women walked off, laughing. Thankfully, their driver was willing to take Gerard's bags so he needn't lug them to the hotel.

Lowell had spoiled him already.

At the Royal, Gerard sent a message to Rainford, then settled in a chair behind a newspaper to watch the lobby. One could tell a great deal about who was in town watching a place like this.

The Marquess of Rainford was dubbed the Ice King for good reason. With his pale hair, lack of bushy facial hair, and appearing sharper than a knife blade in one of his immaculate gray suits, Rainford entered the tavern.

Acting appropriately noble, they repeated their earlier performance, strolling into the tavern as if they were kings and taking a private table. Winter and his companions weren't there yet to notice this performance, but Gerard relied on gossip.

A barmaid hurried over to take their order and to whisper, "They talked of visiting the Old Rooster tonight. The earl won a few pounds on the horses today, and he's promised to introduce your lordship to Mr. Winter."

Rainford slipped her folding money. "Excellent job, Ruby. Warn us if they head our way."

"You play this game too well," Gerard noted. "I expect you now know who owes what to whom by now."

"Pretty much," Rainford admitted. "The American is almost as bad at gambling as Craigmore, but Winter pays his debts. Craigmore doesn't—because he makes promises like introducing me to an encroaching mushroom I have no intention of meeting."

Gerard snickered at his friend's word choice but stayed on topic. "Is there some danger Winter will frivol away his fortune? The lady should be made aware of that."

The marquess eyed him skeptically. "You found her? She agrees to this charade?"

"Of course I found her. Keeping her in sight is the difficulty. She went haring off the instant she hit town. But yes, this is her idea," Gerard admitted irritably. "Never tell her anything is impossible, or she'll do her best to prove you wrong."

Rainford sat back, stretching his lanky frame and grinning. "The imperturbable earl has been perturbed—by a woman. I must meet this formidable lass."

"She imagines herself a master of disguise and is likely to turn up in trousers," Gerard warned, irritated at his irritation. He'd worked hard to earn his implacable reputation.

The idiot medallion in his pocket chortled.

"You haven't answered my question about the American." Gerard shut out the chortles.

Rainford sipped the whisky the maid delivered. "It's hard to answer. He's not precisely a wastrel. And my sources say his income is enormous. But he's not paying attention to his investments. Any downturn—"

Gerard grimaced. "Not what I want to hear. I'll start dictating the settlement terms to my father's solicitor, but we need to look for all possible alternatives. She's counting on a monthly allowance to repair what Craigmore has damaged. If Winter's fortune slips—"

"—she can't marry another and she loses. Understood. What about the other sister?"

"She's a Malcolm who wishes to hide in the country. There is almost certainly something wrong with her, but I've not gained their confidence. She said almost nothing over dinner, and Lady Iona was protective of her."

"I'd like to meet them once this is over."

Since the marquess came from a long line of Malcolm healers, Gerard assumed his interest was medical—not useful for Malcolm maladies. But if it served to distract his friend from the ducal duties looming, Gerard wouldn't quibble.

"I've asked my cousin Phoebe if her country, card-sharp cousin might help us if we arrange a respectable soiree. That may be our last resort though. Do we head over to the Rooster this evening?"

"I'll send over a couple of the men still intrigued by the reward. One is a viscount. That should raise Winter's hopes that he's being noticed. Let's learn how good he is at cards first." The marquess finished off his whisky just as Winter entered the tavern.

The American was still wearing a purple waistcoat over his paunch, although this one appeared to be heavily embroidered in gold, presumably to match his golden-brown tweed coat, which he wore unbuttoned. He scanned the room and found Gerard and Rainford immediately.

"Time to go." Gerard returned his hat to his head. "I'll be at Dare's. Let me know if you need me."

"Playing hard to get is losing its interest." Rainford left coins on the table. "I want to settle this soon."

"A few more days," Gerard promised as they brushed past Winter and his entourage without acknowledging them. "They'll be chomping at the bit."

As they entered the lobby, the street doors opened to admit a slouching, slender man with receding dark hair. In a hazardous degree of impairment but dressed as a gentleman, he handed his hat and gloves to the doorman, who evidently recognized him.

"Uh oh," Rainford murmured. "That's Craigmore."

The faux earl saw them before they could retreat to the stairs. "Rainford, well met! I may have a witness who knows where my daughters are, if your men are still interested in that reward."

Behind him stood a short, robust lad wearing spectacles, a loose wool jacket several years out of date, and a trilby—over familiar dark curls.

SIXTEEN

"Baron Twaddle von Kitsch," her stepfather drunkenly shouted, obliviously introducing Iona to the earl and his companion. "Student at the university. The baron says he has met the naughty pair."

Hiding behind her spectacles, Iona bit back laughter and insouciantly swung her cane as she watched the reaction of the men in the lobby. Lord Ives looked as if he'd like to bite her head off. He'd recognized her instantly.

She assumed the icy-blond gentleman with him was the marquess. He just appeared bemused, as he should be if he knew German.

"Good of you, Craigmore," the marquess said noncommittally. "Should you not follow up the lad's suggestion and save yourself the reward money?"

"They're on their way to Newcastle!" Mortimer cried. "I'm too old to catch up with them. Your lot are better equipped to follow."

In other words, the reward money wasn't his to save, and he lacked the coin to buy a ticket to Newcastle. Iona had anticipated that.

"I'll handle this, Rainford," Lord Ives said, shoving his way past Mortimer to get at Iona, a furious gleam in his eye. "I'll take the baron to the tavern so he can explain what he knows to our friends."

He had his hand around her elbow and was practically dragging Iona toward the door. Since she was eager to escape, she allowed it.

"Excellent, thanks, Ives. Tell Drummond I'll finance his journey if he leaves tonight." Rainford tipped his hat and escaped up the stairs.

"Wait a minute—" Mortimer cried as earl and marquess parted ways in different directions. "I want you to meet—"

Before her stepfather could say what he wanted, Gerard all but carried Iona out the door to the street, avoiding being introduced to the American, she assumed.

"I swear, I should leave you to the purple-vested pig," he grumbled, dragging her down the busy thoroughfare. "Your mother didn't spank you often enough."

"She never spanked us. Our talents often came in useful. You're the only one who sees through me. How could you know it was me behind these wretched pillows?"

"Only a blind man would be deceived!" he shouted. "Baron Twaddle, indeed. Mortimer is a complete and utter fool."

"Well, yes, on this we can agree. That's why I did it. I couldn't resist when we ran into him on the street. By the way, whatever you're paying your valet, it's not enough. This really is a better disguise than I could have created. And we found it all at the second-hand market."

"I'll sack Lowell for this," the earl muttered, signaling for a hansom. "Then I'll kill him. Even university students have whiskers."

"Not necessarily." She rubbed her smooth cheeks. "And if you sack Lowell, I will hire him. Where are we going?"

"You don't have tuppence to hire him. We're going to Dare's. Where did you stash Lowell and your baggage?"

"He's right behind us, acting as a proper guardian. I do believe he carries a pistol." Iona refused to climb into the carriage until the servant caught up.

"You are not redeemed," the earl said coldly to his valet. "Guarding her should mean keeping her out of trouble." He swung into the hansom and took the seat beside her.

The gray-haired valet implacably handed up Iona's parcels. "If you will give me direction, my lord, I will meet you there."

"Nonsense, Lowell. If the earl will quit sprawling in the seat, we can squeeze you in. I'm sure it's just a short distance, and I cannot hold all these packages myself." Iona elbowed his lordship.

The earl scowled and handed his servant coins. "You carry the rest of her loot. We're heading for Viscount Dare's on George Square."

It was Iona's turn to scowl. "You should not be so mean. Lowell showed me the most marvelous market where I could buy pretty gowns so cheaply I needn't sell more pearls! He's a gem among men."

"Pearls? You have pearls to sell?" His lordship looked as if his head might blow off. "Are you receiving anywhere near a fair price for them?"

"Of course. I asked around first. The pearls are precious to me, and I do not part with them easily." Iona settled back on the cushions, adjusting the uncomfortable trousers over the pillow padding as the horse trotted down the street.

The earl rubbed a tic in his jaw. "I suppose you are selling family heirlooms everywhere you go. And you don't think Mortimer will recognize them?"

"If he knew we had them, he would have sold them himself. Besides, he doesn't even recognize *me*. Didn't I just prove that? He's a blind drunkard who spends so much time thinking of himself that he has no time for anyone else. If I walked in wearing a gown and in accompaniment with you or another Malcolm, he might look twice, if only to see what advantage he could take. Therein lies the danger of being seen with any of you." She sat back against the cushion and fiddled with the string on her package.

She could scarcely breathe with his lordship filling up all the space with his sprawling, masculine presence. She had not realized hansoms were so very small. Or perhaps she had thought herself small when she'd last been in one and had learned a better sense of herself since.

"Give me a list of places where you sold your pearls," he said wearily. "When I have the reward, I'll buy them back for you."

"When I have the settlement, I can buy them back myself," she said stiffly, although her heart melted just a teeny tiny little at his offer. She glanced out as the horse pulled them across an enormous bridge, taking them from the fancy establishments on one side of the train tracks to towering ancient tenements and shadowy, narrow streets on the other. "Where is this George Square?"

"Near the university. Don't worry, the area isn't as old as these slums. Have you ever been to Edinburgh?" He took the paper-wrapped packages she was holding and squeezed them on the seat between them, providing a buffer.

A few packages didn't erase his presence, but Iona appreciated that he might be having the same difficulty as she. They should never have exchanged kisses. Apparently, they were addictive.

"When my mother was still alive, we'd come here occasionally. We stayed in a small hotel accessible to the shops and didn't explore much. She'd do her banking and buy us school gowns and new clothes. Nothing fancy, mind you, because that would look like we were lording it over our neighbors. And we needed boots and beekeeping equipment more than gowns." She watched the narrow street until it turned onto a broader thoroughfare.

"It's an interesting city. Phoebe's husband is replacing some of the medieval tenements down by Holyrood Palace. I'd like to explore the grounds once he's removed the debris. Can you imagine the generations of people who have lived here over the centuries?" the earl said unexpectedly.

She cast him a sideways look. "You are interested in archaeology? Is that why you wished to find a Roman fort in Wystan?" She feared if she knew too much about this man, she'd learned to like him too well, but he fascinated her.

"It's a hobby." He shrugged his indifference.

"You're lying," she decided. "Or being less than honest. Your scent changed."

He crossed his arms and stoically faced ahead. "Archaeology requires study. I haven't the time for it."

She bobbed her head. "Now you're being honest. If you only spend a few days a year in Wystan, what on earth else do you do with your time?"

"I'm my father's legs and eyes. He's getting on in years, and I need to know what he knows so I'm prepared to take the reins when needed. Even though I cannot perform my father's duties, being an heir is a full time chore just the same as an understudy in the theater. I should be running for office. I've put that off for too long and will have to consider it in the next election."

She pondered this for all of half a second. "You might make a very good bureaucrat, pushing papers about and shutting the door on annoying people. But politician? I don't think so."

He cast her a narrowed eye look. "I would be perfectly capable."

"I didn't say you wouldn't be *capable*." She gestured impatiently. "But unless your father bought the office, you would never win an election."

Surprisingly, he barked in laughter. "Which is why I haven't attempted it. To lose would be humiliating."

"We can't all successfully sell ourselves to a broad range of people. With your pretty face, you'd do better if they'd let women vote. Until then, push papers."

"You think I have a pretty face?" He raised an eyebrow at her.

"You know perfectly well that ladies swoon over you. You don't need me to feed your monstrous pride. Is this the house we'll be staying at?" Resisting his disturbing presence, she glanced out at the impressive Georgian townhouse across from a very nice park.

He was still chuckling as he climbed down. She scowled at him when he offered his hand and indicated her gentleman's attire. He immediately scowled back and grabbed the parcels.

Another hansom cab pulled up directly behind them, and Lowell hurried down to add the stack of parcels to the ones he already carried.

Verifying that no one seemed to be watching, Iona clambered down. She'd never practiced wearing men's attire but tried to stomp up the stairs as a portly man might do.

The earl snickered behind her.

GERARD KNEW HOW TO DANGLE HIS APERITIF GLASS AND LISTEN WITH AN AIR of boredom as his host and hostess prosed on about their latest charity or favorite opera. He knew how to slouch and hold himself aloof when forced to accompany an uninteresting lady into the dinner table. He had polite, stiff conversation polished to perfection and could swivel from one companion to the other without ever really listening.

He could not take his eyes off Lady Iona Ross in her secondhand gown.

He didn't care if the petticoat was last decade's fullness or the sleeves were the wrong degree of tightness for evening. He supposed the rose-and-white stripe was inappropriate for dinner as well. All he could see were her creamy shoulders and firm breasts rising above the frills and furbelows—and imagine unfastening the cunning loops holding it all together.

He even engaged his host in a discussion of the artifacts found in the medieval tenement demolition and still couldn't reduce his aware-ness of Iona. She talked excitedly with the viscount's wife about a collection of photographs they studied—not giving him a second glance.

He should be miffed that she ignored him, but he suspected she was doing the same as he—attempting to pretend that kiss never happened.

His loins told him otherwise.

Viscount Dare led Lady Iona into dinner, and Gerard held out his elbow for Azmin, Lady Dare. A laughing minx with huge dark eyes, she always appeared to know things he didn't. Women were a damned annoyance.

"We should let Lady Iona wear her male costume when we have some of Zane's students over to dinner, let her learn to blend in," Azmin said in amusement. "We cannot expect her to hide all alone with only us for company."

"I should like to attend the gambling hell where my stepfather and his cronies lurk," Iona asserted as they took their seats at the dinner table. "The sooner I can end his tyranny, the sooner I can go home. I can't be useful sitting here, twiddling my thumbs."

Instead of leaning back in his chair, casually dangling a wine glass, Gerard leaned forward and all but broke the glass stem. "You in no way, manner, or form resemble a man," he argued. "You'd be mocked, knocked down, and thrown out of any gambling establishment. Forget that notion."

"Then I'll wear rouge and kohl and naughty dresses and go as your courtesan," she countered, daring him with those big, liquid-gold eyes.

"I'm not planning on attending gambling hells. I'll be entertaining lawyers. You may go with me, if you wish—not dressed as a man or a courtesan." He stabbed his butter and tore a hole in his bread.

"Certainly. I expect to dictate my wishes for my future. But those meetings cannot last all day. Perhaps I could visit a library and see if there are any newer books on beekeeping." She demurely sipped her soup.

Gerard wasn't fooled. "You will not go dressed as a student!"

"I am not yours to command," she reminded him. "And if they admit females, then I shall happily go as myself. I doubt Mortimer will be looking in the library for me."

Treasure! Use your brain, boy.

He couldn't very well respond to a voice in his head, but he'd dearly like to ask how an obnoxious, penniless Malcolm could be a treasure. Gerard had pretty much determined the old soldier didn't mean real coin, to his disappointment.

"You could wear your student costume and go with Zane and Gerard to the demolition site," Azmin said helpfully. "No one will notice one more student wandering about. I'm not sure what the fascination is with old tools and broken pottery, but there might be hidden coins or jewels, I suppose."

Gerard couldn't help himself. He waited to see Iona's reaction to that insane proposal.

She nibbled her bread and thought about it. "It sounds quite filthy and not the kind of place I would drag my new petticoat, but it should be interesting to see. In fact, I'd love to explore the whole area. It's only a mile from the palace to the castle, correct? I can walk that easily. A guide would be lovely, so I understand the history I'm seeing."

"You're interested in history?" Gerard heard himself saying, much to his dismay. He knew better than to express interest in any topic a woman brought up.

"I enjoyed it in school. I can't say that I've ever been given any other opportunity. So, yes, I'd like to learn more. I simply must be careful not to be noticed by my stepfather or his spies, so the student guise will have to suffice."

His cousin Zane chuckled. "I'd say give her over to Phoebe, but she's up to her ears in animals and students at her new veterinary school."

"And I'm working with the newspaper on an article about the lack of resources for women whose husbands mistreat them. The editor is not wholly sympathetic, so I have to monitor every aspect of the story. It should be done in a few days, but I will be busy until then," Azmin said apologetically.

"I do not expect anyone to entertain me," the intrepid countess protested. "I was hoping perhaps a student of history might be interested in accompanying me."

"If you wore that gown, they'd be most interested," Gerard said dryly. "I don't suppose you can acquire widow's weeds? A nice thick veil should do the trick."

She wrinkled her nose at him. "That's a rather obvious disguise if I'm seen leaving any Malcolm establishment. Mortimer's spies might be watching."

"I cannot believe the sot has the wherewithal to hire—"

The front doorbell resounded through the house.

"We're not expecting anyone." Dare lay down his utensils.

With a sigh, the countess removed her plate and vanished behind the baize servants' door.

A young lad dressed in a uniform arrived with a silver platter. "A message from the Earl of Craigmore, my lord."

SEVENTEEN

"Mortimer knows I'm staying here, and that I brought the baron with me!" Lord Ives rested an elbow on the mantel in the front room after dinner. "How can he possibly have followed us?"

To their hosts, he probably appeared as a model of aristocratic irritation and no more. Iona, however, needed roses to mitigate the scent of his fury so she could pretend he didn't affect her.

She tested the keys of an old pianoforte. "He pays street urchins, probably with the American's money. At home, he'd simply tell everyone he'd not let them hunt on our land if they didn't report our every move. Poor people are very cooperative if it means food in their stomachs."

She regretted bringing this down on her nice hosts and the earl. "I'll go to the flat I've rented in the morning. He's less likely to find me on my own."

"You will do no such thing," Azmin, Lady Dare, protested. "It could be surrounded by thieves and infested with bedbugs. It's not as if your stepfather can break into our house and abduct you."

Iona held her tongue.

The all-too-perceptive Lord Ives noticed. He stopped his prowling to glare at her. With their hosts, he was the very model of decorum and bored aristocracy. She seemed to be the only recipient of his scowls. His attention warmed her all over, especially when he hovered by the piano to select music.

"Abduction is illegal," he said in a practiced, offhand tone. "He wouldn't do that, would he?"

Iona picked out a few notes of the song on the sheet music he opened. It had been a long time since she'd practiced—since school, at least. "When Mortimer emptied her savings, Isobel ran away to a friend's house in hopes of having him reported to the sheriff. Mortimer sent one of our tenants to stop her and bring her home."

The shock had rendered her twin insensible so she could not fight. *Iona* could fight, but she wasn't much good at it when Isobel was used as a shield.

The viscount whistled in surprise. Lord Ives crumpled the music sheet he held.

"We sent the messenger away with a flea in his ear," Azmin said, with an implacable tone that said she'd use a knife on the next one. "This is not the rural Highlands. Our guests are private. But if the urchins recognize your baron's disguise, it's probably not wise to use it again."

"I suppose not," Iona said regretfully. "It was foolish of me to test it on Mortimer in the first place. I should have just taken Lowell's pistol and shot the rat when we ran into him like that. I am not good at thinking on my feet."

"Never give her a pistol," the earl said without inflection to no one in particular.

"The two of you should visit my investment agents tomorrow in your baron guise." Zane poured himself another whisky, then offered the decanter to the earl. "Hugh is on his honeymoon, but I'll send a note to his partners about the baron. Once there, Lady Iona can change into different attire and the secretaries can take her elsewhere. That should discourage any urchins following."

"I'll take my plain gown, and look like one of the servants leaving the building. I really want to explore Edinburgh a bit. And then I should take the train to my flat. I hate that Mortimer forces me to spend my life hiding." Iona crashed her fingers on the keys, creating a discordant clamor in the pleasant withdrawing room.

"Then quit hiding." The earl rejected his host's offer of whisky, sat down beside her, and began playing the song he'd chosen, usurping all the air and space around her with his masculine presence. "You are not even his daughter. You are of age. You are an independent woman. Kidnapping you in Edinburgh is not as easy as it is where he controls the countryside."

Iona pondered the lovely dream of walking the streets as herself, stopping to visit shops and friends, without a care in the world. Someday. . .

"I don't believe I could actually shed blood," she said regretfully. "I'd love to carry a pistol and a *sgian dhu,* but a hatpin is more my style. Or maybe a walking stick. I was brought up in an English boarding school. I never learned how to protect myself against kidnappers. But I don't share your confidence that anyone would care a fig if they saw me being thrown into a carriage."

"You are more comfortable hiding," Lord Ives said in disgust. "I dare you to walk out with me tomorrow as a lady to attend my meeting with the solicitor. I can and will see that you are safe."

She found where he was on the music sheet and attempted to catch up with him but failed. She was too out of practice—in many things, apparently. "I hate ruining my few good clothes. Let me dress in my servants' garb. Then I can more comfortably accompany you to the demolition site. I'll attract suspicion but maybe the urchins will hesitate to report me unless they hear me addressed."

"Shall I call you Sally?" the earl asked, reeking of distaste.

For a gentleman who presented an indifferent attitude, he roiled with strong emotions. It was like smelling a spicy pudding cooking.

"I can provide the walking stick," Zane suggested, grinning. "Do servants carry them?"

"I'll provide ample hat pins," Azmin offered. "I occasionally wear a stiletto in my hair, but yours is too short. Phoebe wears a *sgian dhu* in her boot, but she's skilled, and you're not. We should have her teach you a few street tricks."

Iona hated to disappoint the earl, but she knew her comfort level.

Servant, it had to be. "Thank you. Someday, I would be delighted to take lessons from Lady Phoebe, should I survive this. I appreciate everything everyone has done for me. That includes you, Lord Ives," she added demurely.

She rather enjoyed the complex scent of reactions he emitted. She thought they might just be similar to her own, which meant he was as confused as she was. It was comforting to know an experienced gentleman like the earl could have his moments of uncertainty.

GERARD TOLD HIMSELF TEN THOUSAND POUNDS WAS WORTH LOSING A night's sleep. Maybe the medallion was right and Lady Iona represented a treasure of wealth, if he could lay his hands on that reward. Even half the amount would work wonders on the castle roof.

He stayed up most of the night making lists of demands for her settlement and keeping an eye on the stairs so she didn't sneak out.

He was probably better off returning to London, but he simply couldn't let this go. The beekeeper deserved to return to her hives and the life she wished without an ogre breathing down her neck. He couldn't live with himself if he did nothing.

So he scribbled off notes to his father and his London man of business and various others to let them know he hadn't been buried at Wystan, then after a brief nap, dressed for a visit to his father's Edinburgh solicitor. The marquess had his fingers in a lot of pots and had family all over the north country, so a law firm looking after his interests here proved useful.

Lowell made discreet hints about an excellent tailor with good prices nearby. Gerard ignored him.

Lady Iona emerged in the promised servant's drab. She still took his breath away. Her big eyes sparkled gold from beneath a flat black cap— sporting several decorative hat pins. She'd not bothered with the false hair and had apparently attempted to wash out some of the brown dye. Her pixie curls framed her heart-shaped face, and when she smiled, the sun rose inside the house.

The damned medallion chuckled.

"I'd need to put a bucket over your head to make you unrecognizable," he grumbled. "I still can't believe Mortimer didn't—"

She donned a pair of spectacles that reflected light from the windows, veiling her distinctive eyes. She slumped, curving her shoulders forward and dragging her big straw carryall to her feet. She shuffled toward the door.

"I take it you did well in drama in your boarding school." With a sigh, he opened the door before Dare's servants could reach it.

"Highest grade in the class," she cackled in a raspy voice. "And I'll have to go out the back and meet the carriage at the end of the alley, like any good servant."

"If you don't want to be a countess, you can always be an actress," he grumbled, but she was already half way down the hall. He slapped his hat on, dashed out to Dare's waiting carriage, and ordered it around to the alley before she could disappear again.

Spotting an urchin loitering by a lamppost, Gerard leaped from the carriage the instant it halted and chased the brat off with a few threats. He stood guard to be certain no other appeared until Iona had climbed in —without his aid, of course. Gentlemen did not aid servants. With a sigh of exasperation, he joined her.

"He'll be back," she said complacently. "If he's any good, he'll have notified the rest of his gang, who will be watching this carriage from every street corner. I may not have spent much time in the city, but I know how bees scout. It's a basic instinct."

"I don't care." Gerard sat across from her, grateful for the larger vehicle. But the distance didn't help much. Now that she was out of public view, the little countess sat like a proper lady, her hands on the knob of a walking stick she must have picked up on her way out. "You're the one hiding behind that ridiculous garb. I'd just as soon shoot anyone who approached you."

"Are you carrying a pistol?" she asked with interest.

"I am. And a knife, if you're thinking bloodthirsty thoughts. But like you, I prefer a brass-handled walking stick and my fists." In fact, his fists were itching to plant themselves in her stepfather's fatuous face. That didn't help his humor.

"I shall attempt to stay out of trouble," she said soberly. "I do appreciate all you've done, even if it is in the interest of a reward I fear you'll never see."

"Rainford is investigating the terms of the reward. I have legitimately found you and your sister. We can arrange to meet Mortimer and Winter in some safe place with authorities present. It's your desire to marry the wretch that is causing complications." He sounded stiff, even to himself.

"I apologize. But even should we split the reward, I still need another level of protection before I will feel safe once you have left for London. I know of no other means to make Mortimer go away." She almost sounded regretful.

He'd like to test the knob she was clutching to see if it gave off vibrations like the map she'd drawn, but he didn't feel inclined to explain his curiosity. It wasn't as if he sensed much on anything else he touched, so perhaps it was only Iona's fears he felt.

He wanted to feel her happiness the next time he touched an object of hers.

That twisted his gut. Was *she* sensing *his* unhappiness?

He wasn't a man prone to noticing the sentiments of others. He brushed off his own now. "We'll talk to the lawyers, see what they say."

The lawyers were less than helpful. They agreed to draw up a strict settlement document as requested, but admitted there was very little they could do to Mortimer unless he physically abducted one of his stepdaughters. And then it was up to the criminal courts, which wasn't their bailiwick.

They agreed to ask about Iona's request for her letters patent, but they didn't seem optimistic that it would be accomplished any time soon.

Clenching his teeth, Gerard sent Iona from the solicitor's office in the company of a bevy of maids. For a few coins, the women agreed to lead the drably-garbed lady down to the slums Iona insisted on visiting. Recalling her comment about urchins following the carriage, Gerard sent a message to Dare's driver. Then he folded up his top hat, borrowed a cloak, and left the building from the rear. Taking alleys and cutting corners to the more crowded thoroughfare, he easily caught up with the sauntering women and passed them as if they weren't there.

Lady Iona seemed to be enjoying herself, chattering with uneducated servants as if they were the queen's court. He supposed her sensitivities allowed her to react to how the women felt as much as she did to their words. That would be a useful ability, although as with all Malcolm gifts, there had to be a drawback.

As far as he could tell, his gift was singularly useless, and voices in his head were a distinct drawback.

He left Iona flitting about the shops while he turned down the narrow alley Dare called a wynd—for obvious reasons. The towering tenements had been built along the side of a steep hill on a path fit only for wandering cattle. Gerard removed a glove and circumspectly brushed his hand over ancient stones and ornaments but nothing interesting leapt out at him. He assumed his encounter with Iona's map was a fluke.

Zane was already at the construction site, talking to Andrew Blair, Phoebe's husband, and a man holding what appeared to be blueprints. Gerard acknowledged them with a gesture but left them talking while he wandered into the littered lot that had once held several old tenements. Remnants of the ancient foundation remained, along with construction debris. The medallion in his pocket made no comment.

He kicked the rubble about, looking for anything besides stone and brick. He sensed Iona's arrival before he saw her. It was as if the universe shifted subtly—sound became more acute, light brightened. He heard her converse with Zane as he hadn't heard the male conversation earlier. He knew when she approached, although he hadn't noticed the foreman strolling the perimeter until he looked up now.

"Lord Dare says hundreds of people, including Lady Phoebe and her mother, once lived here," she said in amazement, removing her fake spectacles and putting them in her pocket. "And Mr. Blair started the project after Lady Phoebe's building collapsed. They had a dreadful time finding housing for all the tenants. I cannot even begin to imagine the immensity of such an undertaking." She crouched down to examine a pile of crumbling old brick.

"You'll get filthy," Gerard warned.

She shot him one of those bright smiles that smote his hard heart with a thousand darts.

"Have you ever smoked a bee's nest out of a tree? Sheared a sheep? A

little brick dust is nothing. I am smelling something interesting here."
She poked the dirt beneath the bricks.

"Besides a urinal?" he asked in derision. But he crouched down
beside her and used a sharp piece of wood to dig a little deeper.

She chuckled and let him dig. "I generally only smell live people, as a
bee would sense live flowers. Dead ones hold no interest. But every so
often—a child's loved blanket, a bride's hand-stitched linen—I can smell
emotion embedded in an object. Perhaps a little bit of our souls? I am not
smelling love, though, but a murkier sensation, perhaps some combination of hate and guilt?"

She spoke so easily of her extra sense—as if everyone understood her
ability.

"Not exactly an object one wishes to touch then. How did you learn
what each emotion smells like?" His stick hit a hard object, and he dug
deeper, suppressing any excitement.

"Trial and error mostly. Children learn easily, so perhaps it was like
learning the differences in word sounds."

A lesson he had thankfully missed. He couldn't imagine going
through life sorting out the complicated feelings of the many people
around him.

"Isolation probably helped," he concluded. "It must be easier to sort
and study when there are only a few familiar faces about instead of
hordes."

"I've never given it much thought, but you might be right. The scent
is stronger now. Do you feel anything?"

He thought for a second she was referencing his peculiar ability, but
then realized she meant his digging.

In fact—he *did* feel the object, as he often did when an artifact called
to him. He simply thought of it as an object speaking to him in the same
way an artist might say a subject spoke to him.

Not the same, the soldier protested.

Gerard refused to argue with a voice in his head. That way lay
insanity.

He uncovered filth-encrusted metal. Producing a penknife from his
pocket, he pried around the edges until it loosened. "Possibly a knife,"
he concluded. "I think I see insignia beneath the dirt."

"Kitchen knife or long ago murder weapon?" she asked, as if he'd know.

And he did know, the instant he pried the blade from the clay and held it in his bare palm. "Someone's prized dagger, reluctantly buried after an unfortunate fight."

He regretted his observation the instant he uttered it.

EIGHTEEN

As if just seeing him, Iona regarded Gerard with shock. "You have a *gift*. Or you're a very good storyteller. But I don't smell the lie on you."

Cursing himself, still shaken by his reaction to the dagger, he handed her the filthy object. The tip of the blade had broken. "I doubt it's precious metal," he said dismissively, attempting to brush aside the incident.

"You're only interested in the monetary value?" Disturbed by his reply, she didn't appear to notice that he hadn't answered her observation.

"That would be practical," he agreed. "But no. I'm interested in the history. We could take it to someone knowledgeable, but what would be the point?"

She scraped at the dirt-embedded insignia with a hatpin. "We'll never know the history if you can't read more. I wonder how long ago it happened?"

Knowing better than to expose himself this way, but challenged by her question, Gerard removed the medallion from his pocket. He set it aside so as not to have two nags in his head and took the dagger back. His mind sought an inner voice as he'd learned to do as a curious child.

He had the vague sensation of rude curses but not an actual voice.

"Medieval, like the tenement," he guessed, hoping that sounded as if he could identify the hilt by its looks, which he couldn't.

She reached for the object, and for a moment, both their hands gripped it.

A violent, dimly-lit scene struck him. A whirlwind of anger, betrayal, and pain swept through his head, followed by the slicing of flesh, a cry of anguish, and a wave of terror.

Iona dropped the knife and backed away. "Did you feel that?"

He flung the knife back in its hole and picked up his more sensible medallion to steady himself. The old soldier grunted in his head. Gerard refused to interpret grunts.

Iona snatched up the knife and shoved it in her waistband beneath her bodice.

Bolting down his anger at exposing her to that sordid scene, unable to deny what they experienced, Gerard took her elbow and steered her from the debris. "That's not edifying history. That's human nature at its lowest."

She shifted her straw bag, lifted her too-short skirt, and let him support her across the rocky lot. "That's never happened to me before. You *are* gifted. How does that work? Do you always feel things on objects?"

Gerard cursed his wayward tongue and her Malcolm curiosity. "Until this moment, I have *never* seen things on objects. Let us find the carriage and return to the house for luncheon, like sensible people. I'll send a messenger to your flat to see if any mail has arrived, although I can assure you that the queen hasn't replied. Your letter is still sitting on some underling's desk."

She refused to be distracted. "I had an odd sensation of a knife fight and all the dark emotions one might feel at such a time. It was no cold-blooded murder. Smell was only a small part of the feeling, so I'm assuming the rest was you? You made me *feel* the scene?"

"Odd things happen occasionally," he muttered, hurrying her down the street with only a wave to the others. "There is no profit in them."

She shook her arm free and responded irately. "Our gifts are meant to be used to help others, not to *profit* from them. Did your mother not teach you better?"

"She knows nothing of it, and I'd thank you to not mention it. I have quite enough to do without having people shove their prized possessions into my hands to satisfy their curiosity." He'd heard tales of family members with the peculiar ability to sense powerful emotions on objects. It wasn't a pleasant experience and in most cases, not productive. And it wasn't as if he'd done it. . .

Except when Iona had been involved.

"Yes, I suppose, for a busy, important man, such importunities would be a nuisance, especially if you failed to feel anything," she said stiffly, not sounding as if she really excused him. "Life is all about learning from failure. If you practiced more, you might develop a better sense of the artifacts you seek."

"If I ever had the opportunity to seek them," he grumbled.

"Ah, that is the reason for your wish to go to Italy! Yes, I can see that might be an exciting opportunity to explore your abilities without anyone watching you fail."

"There is nothing there to fail at," he said curtly, insulted. He led her down the street, keeping an eye out for urchins.

"Touching that knife at the same time as you produced visions far more detailed than my sense of smell ever has. It was exciting! Wasn't it the same for you?"

Damn, double damn, and hellfire. Why did she have to be a human lie detector? Once he admitted they had a psychic connection. . . He'd never hear the end of it.

"Yes," he said curtly. "Now, did you want to explore the Royal Mile or do I hail a hackney?"

She shot him an enigmatic glance but politely responded to his suggestion. "Explore, please. There are bees in the steeple of that church. That's a good sign. Let us go in and find something pleasant we can touch. It would be interesting to see if perhaps an organ would produce memories." She hurried into the old cathedral.

Gerard watched the tower warily for bees but didn't see what she saw. He had to admit that St. Giles was an excellent place to explore antiquities, if one could find them beneath the fire damage and debris of centuries of fighting, neglect, and partitioning.

"I doubt the place has an organ any longer," he warned. "Most of the medieval ornament was stripped when Scotland rejected Rome. I don't think touching walls and floors will be of much use."

The old Catholic cathedral had been walled off into four different parish churches. Even finding the original medieval walls might be a challenge. But Gerard assumed the lady was safer here, out of sight of the public, so he followed along as she trailed through the once grand cathedral.

"I'm not accustomed to seeking scents on *objects*." She refused to drop the subject. "How did I sense the knife?"

"My masculine proximity enhances your gift?" he suggested sardonically, using that excuse to take her arm.

Thinking lewd thoughts in church would probably send him directly to hell, but even in drab servants' garb and spouting nonsense, the lady aroused his lust. And he could see her ankles beneath that too-short skirt. She wore stockings with bees embroidered on them, and his imagination traveled dangerous paths.

"Interesting theory but not feasible." She relaxed and leaned into him just a bit as she studied the soaring ceiling and inhaled. "So much sorrow! I was hoping for peace and contentment."

"The old chancel, perhaps? If we go straight back, there might be remnants of the original." Although straight was relative. As they worked their way past partitions to the back of the church, her arm still on his, Gerard realized he was picking up *vibrations*. He could almost feel the memories stored in the ancient walls.

He'd thought he found his artifacts by luck. Had he actually been picking up on their vibrations? Could memory leave physical energy on objects—and Iona was intensifying the effect? Or forcing him to focus on his surroundings more?

And how did that differ from the spirit voices in his head?

She drifted toward the walls, ignoring pews and chairs. "All the old pieces are gone. We'd have to ask the church warden to see whatever they've tucked away. A few of these memorials maybe. . ." She touched a brass plaque of two women representing Justice and Religion. "There's a haunting scent here that I cannot identify."

To humor her, Gerard removed a glove and flattened his palm on the brass. He thought he felt a connection, but it was too complex and didn't speak to him as his medallion did.

Iona laid her bare hand over his, skin to skin.

Satisfaction and peace settled over him. A brief vision of a clergyman in garb too old for him to identify hovered in his mind's eye. The spirit image rubbed the plaque and offered a grateful prayer in mangled English for the end to conflict and. . .

"He's grateful that the sinful Catholic adornments were removed?" Gerard yanked back his hand to free his head of the vision but a headache lingered. "He's *grateful* that they destroyed centuries of history and craftsmanship? That's appalling, not peaceful."

IONA CARESSED THE BRASS, ASTOUNDED BY THE CLARITY OF THAT VISION. "That's religion. Faith is not logical. The poor man sincerely believed the stained glass and statues were devil worship. How sad for him not to understand a human need for beauty and the familiarity of a shared history."

She glanced up at the stunned earl. Lord Ives did not look happy with their combined history lesson. "Our Malcolm ancestors worshipped trees and goddesses, remember," she said with a hint of mischief. "The clergyman would most likely have burned us at the stake for what we just did."

"There are some who would still do the same today," he said gruffly. "People can be judgmental, bigoted, and ignorant about anyone different from themselves. That was even more clear than the knife. I've *never* seen visions like that before. Is that your work?"

"Never? I thought I was simply amplifying your gift the way Isobel and I occasionally augment each other. But you've never seen visions?" She studied the plaque. "Perhaps it's something in the brass?"

"That doesn't explain the knife. Enough of this experiment." He pulled his glove back on. "This does not solve your problem with Mortimer unless we can reach into his head and slosh his pickled brain around. Is he always drunk?"

Sharing a gift with her sister and mother was second nature to Iona.

She was not quite as shocked as he was by the apparition they'd raised. It brought them closer, though, and they both had reason to resist that.

"More or less." Unthinkingly, she hooked her hand through the crook of his elbow. It felt natural somehow. She heard the bees in the steeple humming their approval, so she didn't withdraw it as he strode out the nearest exit. "Since Mortimer's scheming seems more in the moment than long-term, I assume touching anything of his would be fruitless. Perhaps we should learn more about Mr. Winter. It would be good to know that he'll honor any agreement we make."

"I still don't like the idea of you selling yourself to him," he growled. "Even marrying me would be better."

His shock at his own words was easily identifiable, and Iona laughed as they stepped into the brisk autumn day, on a side street and not the busy thoroughfare they'd earlier traversed. "Marrying you *after* we claim the reward and enrich our coffers, correct? Then you'd have to sponsor another come-out for Isobel to choose a husband so Mortimer can't marry her off. And we'd spend the rest of our newly-acquired funds hiring lawyers or killers to remove him from our home so Isobel might return there. It's a very generous thought, my lord, but probably not practical."

Although marriage to the Earl of Ives and Wystan seemed like a lovely dream to her. He was a good man. He owned Wystan, where she could be very happy. He wanted to visit Italy, which she'd love to do—in the winter, when her bees slept.

But he needed wealth, and she didn't have it. He lived in London and would rightfully expect her to do so as well. She couldn't take her bees to London. It took love to overcome such obstacles, and she didn't think the earl had that sentiment in him.

He gloomily pondered her eminently practical response. She could sense his war of emotions. That he *wanted* her enough to even make such a suggestion warmed her all the way through. It was good not to be suffering unrequited lust.

Before he could respond, a towering, heavyset brute in malodorous rags stepped from an alley to block their path. "Unhand her, ye scalawag! Her da wants her back."

The brute grabbed her arm, and more ragged urchins popped out of doorways and alleys, rushing to surround them.

Iona screamed at her highest pitch to attract attention. Yanking the filthy knife from her waistband, she struck the hand holding her. Unsurprisingly, the blade was dull. The heavy fist tightened around her cuff, and he knocked the knife flying.

The normally imperturbable earl roared in a voice so loud it may have shaken a few tiles from the roof.

Dropping his insouciant pose, Ives smashed a gloved fist into her attacker's jaw. He followed the punch with an ungentlemanly blow of his walking stick knob considerably lower, in a place that caused her captor to howl in agony and release her wrist to cover his privates.

While the thug was bent over, the earl slammed the length of the stick on his thick neck, and toppled him.

With her arm free, Iona used both hands to swing her stick at the clamoring urchins surrounding them. A few had cudgels, but with their major opponent laid flat, the earl used his ebony stick as a staff to beat them back. Between them, they held off their attackers, although their foes' strength was in numbers, not size, and they weren't retreating.

While Iona tried to mentally connect with the drowsy bees, one rascal yanked her weapon away. She lost her concentration when another grabbed at her old wool skirt, tugging and pushing and attempting to separate her from the earl. Removing a hatpin, Iona kicked and screamed and stabbed every hand gripping her.

A few bees lazily descended but not enough for Iona to use as weapon. She needed her own queen to communicate her fear.

Lord Ives grabbed an urchin by the collar and flung him on top of the fallen miscreant, who groaned even more. He smacked a few more with his stick, far harder than she'd managed to do, dislodging stronger grips.

Finally, her screams brought men running, and behind them, she could hear the screech of a police whistle.

That shrill signal sent the pack scurrying back into their holes.

Collapsing from emotional exhaustion as much as physical, Iona hugged Lord Ives' waist, clinging to him as he caught his breath. He squeezed her briefly, then set her aside to stomp his boot on the large brute struggling to flee.

When the policeman ran up, the earl pointed at his captive. "He attacked us and attempted to abduct the lady. We have reason to believe he was sent by a man posing as the Earl of Craigmore. As soon as I take the lady home, I'll be down to the station to file a complaint."

Given how she looked, Iona was grateful he did not use her name. Even so, the policeman glanced in doubt at her drab wool.

But he nodded respectfully as Lord Ives casually brushed off his suit coat as if he engaged in fisticuffs on a regular basis. "Yes, my lord. The miscreants do nae usually attack in day."

"The lady does not go out at night for fear of such attacks. Craigmore has apparently become desperate. We'll follow in your path in case they return." Lord Ives briefly squeezed Iona's shoulders, then more appropriately offered his arm.

She needed it. She was still trembling. How had Mortimer discovered she was in town—and learned where she was? They'd been so careful! She was quite certain he had not seen through her baron's disguise and had only intruded on the Dares to see if Ives had followed her false claim.

Several of the passersby who had run to their aid also followed to be certain the large scoundrel did not escape from the much slighter policeman. Iona felt as if eyes stared at her from behind windows up and down the street.

"I don't like this," she murmured. "I don't want to lead anyone back to Lord Dare's."

"Agreed," the earl whispered back.

After depositing the policeman and his captive at the police station, Lord Ives caught a hansom and helped her in. Climbing up beside her, he ordered the cab to the train station.

"If you send me back to Isobel, I cannot appear for the reward to prove you've found me," she objected.

"I am considering leading Winter and Mortimer out to Calder Castle and shoving them off a cliff," he said grimly.

"It might be easier to do so from the fort." She indicated the high bluff supporting the ancient fortress ahead.

"Tempting," he agreed. "But I intend to pretend I'm putting you on a train. You will sneak off further down the cars while I stand there idiotically waving at strangers in the windows. The Royal hotel is just down the block. Do you think you can slip in a back door as if you're part of the staff?"

"Give me your cloak. I'll put it in my bag and wear it when I get off. It's not much, but it will hide me and the bag. I should be able to find a crowd of people to walk with." She was still breathing too fast, and her pulse was racing. That had been much too close an encounter.

She prayed Mortimer knew nothing of her twin's hiding place. There were strange workmen all over the grounds at the castle. She'd have to send a telegram and caution Isobel to stay inside.

Without warning, the earl leaned over, placed his mouth over hers, and captured her breath.

The unimaginable sweetness of his kiss filled her head and drove away any lingering fear.

This was where she belonged.

And she could never have him.

NINETEEN

ALL THE FURY AND CONFUSION OF THE MORNING MELTED AWAY WHILE
Gerard held Iona in his arms. Her kiss soothed the savage beast that had
unexpectedly awakened when he'd seen her attacked. Her breasts
pressing into him caused his racing heart to send blood to more intimate
places than his fists. The world almost made sense when she snuggled
into his embrace.

And then the carriage stopped and she pushed away and looked like
a wide-eyed doe. Not frightened, thankfully, but definitely startled. He
had to remember that, despite her confidence, she was young and inex-
perienced.

Still unbalanced but recovering his usual composure, he handed her
the borrowed cloak he carried over his arm as if their embrace was an
everyday occurrence. "Hold the hood over your head after you don it.
Changing your hair does *not* disguise you. And put those horrible spectacles back on."

She took a breath and nodded, pulling out the spectacles and
fumbling with them. "You'll be in the hotel lobby?"

"Probably hiding behind a newspaper," he agreed, trying to sound
whatever in hell normal might be when his blood raced and his mind
swirled. He climbed out and held out his hand to help her down.

"I will find you." She took his hand and clung to it a little longer than necessary, as if needing to steady herself.

He knew the feeling. Thank all that was holy, there was a train already in the station. She climbed on, leaving him standing there like an idiot, watching the packed car and waving as it pulled away from the platform.

He prayed she wouldn't stay on the train, leaving him behind. He noted its destination, just in case.

Then crossing the track, he climbed up to Princes Street and strode hurriedly for the hotel. He didn't see any sign of a cloaked female in the scattering of passengers ahead, but she'd had several minutes to run ahead of him.

In the lobby, Gerard stopped at the desk to let Rainford know he was there, and to take a room, ostensibly for his sister. The clerk couldn't give him a second room nearby. That fretted at him, but he couldn't endanger friends and family by taking Iona back to Dare's. A large, anonymous hotel somehow seemed safer than a residence Mortimer might recognize as a refuge.

They had to act soon, faster than he liked.

He settled in a chair with a newspaper, watching over the top of it. To his dismay, Lady Alice sailed down the grand staircase. Of course, as long as she was in the north, she'd be visiting her father. Gerard yanked his newspaper up and peered from the side until he saw the lady gliding out the door in a flurry of ruffles and petticoats.

When he glanced at the lobby again, Iona was serenely arranging a bouquet of flowers on a table. She wore her spectacles and a white cap, and in her too-short dress, she looked as if she worked for the hotel.

A wave of relief rolled over him. She'd put him through so many ups and downs this morning that he finally recognized that his habitual detachment was as much a pose as hers—at least where Iona was concerned. He needed to send her off before the pressure of emotions he hadn't known he possessed burst his tightly-bound seams.

Folding his paper, he stood up and stopped near the bouquet to check his watch. "Room 110." He left the key on the table and took the stairs up.

He almost had a heart attack when she didn't immediately follow. He paced the hall, caught Rainford loping down the stairs, told him to wait in the tavern, and had almost worn a rut before he saw Iona hurrying from a hidden door at the end of the hall.

She was carrying the cloak, walking stick, and her bag this time and had discarded the little white cap.

"That was a most edifying adventure," she announced as she held out the key to him. "I could take a position here arranging flowers, I think."

Refraining from rolling his eyes, Gerard unlocked the room and shoved her in before anyone could see them.

He resisted the urge to wrap her in his arms again and watched as she perused the small chamber.

"Very nice," she declared. "I cannot stay here, of course. I really should go to the room I've paid for."

"For the moment, no one knows where you are. Let me talk to Rainford to see if he's discovered anything new. I'll have tea and sandwiches sent up. Dash off a note to Azmin and Dare letting them know you're safe. I still need to file that police report, so I won't be back as quickly as I'd like."

"Will you send a telegram to Isobel warning her to stay inside?" She folded her hands at her waist and watched him anxiously.

"Of course, good idea. Anything else?"

"Lady Alice is here," she pointed out, irrelevantly.

"Everyone who is anyone is apparently here. That is the point of places like this—to see and be seen. I've told the clerk you are my sister. I think I should send a dressmaker over. If you are to appear as my sister —or a countess—you need something better than that rag."

She opened her straw tote and shook out a rumpled cotton gown of demure green and gold print. "I'll ask the maid to have this pressed. With a bustle and underskirt, it will look respectable."

"One of Lowell's choices? Then it might work. I'll have someone collect it. You're safe here. Can you *not* buzz about for a few hours, until I return?" If she wasn't here when he got back—Gerard wouldn't let her see his fear, but she probably sensed it.

"If the reward exists, you'll have it," she assured him.

She'd read his fear wrong, but nodding as if he were reassured, he walked out, waiting until he heard the key turn before trotting downstairs.

Leaving his messages at the desk—it was amazing what one could command with a few coins and a title—Gerard hurried on to the tavern.

"Word is that you've brought in one of your sisters," Rainford said the instant Gerard pulled up a chair. "I've met your sisters. There is no way they would have arrived without a parade of baggage, children, servants, and a twelve-piece band. I assume our heiress is now in residence."

"Damn, I hate this town. Give me London any day." Gerard took the drink the waitress instantly brought over. "Tell me we can set up a meeting tomorrow and claim the reward."

"The money is there," Rainford agreed. "Mortimer is increasingly desperate. Word is that Mr. Winter is no longer inclined to believe the twins exist."

"The reward is not tied to marriage settlements?" Gerard verified. He really wanted to throttle Mortimer before presenting Iona, but that was his newly discovered savage beast speaking.

"Not as far as I can ascertain. Mortimer may insist that the ladies be handed into his care, but I'm fairly certain we can provide sufficient objection. That still does not mean the twins are safe to go home."

"No, we need to remove Mortimer from the picture. To that end, how did Drummond fare at the card table last night?" Gerard forced himself to sip his drink until his lunch arrived. Iona was safe. He needed to keep his distance—and his head.

"Mortimer is a drunk and plays like one. Winter appears tired of bailing him out. Tempers are running short. I don't think it would be difficult to force Mortimer to sign the twins away. *Enforcing* the agreement, of course, is a different matter. You may need the reward money to pour him on a ship leaving for Australia."

"There's one in port now, sailing in a few days for the Far East," Gerard offered. "We think alike."

"Ho! Leave him with the Chinese where he can't speak a word. Even better. So how do you wish to work it?" Rainford sat back, calmly sipping his whisky as his lunch was set before him.

"We'll have to prove we have at least one twin and hold the meeting in a solicitor's office tomorrow." Gerard had planned this carefully, but he waved his fork about as if he were thinking aloud. "Perhaps play a card game with them tonight to convince Winter we're the genuine article. Give them a little hope and pry Mortimer off the girls' back for a day or so."

"Take the money and run?" Rainford suggested.

Gerard scowled at his facetiousness. "Take the reward money, then offer a chance to win it back."

The studious marquess beamed. "Put Mortimer deep in the hole, and force him to sign the agreement to leave the twins and their property alone."

"Then get him drunk and carry him to port," Gerard finished, knowing it would never be easy. But at least it was a plan.

"Leave Winter to court the lady?"

"That," Gerard said gloomily, "is the fly in our ointment. He must have some plan to force her hand. And she's not a countess yet. The title is still in abeyance. We can't predict how either of them will react."

Rainford bit into his beef as if it were nails instead of tenderloin. Gerard knew how he felt—only worse.

AT THE KNOCK ON THE DOOR, IONA FRETTED OVER LETTING ANYONE IN. HAD the maid already pressed her gown? She didn't know what to expect of a luxurious hotel like this one. Even the soap in the washbasin smelled of lovely herbs.

"I have your gown, my lady," a female voice said from the hall.

Iona grasped her walking stick and a hatpin. The attack today had shaken her. She'd known Mortimer was capable of it, but she had thought they'd been so careful—

Easing open the door a crack, she glimpsed a dour matron holding the secondhand gown, followed by a bevy of young women carrying measuring tapes and baskets of trimming and fabric—seamstresses?

"His lordship said you'd be needing a wardrobe to fit this size." The stout matron shoved in, holding up the gown Iona had sent for pressing. The stranger gestured for her army to take their places around the room.

"We can fit you up with a few ready-mades. You're a small size, so we can take down several. Anything fancy will be longer."

She threw the cotton print over the bed and studied Iona with expert eye. "Let's get you out of that rag. Travel is dreadful these days, losing a lady's luggage like that."

Not knowing whether to be thrilled or angry at the earl's tale-telling and presumption, Iona let the plain-spoken seamstress bully her into a fitting. Was this how a lord made a woman into a mistress? Sweet kisses, a secret hideaway, unexpected gifts?

That kiss in the carriage—she'd been too caught up in the pleasure to read his reaction. Or perhaps his scent of desire had blocked all else. But bringing her to a hotel room and providing her with a wardrobe. . .

She didn't think she'd object too much to being the earl's mistress—except it didn't solve any of her problems. She needed to be back with her queen by spring. It would be better if she could ensure the hives' safety over winter—which was the most she could hope for.

The gowns the modiste produced were simple but of excellent cloth. Iona rejected two in colors she didn't wear but accepted two with interchangeable colors, bodices, and skirts. One of the younger girls stitched up the secondhand gown so it fit perfectly, giving her a third choice.

By the time Lord Ives returned that evening, Iona was hungry, tired, and dressed in the simple gown with the pretty gold bouquet print. The dressmakers had added a fashionable apron bodice in a deep green and a frill of lace for the neckline.

The workers were already packing up their bags. The modiste promised to complete the other gowns by tomorrow and ushered her charges away.

"Lord Ives," Iona said stiffly once they were alone, uncertain how to approach him after his generous gesture.

"I wish you would call me Gerard," he said. "There are far too many of us to wish to be called Ives by people I've come to know."

He didn't even notice Iona's pretty attire. Warily, she nodded, "Very well, *Gerard*."

He nodded and began pacing the tiny room. "I've filed a report with the police but I won't count on them arresting Mortimer. I can't leave you alone all evening. We've decided you'll be safe with Phoebe's aunts for the night, if we can smuggle you in without anyone noticing. I'm hoping we'll keep your stepfather busy at cards this evening so he won't think to hire anyone to look for you."

"Unless Lady Phoebe has a flock of aunts, I'm assuming you're taking me to the School of Malcolms? Surely they must be full to bursting and run ragged at the start of a school year."

Miffed that he didn't notice how nice her stylish gown fitted, Iona swirled around, letting the skirt fly above her newly trimmed petticoat. Her short gowns were practical, but this bit of confection appealed to her long-denied feminine nature.

"They're expanding the school into the next building. There's room," he said curtly, keeping his gaze above her head. "Tomorrow, we'll meet with the solicitors to claim the reward. We're hoping to have Mortimer sign a document relinquishing all claim to you and your property. I won't promise anything except a second plan if he does not comply."

"It won't work, of course. I'm certain Mr. Winter has promised to pay off Mortimer's debts in return for my title. But you'll have your reward. I suppose these gowns can be considered an expense of doing business, *Gerard*."

She taunted him a little, stepping close to his proud figure and drawing her finger down his waistcoat buttons. He was very much the proper gentleman in silver-blue today, a shade that went well with his dark coloring. "You can be free of me tomorrow," she said a trifle wistfully.

He grabbed her invading hand and seemed set to push it away. Instead, he wrapped it in his long fingers and pressed her palm to his chest, where she could feel his heart beating. "I'll never be free of you. You'll haunt me like all the other voices in my head. But I won't be leaving until I know you and your sister are safe."

Aroused by his scent and proximity, she slid her hand away. "Heroic of you, I'm sure," she said sadly, not thrilled to know she'd caused him grief. "I'd rather you promise to take me to Italy as long as we're talking fantasy. I really do not expect you to take care of me. You have enough to do."

He finally turned his gaze downward, and she sensed his churning conflict. She shouldn't do this to him, but she wanted so much and could have so little— She drowned a little in his dark, troubled eyes.

Then he yanked her against his hard body, so she could feel his conflict as well as smell it.

"This is the reason I'm taking you to the school," he muttered, bringing his mouth down on hers.

She wanted this so very much—

TWENTY

GERARD KNEW BETTER THAN TO KISS THIS WOMAN HE CRAVED, ESPECIALLY IN a private room. He had experience and understood how easily the flames of lust could soar into a conflagration.

But by tomorrow, Iona might be gone. He would never have another chance to touch and hold her, to explore the richness of her kisses or the lushness of her curves. In that foolish gown, her breasts rose above the neckline, taunting him with their perfection.

He wanted her to remember him as he would always remember her.

He didn't need the voice in his head to mutter *stupid*.

But he couldn't resist her enthusiastic response to the thrust of his tongue. She didn't back away when he held her close but clung tighter. He ran his questing hands down her back, to the annoying bustle that prevented him feeling her natural curves. He couldn't undress her. . . but he wanted to.

Undeterred, Iona worked her fingers beneath his waistcoat, scorching him through his linen. How would it feel to lie with her all night, her nakedness against his? Instead of her usual roses, fragrant herbs wafted from her skin, and he wanted to taste her all over. He longed to see how far her boldness would take them.

He carried his kisses along her jaw, to her ear, and she pressed closer, moaning encouragement. The fool woman knew no fear. He was a man with tight control, but not all men would respect her innocence. To prove to himself—and to her—that this had to stop, he caressed her breast above the corset, where he could relish her softness.

She practically climbed up him, covering his jaw with kisses and letting him take his fill. He was so engorged, he feared he'd rip his trousers. She didn't even know to be afraid.

"Damn, I know I'll regret this," he whispered as he lifted her against the wall. He buried his face in the enticing curve of her neck, planted kisses on the ripe curves above her lace. She wrapped one leg around him as she had before, instinctively pulling their hips together.

He wouldn't take her like this. He wasn't that kind of cad. But he pushed her skirts up, rubbing his thumb along the fine linen of her drawers. He would buy her silk, if he could.

At the intimacy of his caress, she didn't shove him away but arched into him, almost begging for the caress he craved as much as she did.

All the voices in his head stilled as he located the slit of her drawers and rubbed her where she was wet and willing. It would be so very easy. . .

Gerard steeled himself, refusing to take advantage of an innocent who had no clear idea of what she was doing. Kissing her, he used his fingers to teach her, until he was muffling her screams and holding her as she bucked into his searching hand.

He continued to hold and kiss her as she melted and went limp. He let her skirts fall back in place. Once she merely leaned into him, shuddering slightly, he stepped away.

"That is only a sample of what a husband can give you. Do not throw yourself away," he warned, stepping over to the washbasin to clean up and steady himself.

When he turned back to her, he saw a tear streak down her cheek, but she was already straightening her attire. She swung to check her hair in the mirror, rubbing surreptitiously at her eyes.

"I will find lovers," she said boldly. "I will be like a man and take what I want."

"Women have babies." The thought of her in a brute's arms caused him to run cold, but he had no right to dictate her future. "Women cannot behave like men."

"Your aunts will welcome me at Wystan," she taunted. "They love babies. And they will teach me how not to have them. Why should I be tied down to one man?"

He could see it now—she was entirely right. He might go to Wystan one day and see her coddling another man's baby, and his tenants cooing over it as if it were their own.

"Because you are loyal and loving and being tied down happens. Come along, we need to take you to the school before it's dark. I have to meet Rainford." Gerard picked up the cloak and helped her into it.

She silently fastened the hood and waited for him to grab her satchel. She refused to take his arm as they stepped into the corridor. "I'll meet you at the train station." She walked rapidly toward the servants' door.

The entire hall smelled of sex to him, but at least her cold taunt had made it possible for him to move without crippling himself.

The philosophical soldier in his head remained silent.

IONA SAT AS FAR FROM LORD IVES AS THE HANSOM ALLOWED. SHE WAS A wanton. She should be thoroughly ashamed of herself—but she had enjoyed every second of that marvelous encounter and wanted *more*. If just touches could produce such exalting sensations—what would actual coupling be like? She grew up on a farm. She knew there had to be more.

But Lord Ives was an automaton with clockwork control of himself. She ought to be glad of that. If he controlled everyone else the way he did himself, he'd succeed at obtaining the reward and setting her free.

That was almost a depressing thought. She knew money wasn't the end of her problems. But her time with Lord Ives had taught her a great deal. She'd needed to learn who she was, what she wanted, and she was gradually coming to understand herself. Almost.

She simply had to forget her irrational longing for a man she couldn't have—an automaton she shouldn't want. So she had a few lessons to learn yet—like how to control her roiling emotions the way he did.

At the school, he introduced her to Phoebe's aunts. The older women were complete opposites of each other. Lady Agnes was short and welcoming, and Lady Gertrude was tall, stout, and formidable. While they exclaimed over her likeness to Isobel, they reminded her of the ladies at Wystan, and she felt at home.

Iona allowed herself to be swept into the world of women without a second look back at the dashing Lord Ives, who held her future in his hands.

For once in her life, she had to trust someone other than herself. She couldn't think of any better place to start than a man who could turn off his emotions like a spigot.

IN ILL HUMOR, GERARD DESCENDED THE CRUMBLING STONE STAIRS TO THE ill-lit interior of the Old Rooster tavern. He knew he'd done the right thing by leaving Iona untouched and taking her to the ladies at the school. But afterward, she'd treated him as if he were an old coat she'd discarded.

Far better that way, he realized. They needed distance before they committed an irrevocable act. Logic didn't improve his humor.

Rainford was already there, commanding a table, wearing his evening tails and appearing the glamorous and fabulously wealthy lord that he was. Young Viscount Drummond was with him, gathering players he'd apparently met on the previous evening. Gerard hated gambling, but he'd donned his dinner clothes to look the part of dissipated aristocrat with gold to waste.

The players all slapped him on the back and steered him toward a chair in a prime location in the gas-lit, whisky-stench of the ancient cellar.

Rainford held him back for a minute to murmur, "I've met with the Queen's secretary. He's located the lady's request and will expedite it through the committee. It will give one of the twins some amount of legal power once this all falls out."

"Brilliant, thanks." Gerard pounded the slender marquess on the back and shoved him into his chair.

Rainford had done all the work. Gerard felt like a sponger—until

Arthur Winter and the drunkard Mortimer arrived. They gave off such strong vibrations of excitement that he didn't even need Iona at his side to notice. Or maybe thinking of Iona brought his focus to pinpoint acuteness.

It was very possible he'd shut out people and their interfering *energies* in order to accomplish the many tasks he set himself. In the process, he'd shut out this part of himself as well. He wasn't entirely certain he wished to go through life noticing *vibrations*, but for Iona, he'd concentrate as if people were antique objects of interest.

Crossing one leg over his knee and leaning back in his chair, he assumed his best air of boredom and disdain as Drummond introduced his gambling mates from the previous evening. Gerard shrugged when one of the others suggested the newcomers join them.

Winter practically rattled the table with his eagerness. A stout young man, wearing tailoring finer than Gerard could afford, the American beamed delight from a cherubic face it was hard to dislike. He was quite possibly as much a victim as the twins.

While Winter lavished them with gratitude for allowing him to join such exalted company, Gerard watched his companion, the supposed Earl of Craigmore. Mortimer wasn't too far into his cups yet. He had probably once been a handsome man but dissipation had carved lines in his face, shadowed his eyes, and sapped his body. A receding hairline and untrimmed sideburns and mustache created a caricature of a degenerate villain.

It only took a few rounds of cards to determine Mortimer was cheating. Gerard fingered the cards the villain handled, focusing on the energy they emitted and not how he played. As Iona had said, her stepfather wasn't much on planning more than the moment. His vibrations were so shaky and crude that even Gerard's newly discovered talent could translate them as fury and frustration—and fear.

He didn't need pulsing air to tell him Mortimer was quite capable of doing damage if he didn't have what he wanted.

The old soldier in his head grunted agreement. . . and interest. It was worse than having his father in his head.

After a few more rounds of play, Gerard almost began to like the eager young American. On Winter's cards, he picked up languid shreds he interpreted as boredom and impatience, presumably with Mortimer. Again, he didn't need vibrations to discern the wealthy American's unnatural interest in young Drummond. *Damn.* This business of reading others was worse than sitting down to a gossip fest.

Irritated, Gerard laid down his cards, literally and figuratively. "I'm ready to call it a night, fellows, sorry. Craigmore, I believe I've found something of interest to you. I'm seeing your solicitor in the morning to verify that all is above board. It was good having a chance to meet you first."

He tapped on his hat and stood, leaving the fake earl and his wealthy friend looking startled and shoving back to follow. Rainford and friends prevented them from doing so.

Gerard had no doubt that he'd be tracked the second he climbed the cellar stairs. Insouciantly, he summoned a hansom and took it to the hotel. He had no fear for himself, but he may have just dropped a bomb that would have repercussions.

Mortimer had seemed dangerously desperate. Would he try to find Iona first? If the false earl thought he could pry a large marriage settlement out of Winter, he'd want as much control of Iona as he could. That wouldn't happen in a solicitor's office with Gerard watching.

Wrapped up in his thoughts, Gerard forgot to be wary once he reached the relative safety of the busy hotel lobby. It was early enough in the evening for guests to be returning from dinner or leaving for entertainments. Heading for the stairs, he nearly tripped over a ruffled red train.

The wearer of said train swung angrily, then said in disgust, "Lord Ives, of course. Why aren't you in your sty where you belong?"

Lady Alice. He really didn't have time for flirtation or argument. Volatile Alice was capable of either without a moment's notice. They'd been lovers a few times, years ago, but mostly they were childhood acquaintances who occasionally leaned on each other. And she apparently thought him dull enough to marry her if pressed. He knew to be wary now.

He offered his usual smooth apology, a smattering of flattery, and kept his eye out for her escort. But when it became plain she had just returned from dinner with her father, a little imp in his head kicked cans until he woke up.

Mortimer's spies were waiting for Gerard to lead them to Iona. If he stayed in the hotel, they might tear the place apart in search of her. If they had anyone watching the school, they may have seen Gerard arrive with a cloaked female and not depart with her. Thugs might attack the school.

He hoped the school had the resources to protect Iona for an evening, but why leave it to chance?

"How interested are you in helping the ladies at Wystan who helped you?" he asked bluntly. Alice was self-absorbed but not heartless, and she owed him for that earlier embarrassing contretemps.

Her eyes widened. "You're actually *speaking* to me, not just uttering inanities?"

Gerard waved an impatient hand and played on Alice's usual ennui. "Obviously. It's only a small favor, to aid a young Wystan lady being pursued by an unwanted suitor. You'll benefit from it, I assure you."

"Deceit *and* a reward," she almost purred. "I can do that. If this will settle any debt I owe, what do I need to do? And how long will it take?"

He produced Iona's room key. "I need you to change into something drab, perhaps from your lady's maid, if necessary. If you have a hooded cloak, wear that, or I'll borrow one." He wagered the lady knew the need for hooded cloaks and kept one on hand. "Then go to this room and wait for me. How long do you think that will take you? I shall try to be up there shortly after."

Once they settled on a time, he explained his plan. His cousin Phoebe and her husband wouldn't mind harboring a guest for the night. And the Blairs knew all the right people in Edinburgh who would appeal to Lady Alice and her miser of a father.

Preventing Mortimer's hooligans from attacking might be a different problem, but the Blairs were better prepared than a school full of young women. Their affluent street had watchmen and street lights. Plus, Phoebe had animal guards that could sniff out strangers and terrify attackers.

He was almost starting to appreciate his family's odd abilities. Perhaps he needed to pay more attention to his own.

The old soldier in his head muttered irascibly.

While he waited on Lady Alice, Gerard sent a messenger to warn the Blairs of his plans. So when they arrived after dark, his drama-prone cousin was at the door to greet them. For the benefit of any onlookers, she announced, "Gerard, how good of you to introduce us to your new lady friend! She will be more than safe with us, I assure you. Come along, my lady. We have a room all prepared and hot chocolate just waiting for your arrival."

Alice shot him a dirty look, but he'd explained who the Blairs were on the ride over. For the introduction to Blair's wealthy coterie, she'd hold her sharp tongue and drink chocolate.

While the women hustled upstairs, Andrew Blair appeared from his workroom in back. A large man in an oil-stained shirt that revealed he was no stranger to hard work, he polished a piece of metal. "We're old hands at skullduggery," he reminded Gerard. "You needn't worry. Phoebe's animals are all alert and waiting to take a bite out of any intruder."

"I've had the biggest thug locked up. I don't know if Mortimer has found any more larger than a street urchin, or I'd say have the beasts aim for the testicles." Worrying about Iona left Gerard short-tempered.

Blair chuckled. "We've alerted the night watchman. He's had some experience too."

"Raven says there are two strangers coming down the alley," his animal-mind-reading cousin called down. "Signal Henry and Wolf, please."

"Stables," Blair said crisply, nodding to a footman stationed in the hallway.

Reassured somewhat by this sign of preparation, Gerard shook his head in disbelief. "I'll give Mortimer this much credit, he's done his research. Or someone has, if they know every Malcolm hiding place in the city. If we tie up this pair, do we hope that will prevent others from arriving? I've not your experience at skullduggery."

Blair shrugged. "An organized gang might eventually realize this pair hasn't reported in. It won't matter. The animals are alert all night and will hear any newcomers. Go back and get some sleep. You look as if you've been a round or two in the ring."

"That's at least clean fighting," Gerard muttered, tipping his hat back on. "I think I'll just go back and punch Mortimer in the jaw and end it all."

"No reward in that," Blair said cheerfully. "And you'd have to kill him to end it all."

And without the reward, he wouldn't have the funds to pour the bastard onto a ship.

Growling as irascibly as the old soldier in his head, Gerard stalked out. Calling up the imperturbable, gentlemanly demeanor for which he was known, he tipped his hat to the watchman and strode down the street to walk off his temper.

The old soldier muttered something that loosely translated as *stupid turd*. Then added, *Wealth isn't in coin*, before falling silent again.

Well, fine time to tell him that. "You mean there is no treasure?" Gerard shouted at the empty street, startling roosted pigeons.

Did not say that.

No more listening to stupid coins and ancient voices.

Noticing an odd vibration on the night air, he swung around and caught a tall, ragged adolescent raising a cudgel. Just what he needed.

He kicked the lad in the nuts and walloped him with his walking stick.

TWENTY-ONE

"I'M COMING WITH YOU." IN THE SCHOOL OF MALCOLM'S SHABBY FRONT parlor the next morning, Gerard's Great-Aunt Winifred adjusted an old-fashioned straw hat on her graying blond hair. "My nephew has blind spots a mile wide."

Iona shook out the folds of the gown that had been delivered early this morning. A lovely gold-striped skirt with a toffee-colored bodice and a prim train, it was the most delightful attire she'd owned since her come-out. "No, Lord Ives simply has different priorities. Sending my new gowns here was thoughtful, and the kind of mundane detail that keeps his world running smoothly. We cannot expect him to understand our concerns can't be solved with a new gown."

Winifred was so much a part of Wystan that her arrival at the school had startled Iona, but she was grateful for the older lady's sturdy presence. Perhaps if miracles happened and all went well, they could buy presents for the other ladies and travel back together. She'd love that.

She knew the chances of it happening were next to nil.

"It's the mundane that blinds him," Winifred muttered, stabbing a hat pin into the straw.

"Men are like that." With her gray curls and earrings bobbling, Lady Agnes adjusted a fold on Iona's new attire. "Especially *Ives* men. It's hard for them to grasp all the nuances of the world they inhabit when they only think in steps to the task they wish accomplished. My son can see ghosts. Do you think he bothers to discover why they appear to him? Unless they're offering him an architectural drawing, he's not interested."

Iona chuckled. Lady Agnes's son was Max Ives, the engineering husband of the Malcolm Librarian. She remembered Lydia laughing at her husband's obliviousness. Being able to talk with other Malcolms renewed her confidence, even if her gift paled beside that of others.

"Well, one of us has to open Gerard's eyes," Winifred said, still not completely appeased. "You can be certain he's only thinking of money and not the futures of Lady Iona and Lady Isobel. Imagine, letting a lady marry an uncouth American just so her sister can be safe! Honestly, I don't know what the boy is thinking."

"I am the one who wishes to marry for wealth," Iona reminded her, smiling at the lady's defiant defense. "I have no need of a worthless title, but I have a great deal of need for the wealth that Mr. Winter can provide. Let us not argue the matter. Lord Dare's carriage is waiting."

Lady Winifred huffed, then took Iona's arm down the steep school stairs to the street. Iona noted with interest that the earl's diminutive valet sat beside Lord Dare's driver, armed with a rifle. He greeted her with a tip of his hat but continued scanning their surroundings. That made her nervous enough to look around as well.

What had Gerard learned last night that had him fortifying carriages?

Smelling nothing untoward, she allowed a footman to assist her inside after Winifred. She knew they did not have far to go, but after yesterday's experience, it had become apparent that a carriage was safer than walking.

Lord Ives was not inside the carriage, to her disappointment. But as soon as it halted in front of a towering brick building with a neat iron plaque at the entrance, the earl appeared in the doorway. He hurried down the stairs, a brass-handled cane over his arm. She feared the bulge in his coat pocket might be a derringer. What on earth had happened?

She took his offered hand and didn't dare ask. Her heart pounded faster—out of fear of this next step, or his proximity, or both. He swiftly hid his surprise when Winifred popped out of the carriage.

"Interesting chaperone," he murmured, dutifully waiting to escort his aunt up the stairs.

"Try talking her out of anything," Iona murmured back. Now that he'd steadied her with his presence, she decided her racing pulse was in anticipation of gaining a very large sum of money. The moment was almost upon her. She gripped the earl's arm harder.

She would not think about never seeing him again.

"I hope your journey was not too difficult, Aunt Winifred," he said as they climbed the stairs to the solicitor's floor.

"Travel is always difficult, as are men and most of life. If everything was easy, we would never learn, would we? Now let us proceed so we may take Lady Iona back to Wystan, where she belongs." On the landing, Winifred tapped her foot.

Lowell, the valet, opened the office door and bowed for his betters to proceed him. Iona noted he, too, carried what appeared to be a pistol in his coat, although he'd left the rifle in the carriage. She shuddered and allowed Gerard to rush her past the receptionist.

"What trouble are we expecting?" she asked as they reached the glass-paned door with the solicitor's name painted on it in gold and black.

"Your stepfather is in deeper than we thought," was all he had time to say before they were inside.

How did one go *deeper*? Deeper in debt, perhaps? What else was new? Puzzling out what he may have meant, Iona held out her gloved hand to greet the solicitor who had agreed to handle the reward money, ostensibly for Mortimer. Since the office was a respectable one, she'd surmise Arthur had chosen it.

"Lady Iona, it is a pleasure," the gentleman said. "Please, have a seat. Your father should be here shortly to confirm your identity. And your sister is well?"

"Quite," Iona said, sitting stiffly in the chair so as not to crush her new bustle. She handed over the letter from Isobel, witnessed by the librarian and her husband, to prove her twin's existence. "I cannot say why our stepfather is at all concerned, but it was good of Lord Ives to find us and let us know."

That set the solicitor back a bit. "Yes, well, a father must be concerned. . ."

"Let us not pretend any such thing," Gerard said, taking a chair near the desk after seating his aunt on a sofa. "Mortimer wishes to sell one of his stepdaughters. The twins objected. The offer of a reward changed Lady Iona's mind and brought her here. Lady Isobel is content where she is. You are to see that the reward is given without strings attached and the lady is free to leave. She's of age and independent of her stepfather's care. My aunt and I are here to assure that no undue pressure is applied."

"Yes, well." The lawyer polished his spectacles. "As to that, I have no grounds to speculate. I am merely here to transfer the funds upon the approval of Lord Craigmore."

"Ralph Mortimer," Iona corrected. "My *father* was the Earl of Craigmore. The impostor claiming concern is not my father. He is a wart on a toad without a farthing to his name."

The lawyer looked relieved at a knock on the door. "Yes, Brown, what is it?"

The secretary who had been at the front desk peered in. "The Earl of Craigmore and Mr. Arthur Winter are here, sir."

Iona tensed. She glanced at Gerard. He sat with long legs sprawled, hands crossed over his chest, looking as if he might nod off at any second. She almost laughed. Now that she knew him, she knew that pose smelled of dangerous wrath.

Her stepfather slouched in, smelling of the dreadful shaving soap he'd taken to using once he learned of her talent. She had to give him credit for recognizing that his wife wasn't entirely normal, nor were her daughters. The man might be a craven weasel, but he had an animal's instinct for survival.

Mr. Winter tipped his expensive hat to her and bowed admirably over Winifred's hand when introduced. She could not fault Mr. Winter for having too much money. But she could fault him for lacking the sense to understand that aristocrats were no different from anyone else. A title did not make a gentleman out of a toad wart.

"Lady Iona, it is good to see that you have come to no harm from your little misadventure. I am truly grieved that you may have taken my proposal in the wrong way." Winter took her gloved hand in his. His scent was more of bewilderment than harm. His grip was flaccid in comparison to Gerard's.

She withdrew her hand. "I am not a child. I have every right to visit family without being hunted like vermin."

Mortimer wisely stayed silent, only answering the solicitor's questions and signing the paperwork allowing the reward to be released to Gerard. He immediately produced a document transferring half the funds to Iona and had the solicitor witness them. He was indeed very good at mundane details.

"That's not enough to pay the estate's debt." Mortimer finally spoke. "We'll have to let the place. You'll have to move your belongings elsewhere, including those infernal bees."

Iona tightened her grip around the document Gerard solemnly handed her. His anger had coalesced into a sharp odor much like that of burning gunpowder. She tucked the document in her bag without looking at him.

"The estate's debts are yours, Mortimer, not mine. Lord Ives has been generous in offering me a share of the reward to show myself here. I will not insult his generosity by giving it to you."

"You're a bloody countess," Mortimer shouted. "You cannot abandon your land!"

Thankfully, Lord Ives chose to lean back in his chair and let the fireworks explode without his aid. She loved a man who knew when to stand back.

"I can and will abandon anything your touch has rotted, Mortimer. For Isobel's sake, I will consider the marriage settlements Mr. Winter offered," she acknowledged. "Lord Ives had his solicitor draw up the codicils I require. In preparation, I have requested that my mother's title be restored in my name. I cannot promise when that will happen."

Mr. Winter lit up as if she'd handed him the keys to a kingdom. "I am beyond delighted, my lady! You will never regret this, I promise. I will shower you with everything you can ever wish and see that your sister is surrounded in comfort."

Iona offered a tight smile. She regretted it already, but she ignored her grinding insides. "That will mean hanging Mortimer from the highest tree, so do not be so generous in your promises."

Gerard unfolded from his chair, offered Iona his hand, and addressed Mr. Winter. "Tell me where I should have the lady's requests for the settlement sent so you may peruse them at your leisure, sir."

No hand had ever felt so wonderful as his when he clasped her fingers and assisted her from her chair. Clutching her bag with the precious bank note, she was almost knock-kneed in relief. The earl, of course, was focused on Mr. Winter.

"I'll be having a say in what's fair and proper for the settlements. She'll be leaving with us, my lord," Mortimer insisted, confronting them belligerently. "That's what the reward was all about—having my daughters back with me. And I don't have the other yet."

"You won't have the other," Gerard corrected harshly. "You do not *have* Lady Iona. She is not yours to possess. I thought we made that clear. The ladies are safe. They are of age and independent of your will. From here on, Lady Iona will only correspond with Mr. Winter. You are free to go to hell."

"Now wait a minute!" Mortimer bunched his fists.

Mr. Winter settled a gloved hand on his shoulder. "You will be appropriately reimbursed, my lord, as promised. There is no need to antagonize my fiancée."

Iona winced at the appellation. She might as well become used to it.

Winifred rose to her full stout height and stood between Iona and Mortimer. "Now, we will be off to the bank. Gerard, call for the carriage, will you, dear? We have a trousseau to prepare."

Without looking back at her fuming stepfather, Iona obediently followed his lordship and his aunt out. In truth, she could not have moved on her own.

She longed to be like her queen bee and hide in her hive.

GERARD SLAMMED THE LID ON HIS DISGUST AND FURY AND BUCKLED IT closed. He led the ladies to the bank where Iona deposited her funds in the name of her and her sister. The amount was meager given the expense of operating an estate. He felt guilty about keeping his half, but if she meant to marry that. . .

He couldn't even think of it. He wanted to exterminate Mortimer, but Winter was an effeminate sod who would probably treat Iona like a princess. Not that a woman with her lusts would appreciate that, but it was her damned choice.

What he and Blair had learned last night from the miscreants who had dared follow and attack him chilled his blood though. He could keep his fury with Iona down while he watched every man around her with murder in his heart.

Winifred nearly beat him over the head with her umbrella when he insisted on taking them back to the school.

Iona perceptively took the umbrella away and made room for him inside Dare's carriage. "What is it, my lord? Has Mortimer made threats already?"

She was officially affianced to another. Gerard didn't want to be that close to her again, but he had no choice. He sat next to his aunt on the forward-facing seat though. "Your stepfather has gambled himself into a hole so deep, he cannot climb out. It is not just debts to gentlemen, but to nefarious characters he had no business gambling with. If he does not pay them back, they are likely to kill him and come after you and your sister next. That's why there are eyes on us everywhere we go."

Winifred swatted him again. "That's reprehensible, Gerard. You had no right to terrify a young lady with such sordid stories. You should be ashamed of yourself."

Had it been any other woman, he would have politely held his tongue. With Iona . . . he could not play charades. She knew when he tried to hide anything and would despise him for being less than honest.

He watched as she took a deep breath and processed his news. She looked like a delicate butterfly in that frilly bodice, with wings of striped skirts billowing around her. He wanted to be the man to strip her from those fripperies and expose her naked skin to the air as it should be.

"You have a plan?" she asked steadily.

"I do, but it means keeping you locked behind closed doors until we have Mortimer safely on a ship sailing to China. I've sent warnings to Max to do the same with your sister." He awaited her verdict.

"China! That is creative, but I don't like the idea of placing you in any more danger, my lord," she said slowly, as if thinking aloud. "Your good deed is done. Isobel and I are considerably richer. I should appeal to my future husband for protection."

Gerard nearly broke his walking stick in half while he tamped his fury back in place again.

Winifred spoke before he could. "Don't be ridiculous, child. You cannot marry that man-milliner. You will be fine living with us. Gerard can bring his many cousins to visit and perhaps you'll find one of far more use than an American in search of a title. We should simply take the train and leave town now."

"Man-milliner?" Iona's lips twitched. "I do not think I wish to know the definition. You heard Mr. Winter. I need only ask and he will provide anything I wish. I could ask to be surrounded by guards. I really cannot expect Lord Ives to delay from his other duties any longer."

"Give me tonight," Gerard insisted. "I have everything in place. I want to finish this once and for all. I could not live with myself knowing you cannot safely return to your own estate because I did not follow through."

She made a moue of distaste and studied the street they traversed. "I need to learn to act on my own again. Could we stop at the church for a few minutes?"

"The church where the gang's bullies have already attacked us once?" he asked, unable to hide his incredulity.

"Yes, please." She folded her hands in her lap, looking like a demure princess and not the stubbornly perverse beekeeper she was.

Beekeeper, of course. He refrained from rolling his eyes and ordered the driver to halt at St. Giles. In his lust, he'd forgotten that this was a woman who commanded bees. And he was a man who might die from stings. Charming.

Dangerous the old soldier said in satisfaction.

Gerard didn't appreciate the notion of the butterfly countess being dangerous—but the spirit was right.

Iona was not only dangerous, she could be deadly if she applied her mind to it.

And he had no control over her.

Against his better judgment, he left her in the hands of his aunt and the intrepid ladies of the school.

TWENTY-TWO

FIGHTING THE GLOOM OF WATCHING LORD IVES DRIVE AWAY AFTER LEAVING her at the school, Iona shrieked in delight to discover Isobel waiting for her in the parlor. They hugged and danced around like maniacs to the amusement of the older ladies.

"You shouldn't be here," Iona cried. "You need to be safe with Lydia so we needn't worry about you!"

"So I can worry about you?" Isobel hooted in derision. "I have been crawling the walls in fear knowing your impulsiveness."

"I am not impulsive. I plot very thoroughly." Iona removed her gloves and allowed herself to be shoved to a seat while tea was served. "I am glad you are here but wish you'd waited a day."

"Tell us what is happening," Lady Agnes insisted. "Perhaps we can be of assistance."

Iona let Winifred enthusiastically explain the morning's events. Lady Phoebe and Lady Dare arrived to join them. At hearing about Mortimer's gang, they were appalled.

"This is insupportable," Phoebe declared. "Just as we're trying to clean up the slums and restore this part of town, criminal gangs think they can move in? They'll be taking over the palace before we know it!"

"I don't think we need to worry about the palace," Azmin, Lady Dare said, suppressing a grin at Phoebe's dramatics. "But we do need to protect the school and the twins if their stepfather is involved with dangerous elements."

"I know one of the books I left downstairs had information about the city's lowlifes. Let us see what information it can provide." Phoebe stood. "Come with me, Iona, and help me find it."

Without waiting for a reply, she marched from the parlor. Startled, Iona hurried after her, half-running to keep up with Phoebe's long-legged strides. They took the stairs down to what once might originally have been a ground-floor business and was now the school's library.

"You have a recent book on thieves and gamblers?" Iona asked, unable to hide her doubt.

"Of course not." Phoebe strolled through the stacks, caressing their spines. "I could see you plotting. My aunts tend to be. . . perceptive. It's best not to give them any inkling of what you're planning. I know this city inside and out. Use me. Do you know where they're gambling?"

"I heard the Old Rooster mentioned. But you have a husband at home, and animals that depend on you. I cannot ask you or anyone to help me. I am not at all certain even I can help, except I can smell treachery and perhaps offer warnings."

"And Ives are impervious to deceit. Gerard will only think in terms of honor and proper documentation and the like. Fortunately, Andrew understands I go my own way as he does. My husband is the epitome of a very modern gentleman."

Phoebe pulled a book off the shelf. "Here it is. I did not lie about the book. It exists. It just won't help. Were you planning a visit to the Rooster?"

"Or waiting outside. If Isobel were a little more stable, I'd have her watch the back exit, but I fear she'd faint before she could signal me."

"The two of you together would be too noticeable, anyway, as would I or Azmin. We've attracted a little too much notice, and those who hide in the dark know to avoid us. But I can wait in a carriage nearby, listening to the minds of my pets for anything untoward. I'll bring Wolf and Raven to guard outside and perhaps locate another creature or two for inside. You could wait with me."

Iona took the book and flipped pages. "I am better stationed where I can smell people as they pass by. Isobel has some of the same ability. Not as strong, I fear. Her gift lies elsewhere and is not useful in this case. Perhaps if she sat with you, though, she might note any strong suspicious scents."

"And where will you be?"

Iona rubbed her palms against her skirt. "I'm hoping to pose as one of the urchins. If I could have your dog with me, that would be perfect."

"No, the street urchins all know each other. You'll have to wear a uniform and pose as a groom or some such. You can linger near the front entrance, and we'll park the carriage at the alley in back. But if they're not in that tavern. . ."

"Someone needs to verify it, yes." Iona nodded vigorously, delighted to have a partner in crime. "Perhaps your husband or Lord Dare could speak with Lord Ives."

"All we have to do is smuggle you out from under my aunts' noses," Phoebe crowed happily.

"*All*, she says," Iona muttered, but her thoughts were already racing ahead.

~

"You will not attend, Rainford," Gerard insisted, shrugging away his valet to tie his own cravat. "You are your father's sole heir. A dukedom dying out because of a knife fight is simply not done."

"I imagine it has," the marquess said thoughtfully, tapping his walking stick on the hearth. "Duels, swordfights, war, that sort of thing. And there's always my cousin."

"Not done," Gerard repeated. "Mortimer has taken up the challenge I sent. Blair has offered to attend with me. I think he's had quite enough of Lady Alice's arrogance. I only expected her to stay with them a night, but she's apparently taken a liking to their household and won't leave."

Rainford chuckled. "That was cruel to inflict her on the innocent. We should introduce her to Mr. Winter. That would cure him of his lust for titles."

Gerard lifted his chin and allowed Lowell to adjust his collar. "Not a bad idea. Alice's father could persuade the rich American to contribute generously to some cause of the queen's, get him noticed, knighted. . ."

"Dream on. The American is claimed, and just because you don't like it doesn't mean it won't happen. I don't know why you're going to this effort for a female who needs to marry wealth."

Stupid bastard the old soldier muttered. Or maybe that was Gerard's own opinion of himself. It didn't matter. Five thousand pounds burned a hole in his pocket. He could fix Wystan's roof before the snow flew. But he knew what was right. He would finish this first.

"It will give me satisfaction to see a man who has made lives miserable be tossed into misery of his own." Satisfied with his appearance, Gerard picked up his hat and stick. "Off you go, Rainford. Give my greetings to your father. Choose your bride. I'll expect notice of an heir this time next year."

The very proper marquess made a rude noise and sauntered out after him. Checking his weapons, Lowell locked up. A sharpshooter valet wasn't of much use in a crowded tavern, but one never knew when one might come in handy.

Leaving the marquess to go his own way, Gerard and Lowell took a hansom across the bridge to the old side of town. Stepping down at the tavern, Gerard tried to attune his senses to his surroundings as he had the prior night, but his thoughts were too cluttered.

Why was he really doing this? Surely not for a woman who intended to marry for money and march out of his life? For justice, maybe. Because he was damned bored with his life, more likely. That didn't mean he should put an end to it by stepping into a den of thieves.

Undeterred, he took the stairs down to the gambling hell, Lowell on his heels.

Viscount Drummond and a few of his friends were waiting, as were Andrew Blair and Zane Dare, who preferred to be called doctor and not viscount. Since Mr. Winter and his penchant for titles wasn't about, it didn't matter what Zane called himself. Mortimer was their mark, and he was already there, three sheets to the wind.

"You stole my daughters," Mortimer slurred. "I want them back."

"And you think winning at cards will persuade them to return to you?" Gerard couldn't in all good faith trounce a drunk. He'd hoped Mortimer would attempt to stay sober enough to play. "The best you can hope for is to win back the money."

"If it weren't for you, they'd be back! It's their mother's land." Slouched in his chair, Mortimer glared belligerently through half-lowered lids. "I should swab the floor with you. But I'll let them fellows do it. They're not happy with your interference."

Gerard felt a chill down his spine. Andrew and Zane straightened and pushed back their chairs. His valet emerged from the shadows, his hand ready on his pocket. Gerard didn't have to turn around to know the room was clearing—except for the bad vibrations at his back.

He should have gone to Wystan.

Judging distance from the tremors of violence, Gerard dropped into a crouch. Using his newly-purchased sword stick, he spun around and swung at the wrinkled trouser legs approaching. Screams of pain drowned in the explosion of gunfire over his head.

The tavern erupted in fists and cudgels and knives. Cursing, regretting that he'd dragged his friends into this, Gerard focused on his goal—Mortimer. The ship sailed in the morning.

Dodging cudgels, fighting dirty and landing crippling blows with his stick and any body part that sufficed, he finally reached the fake earl and bunched the cad's waistcoat in his fist. Staying low, he yanked Mortimer out of his chair and down to the filthy floor. The drunk attempted just enough of a fight to justify breaking a fist against his jaw. He slumped.

A knife slashed downward, but sensing the motion, Gerard rolled from the blow. He whistled at Lowell, who ducked and sidestepped and joined him in grabbing Mortimer's coat.

Zane and Drew flanked them, protecting their backs with fists. More scoundrels blocked them.

"Dammit, why can't anything be easy?" With a sigh, Gerard stood up abruptly, smashed the knob of his stick against a whiskered jaw, and jabbed the knife end at a dirty trouser leg.

~

THE ENORMOUS WOLFHOUND AT IONA'S SIDE CAME TO ATTENTION AT THE crack of a gunshot.

Uncomfortable in her ill-fitting boy's clothes, she straightened from her post in a doorway to study the lamp-lit street. Gunshots weren't good. She had only the small knife Azmin had given her.

Phoebe's raven screamed a warning overhead.

Iona opened her senses to the wind. She'd already identified a carriage waiting down the street as Viscount Dare's. Several of the men entering the tavern stank of hunger and a scent she could only call vile— not exactly deceit but worrisome. But she really needed to be closer to smell more.

Leaving her niche, she edged nearer to the stone cellar stairs leading down to the tavern, close enough to hear the shouts and groans. Heart in throat, she debated descending. Her meager gift wasn't of much use indoors—and apparently not much use at all if she didn't recognize the scent of violence.

To Iona's disgust, Isobel ran from her hiding place around the corner. She'd insisted on accompanying Phoebe over Iona's strident objections. Just as she appeared, men from the cellar began pouring up the narrow tavern stairs in a great hurry.

"Phoebe's rats or mice or whatever say there is a tremendous brawl in the tavern. The rodents are apparently getting drunk on spilled ale. What do we do now?"

Panic? Iona pulled them both flat against the wall in the doorway where she'd been hiding and pointed down the street. "That's Lord Dare's carriage. Stand near it until we know what's happening. I may need to send Wolf into the tavern, and it would be good to know you're nearby to back me up."

Isobel was a bookkeeper with a mind for money. Warfare was beyond her understanding. She nodded agreement and retreated to safety.

Iona steeled herself to go inside—until the fight burst through the door. In the shadows, she couldn't discern villains from heroes. In the melee of torn coats and flying fists, she could only sense Gerard's fury.

If she was not mistaken, that was him dragging Mortimer up the stairs.

She didn't have Phoebe's ability to give Wolf orders. He was only there to protect her. She hadn't planned for a brawl where she couldn't separate one man from another. She winced as a blackguard attempted to jerk Gerard back down the stairs. The earl had to release Mortimer to swing his fists. She could almost feel his pain.

He was hurt!

"C'mon, Wolf, let's smite a few rodents." She ran toward the melee, determined to pry Lord Ives from disaster.

Throwing punches over an insensate Mortimer on the stairs, the damned earl didn't even notice as she and Wolf grabbed her stepfather's coat. Gerard's unprepossessing valet dodged flying fists to add his strength. Together they dragged the sot up the rest of the stone stairs, while the earl clouted and kicked the hirelings back down. Iona was grateful for her boy's clothes. No one gave her a second look.

Once they had Mortimer sprawling on the cobblestones well away from the entrance, Lowell dived back into the fray, attempting to part Lord Ives from the throng.

Gerard was now fighting his way back *into* the melee. "Drew and Zane are still in there!" he yelled at his servant over the noise of the fracas.

Well, rats, Phoebe wouldn't like that. Neither would Azmin. As more men spilled up the stairs, flinging fists and cudgels and knives, Iona began to hum under her breath. She just needed Gerard out of there. . .

She tugged Wolf's collar, causing him to yip. A moment later, he howled—Phoebe was telling him something.

At the sound, Gerard glanced over his shoulder. She prayed he recognized the wolfhound. From his scowl, she gathered he did, but he didn't see her. He returned to beating off attackers. Was that a sword at the end of his stick?

She couldn't think curse words and concentrate on humming.

To her relief, the mob finally pushed his lordship back to street level.

Sensing a confusion of fury and. . . blood thirst?. . . approaching, Iona swung around, still humming. More men spilled out of the alley. To her utter dismay, at the sight, Isobel crumpled beside the carriage. Telling herself it was just her sister's reaction to fright, Iona released Wolf and prayed.

The dog eagerly leapt to guard her against the new ruffians rushing toward the tavern entrance.

To Iona's relief, the rather large Mr. Blair and the professorial viscount finally emerged looking bloodied but determined. Blair held a smoking pistol and appeared prepared to commit murder. But the three gentlemen were completely outnumbered.

And Mortimer was climbing to his knees, reaching for his pocket.

TWENTY-THREE

GERARD BREATHED IN RELIEF AS ZANE AND BLAIR FOUGHT THEIR WAY OUT OF the hole, both appearing to be mostly in one piece. If he were a gambling man, he'd wager the big Scot inventor had brawling experience. The good doctor, however, merely possessed an instinct for survival and a wicked temper.

Sensing the vibrations of blows before they landed had Gerard ramming his stick backward while swinging his fist and his boots to clear a path for his friends. Clutching a villain by the throat, he received a vibration so violent that he had to glance behind him—to see a band of hoodlums hoisting Mortimer to his feet.

The pistol that Iona's stepfather held was waving in Gerard's direction. Behind him and on his other side, he sensed more pistols being drawn. Bullets aimed at him would hit the cellar stairs and quite possibly his companions.

A woman screamed—in fury. *Iona.* He'd recognize her voice anywhere.

Well, hell.

Acting on what his senses told him—that they were outnumbered and targets—Gerard dived headfirst down the stairs, arms stretched to shove everyone backward. Just as he landed in the midst of the fracas, a barrage of bullets hailed over his head.

He stiffened as pain dug into his shoulder, but he scrambled to prevent breaking anyone's head. Another pain scorched across his scalp, and he lost the power to fight, collapsing into the tangle of bodies at the bottom of the stairs.

Through the ringing in his ears he heard someone shout "Bees!" And then police whistles shrieked.

He glanced up just enough to see a cloud of bees swarming through a halo from the streetlight. At night. In the cold. His vision was blurring. Perhaps he hallucinated.

As someone cursed and attempted to lift him, he could swear he saw bees covering every inch of the ugly coat Mortimer had been wearing. The shrieks of the thugs attempting to drag the twins' stepfather away were music to his ears as darkness closed in.

THE EXERTION OF CALLING THAT ANCIENT, ENORMOUS NEST OF NEARLY dormant bees left Iona staggering. But she'd seen Gerard fall. She had to reach him while driving the bees in the opposite direction—after Mortimer.

Wolf snarled and snapped and prevented the shooters from going near the cellar stairs. Iona slipped around him as police whistles sent most of the crowd fleeing into the shadows. A few lingered helplessly near the shrieking figures of men covered in bees, but they, too, melted into the darkness as policeman ran down the hill.

Iona had almost reached Gerard when someone grabbed her from behind.

"You can't lift him. Go home with your sister, my lady. Let us handle this." Strong hands lifted her and shoved her toward strangers.

Mortimer's screams had died out. The bees streamed after two figures fleeing down the alley. Her stepfather didn't flee with them.

Iona thought she recognized Rainford's ice-blond hair and lean form descending after Gerard and the others as she stumbled backward in the hands of strangers. The marquess was a physician and healer, she vaguely recalled. Of course, Dare was a physician too, but he was down those stairs. . .

Her heart screamed to stay, even as she was carried away. With the bees buzzing in her head, she had no ability to fight.

"Never saw anything like it," one of her protectors drawled.

"It was if he had eyes in the back of his head," the other replied, sounding bewildered. "He swung before they did, and clipped the ones behind him at the same time. Then dived *before* the bullets flew. Ain't possible."

Iona tried to puzzle out the topic, but her head buzzed. She'd released the bees, but there were a lot of them and they lingered. She had to keep them from Gerard.

"Reckon he's like his witchy mother?"

Finally understanding, Iona shrugged off the helping hands. "You had better hope Ives has abnormal talents so he may live to rescue others someday. He's a hero."

If the gentlemen looked startled, she didn't know. Apparently awake again, Isobel ran toward her, and Iona stumbled over to hug her twin.

"Is that Dare's carriage?" In relief, Iona dragged her sister toward the impatient horses. "Will the driver take us to Lord Dare's home? I believe it's closest."

The strangers dashed up to assist them. "The marquess said we're to take you back to the school."

"That will only delay our arrival at Dare's," Iona said dismissively. "We need to be with Lady Phoebe and Lady Dare, and I'm quite certain they won't be at the school."

"You can't—"

"Oh, dear," Isobel interrupted their protest with a groan. "*Please,* never tell my sister she can't."

Smiling grimly, Iona shouted at the driver. "Take us back to the viscount's, please. Lady Dare will need help." Iona slammed the door on their white knights and hung on so they couldn't open it.

"You might want to help the police haul off the miscreants," she called to her disconcerted rescuers as the carriage began to roll.

"Malcolms," she heard one of the men say in disgust. "You can't reason with them."

"Ives is a *Malcolm*," was the last grumble she heard as she settled back against the squabs.

The earl had made a rather public display of his unreasonable heritage this evening, Iona acknowledged. Although, as far as she was concerned, the Ives brawling was more unseemly than dodging unseen bullets and fists. Still, if these men had actually paid attention and understood what he'd done, it might affect any diplomatic career he envisioned. She had brought him nothing but scandal.

"What happened to Mortimer?" Isobel whispered, interrupting Iona's gloomy thoughts. "Will he live?"

Thinking of the still figure abandoned on the street, Iona shook her head. "I don't know. He tried to shoot Lord Ives, and I became angry. I may have killed him. I almost hope he's dead if he has harmed Lord Ives and his friends."

Isobel squeezed her hand. "Don't. Let us believe they are all fine."

If the hustle and bustle of the Dare household meant anything, they *weren't* all fine. The marquess's speedy carriage had evidently arrived before they did.

A towering giant of a footman let them in. In the parlor, Lady Dare, garbed in one of her infamous saris, barked orders at young men twice her size. Dare's medical students? The men rushed to do the lady's bidding, joining the servants carrying water basins and bandages.

Lady Phoebe's voice carried from down the corridor. What appeared to be a squad of urchins jumped and ran out the back door upon her command. There didn't seem to be anything Iona could do. Wearing the uniform of a groom, with a cap on her short hair, she might pose as a servant. But she couldn't abandon Isobel, who looked pale enough to faint again.

"Suggest to Lady Dare that you fetch Lord Ives' Aunt Winifred. She's a healer of sorts. She can sit with the patients while the others rest." Iona maneuvered her sister toward the parlor while staying in the shadows.

"And what will you do?"

"Carry water basins and bandages." Abandoning her twin, Iona scurried to the back stairs and the steady stream of servants hurrying up and down. No house had enough servants at times like this. These appeared to mostly be worried kitchen staff. Iona grabbed a tea tray cooling off on a table and hustled up the stairs with it.

Most of the activity seemed centered at the top of the central stairs, so she balanced the heavy tray down the upper hall in that direction.

She could hear Lord Dare's voice shouting orders, so he, at least, was alive—and cursing. He was a physician. She wouldn't worry about him.

Closer up, she could hear men consulting in quieter voices. The marquess? He, too, was a physician and reportedly a Malcolm healer. She eased nearer that conversation.

"Look for an exit wound. If there is none, you'll have to cut into that hole and remove the bullet. Have they taught you that yet?"

Iona winced. But surely that meant either Phoebe's husband or Gerard was still alive or they wouldn't be operating.

A pair of gangly students abruptly emerged from the nearest chamber, off to dig into a bullet hole. Iona took a step back but they scarcely noticed her as they dashed the other way, past the door where Dare was shouting at his minions.

The marquess might recognize her, but she had to know—

Boldly, she carried the tray into the chamber he occupied.

Lord Ives lay half naked on the bed. She almost swallowed her tongue at the sight of broad, muscled shoulders and chest, except the blood everywhere had her swaying as badly as Isobel.

His valet—his own wrist heavily wrapped in bandages—attempted to remove his employer's boots. A frightened maid dabbed at the blood running from the earl's shoulder. The marquess alternately sponged blood from his patient's hair to find the wound while attempting to staunch the bleeding gap revealed.

Iona had seen wounds sutured. She didn't like watching, but she knew what it involved. She hardened her senses against the roiling odors of pain and fear. At least Gerard was unconscious, and it was only the servants she sensed. The marquess was oddly—odorless.

Setting the tray down, she washed in the basin by the table, picked up a roll of gauze, and made a thick compress.

Barely looking at her, the marquess nodded approval. "If you can press down on that part, I'll start work on this end."

Iona stayed silent in fear that any moment he would recognize her.

Another student rushed in to help with the shoulder wound. The maid retreated to help Lowell with the boots.

Another student arrived and was sent for clean water. The marquess calmly stitched at the head wound.

Lord Dare walked in just as Iona stepped back to allow Rainford to finish stitching. The physician/viscount wore his shirt unfastened and a bandage around his torso, but he seemed otherwise able and willing.

He glanced at Iona, and she was sure he recognized her, but he said nothing as he took over treating the shoulder wound.

Iona hovered in the shadows, praying. She tried to concentrate on the earl's splendid muscles, but mostly, she watched him breathe. It wasn't steady. He appeared to be gasping but that didn't seem to concern the men. She took a breath for each of his, willing him to live. She tried not to watch too closely as one of the students sponged off all the blood.

"Drew has a bullet lodged in his thigh from a ricochet." Lord Dare began winding gauze around the earl's shoulder. "You should probably look at him next. I just have cracked ribs."

"Ran into a chair, did you?" The marquess knotted his thread and held out his hand. Iona hurriedly handed him a clean bandage. "And Drew couldn't pry his pistol out of his pocket?"

"It's either that or tell the police Ives knocked us flying to protect us from a hail of bullets he couldn't have seen coming. Your choice."

Iona felt as if their words were directed at her. She hadn't helped Gerard do any of that. All she had done was try to murder a man with bees.

Bees. There had been lots of bees. They shouldn't have been near the earl. . .

She had nothing to offer to explain what he'd done.

"Exceptional hearing," the marquess suggested when she didn't claim responsibility. "But the chair and pistol will satisfy the authorities."

Iona wanted to shout *That won't get those monsters hanged!* But she didn't know how the law worked. The thugs might hang simply for carrying weapons—provided they were caught.

Rainford washed his hands and finally glanced at Iona. "That's what you'll tell everyone, right? Ives likes his privacy."

"I was there. I saw it all," she agreed solemnly. "Lowell did, too." She nodded at the valet.

Lowell set down the boots he'd finally pried off. "Broken chairs all over. Scoundrels flung them about. Pistols fire when that happens."

"Right. Let's take a look at Blair. Tell us if this scoundrel wakes." The slender marquess picked up his bag of supplies and stalked out, looking almost regal in his evening tails.

"He'll make a proper duke one day," Lowell said in admiration as the maid and students followed the physicians. Lowell was no fool. He recognized her too.

Iona wasn't interested in the handsome marquess or his future dukedom. "I sent for Aunt Winifred. She's a healer, but Lord Ives won't appreciate her."

Lowell furrowed his already wrinkled brow. "Head wounds can be bad. More important that he gets well than mad. You oughtn't be here."

"Just until Winifred arrives," she promised. She nodded at the valet's bandaged wrist. "You probably need a stiff drink and some rest. Does that door over there lead to a dressing room?"

Lowell peered in. "With a cot. Why don't you wait there?"

"I'm not injured. You are. I smell whisky in that teapot. It's cold. Does that matter?"

Lowell looked longingly at the tray, then back to his employer.

"Take it. That's an order." Looking less like a countess than she ever had, but commanding as if she'd been in authority all her life, Iona pulled a chair up to the bedside. She felt half naked in boy's trousers. And she was shivering, probably from shock, but she refused to show weakness.

"He'll have my head," the servant muttered, but accustomed to following orders, he poured a cup and carried it to the antechamber.

He came back a moment later carrying a quilt. "You need it more than me." He dropped it in her lap.

When the room was finally clear, Iona crept closer to the bed.

Gerard's head and shoulder were swathed in bandages. His

breathing was ragged. She touched the strong column of his throat but she was no doctor. She couldn't tell if it was closing up.

Holding a lamp closer, she forced herself to look away from his naked chest and explore the more likely places for bee stings, like his hands and wrists.

And there they were, two swelling welts on his battered fists.

TWENTY-FOUR

Sun-drenched marble met the golden sand. In the distance, azure waves lapped. Was that a palm tree? A siren's song called. Gerard climbed over the ancient ruins. . .

Blood dripped from the columns, sinking into the pitted surfaces and staining them crimson.

"I need honey from *my* hive." Frustration tinted the siren's voice.

Gerard tried to locate the source but struggled against the murky water closing over his head.

"We can telegraph them, of course, but it will still take a day or two to ship it here. It will be simpler to take him back to Wystan."

Winifred? His aunt was in Italy? Why? Her son! Right, her son needed a sunny clime.

He dived under the water again. Why was he in the water?

"The books recommend inhaling cannabis or lobelia fumes for lung disorders."

Rainford? Was that Rain out there?

"The books are written by dolts who recommend coffee for insomnia. It's a bloody bee sting." *Dare.*

Then he wasn't in Italy? On what golden shore did Roman ruins exist in England?

He tried to speak, but his throat closed up, and he heard only a raspy breath.

"He's coming around!"

Iona. That was definitely Iona, not a siren. Still, a vision of a goddess wrapped in white linen swam through his watery vision.

"My mother's herbal agrees with Lady Iona," Dare's voice continued. "Honey is the best cure if he's sensitive to stings. He's not feverish any longer, so this jar is working."

"Gerard?" Iona's voice coaxed him back to the surface.

"Don't wake him until I check this wound."

Pain shot through his head, and he sank below the waters again.

When he woke next, his head throbbed, his eyes seemed swollen shut, and his shoulder needed to be hacked off before he could move.

"Our healing abilities are helping," Winifred said soothingly. "The earl is still breathing, and that's what matters."

"I almost killed him."

Iona sounded so mournful, he wanted to reach for her, but he couldn't move.

"His own blockheadedness did that," Winifred said with scorn and affection. "He had no business entering that den of thieves."

"He wanted to protect us from Mortimer. We would have been fine once I married Mr. Winter. Mortimer couldn't have touched us then."

"Blockheaded," Winifred repeated emphatically. "Ives are like that."

Gerard wanted to laugh but could only manage a hoarse rattle. He was still an Ives in her eyes, then, not an insane Malcolm who knew things he shouldn't.

A small, cool hand caressed his brow, and the scent of roses wafted around him. He desperately needed to open his eyes but they wouldn't cooperate.

"Will he really be all right?"

"He'll be sore for weeks. Go with your sister. It's better this way."

What would be better? *He* wouldn't be better. He tried to tell her to stay, but the best he could do was clench his fingers into fists.

A soft kiss pressed his cheek, and then the roses were gone.

∽

"WHERE IS SHE?" GERARD MUTTERED, RUBBING HIS NEWLY SHAVED JAW.

"Who?" Lowell fussed with cleaning off his razors.

Gerard tried to rip off his valet's arm, but his grip wasn't strong yet. Lowell easily yanked away.

"The beekeeper?" The valet shrugged. "With her sister at Calder, last I heard, preparing for her nuptials."

Gerard ground his teeth. He'd recovered enough to resist being shipped off to the wilds of Wystan, but it had taken a week before he had the strength to sit up and breathe normally. A *week*. She could be married already.

"Mortimer is still alive then?"

Lowell tucked away his instruments. "Mighty sick, last I heard. Your friends swore to the coppers that he was the one who shot you, so they locked him behind bars. The American hired lawyers to bail him out. They're still arguing over whether he's a peer and entitled to privileges."

"He's no more than the younger son of a viscount. Can't they read? I want him transported." But that was fury speaking. Mortimer had not been the one to shoot him. The cad had been flat on his back, covered in bees at the time.

Iona was marrying wealth, as she'd wanted.

He should take his reward and order the roof repaired at Wystan so he didn't have to worry about throwing out the ladies just yet. Transporting the library would be hell anyway. He didn't think saving the orchard would save the castle in the long run, but maybe he'd find a wealthy heiress to marry. Then he could live in London, hoping Iona was safe under Wystan's new roof.

He'd be dead by now if Iona hadn't taken down Mortimer. She'd saved his life with *bees*.

The soldier philosopher in his head said nothing, and Gerard realized the medallion wasn't in his pocket.

"Where's my lucky piece?" he demanded.

"Wasn't so lucky now, was it?" Lowell said complacently. "It's in a drawer with all your other bits and pieces.

He should probably leave it there, but what if he no longer heard voices? His head still occasionally throbbed when he didn't rest enough. Was there any point in going to Italy if he couldn't hear the voices?

Did he actually feel *disappointment* that he might not have a gift for seeing the past? His head must still be muddled.

"I'm still alive, aren't I? Find out when the wedding is scheduled and where it will be held. If Mortimer is still alive, he'll find a way to drain her coffers just the way he's done Winter's. His thieving cronies will be sure that he does."

"The problem isn't yours," Lowell reminded him. "Your friends are still hobbling about after that last fracas. You can't ask them to do more."

He'd already had visits from Zane and Blair and knew they were recovering and enjoying the coddling of their wives, despite their protests otherwise.

Gerard didn't want to be coddled. But he didn't want a woman as passionate and courageous as Iona to marry a milksop either.

He wanted her for *his*.

That realization had him breaking out in a cold sweat.

IONA FINISHED REPAIRING THE HACKLE COVERING A CALDER HIVE AND WIPED a straying hair from her face. Her hair was starting to grow out. Perhaps she should have it trimmed off again. It was so much easier not dealing with the heavy length—and it wasn't as if her fiancée cared if she wore snakes on her head.

A golden leaf fluttered past. It would snow soon. She needed to leave before then. Arthur could stay and petition the queen all he liked. She wanted to return to the comfort of Wystan and lick her wounds.

And use Arthur's wealth to improve lives, she reminded herself sternly. He'd agreed to her settlement, poor fool.

Isobel raced down the hillside, waving a letter, her dark skirts fluttering in the breeze. Iona had no curiosity about its contents. Everyone in her world was safe and accounted for. Even Gerard was reported to be up and about.

"It's from Balmoral," Isobel cried as she came closer. "The queen agrees to take the title from abeyance. She wants to speak with us!"

Ah well, Iona could gift her fiancée with her title in exchange for his wealth. She had no idea how to go about rewarding him with a title of his own, but perhaps the queen could help. Or her staff. "I daresay the queen doesn't wish to see us. It's probably an interview with a secretary." She took the letter and skimmed the contents.

"It doesn't matter. We can go to Balmoral! I've always wanted to visit. They say it's even larger than Holyrood!" Isobel practically danced in anticipation.

"A lot less historical." Iona folded the letter and handed it back. "I hadn't realized you were interested in palatial mansions. Perhaps *you* should marry Arthur. He wouldn't know the difference."

Isobel laughed. "I don't want to live in a mansion or with Arthur. But I might learn things from the estate. And I can wear one of your new gowns!"

"You can have gowns of your own. Did you think I'd let you go back home looking like a ragpicker while I dressed in silk? We are to be very wealthy." She took Isobel's arm and steered her toward the librarian's castle.

"I can't go home if Mortimer is still about," her sister said mournfully. "Although I like it here very much. I don't think Lydia or Mr. Ives will let him come near me."

"I have taken a lesson from Lord Ives, and I'm making arrangements." Grimly, Iona marched up the hill. "I will simply not be as polite about it. Now that we have funds of our own, I intend to use them wisely. Once I have Arthur's, I'll fritter them."

"I don't know whether to laugh or be afraid."

"Mortimer should be afraid. You should laugh. I now have friends who can tell me when ships leave for China and Africa and South America. It's only a matter of choosing between Edinburgh and Glasgow. The train goes both ways from here, so I think I'll give myself a wedding present, pour laudanum into his drink, and see that he's on one."

"Won't he wake before he reaches the coast ? How will you put him on a ship?" Isobel stopped in the courtyard to watch her worriedly.

"Hire men." Iona had spent lots of nights plotting. "If I have to spend every penny of my money, it will be worth it. Once he's gone, we can keep what we earn."

"We won't need to earn anything if you're wealthy," Isobel reminded her. "But I should like to see if I can make the estate pay for itself again. I like your idea so well that I might even go with Mortimer to be certain he sails away."

Iona hugged her. "And then we'll go to Balmoral!"

"I think I shall like being an independent woman. Perhaps I shall travel, too." Isobel straightened her shoulders and marched toward the house.

"Probably not a wise idea until you're cured," Iona called after her. Isobel ignored her.

Iona didn't much care if she was independent so long as she had the wealth to do as she wished. Perhaps she would follow Lord Ives if he went to Italy. Wouldn't he be surprised?

The question was more—would he be pleased?

She hadn't heard a word from him since he'd been reported as recovering.

Once she was married, she could take lovers, she supposed. She just didn't think she'd find anyone who interested her in the way Gerard did. Simply thinking about him. . . left her weak with hunger. She hoped he felt the same.

He'd never admit it. He'd hide behind his aristocratic boredom and not acknowledge her existence once she was out of sight.

Arthur strolled out to greet her. He was currently experimenting with wearing tweeds, breeches, and boots like a country gentleman. He'd even gone hunting and brought home a goose. Already bordering on stout, he reminded her of an overgrown St. Bernard puppy, eager to please and to play.

"I hear we are to go to Balmoral," he said proudly, offering his arm to escort her inside.

It had not once occurred to her that he would go with them, but she supposed he would be her husband then. She had just thought he would wander off and do whatever it was wealthy men did, but of course he would hope to hobnob with royalty. That was why he was marrying her.

Once inside, she was swept into the wedding planning that she had tried to escape by visiting the bees. Lydia the Librarian loved big gatherings. Iona had persuaded her to keep the guest list small and exclusive, but the public rooms were filling with ribbons and bows—and flowers now, apparently. Big bouquets of autumn colors adorned the drafty great hall. They didn't have the perfume of roses, of course, but Iona loved all flowers.

"And look," Lydia cried as she proudly showed off her efforts. "Phoebe sent you a kitten! She says she heard you never had a pet."

Iona gasped as a tiny golden kitten was dropped into her hands. The kitten crouched and solemnly studied her. She studied him back. He had golden-brown eyes, like hers. Phoebe had noticed her eyes?

Except—she couldn't remember telling Phoebe that she hadn't had a pet. *Gerard*. She had once, a lifetime ago it seemed, told him. Her stupid hope jolted into existence again.

"Hello, tiny little one," she murmured, stroking a small head with a fingertip. "I trust you don't eat bees."

"Cats don't eat bees," Arthur scoffed. "They eat mice. We'll need a barn to keep it in."

Iona chilled. He didn't really think she meant to live with him, did he? Big puppy dogs might. She grimaced and gently reminded him of her plans. "I shall take him to Wystan with me, and he may sleep in my room. If there are any mice there, he's welcome to them."

Lydia, her pregnancy more noticeable than a month ago, beamed in delight. "Mrs. Merriweather adores cats. Tiny will be one very pampered kitten."

"Perhaps I shall call him Kingsley. He won't always be small. Come along, King, let's see if you like my bridal gown." Iona sailed off, leaving Arthur to his own entertainment.

She feared she bewildered him. She'd never meant to hurt him. But she wasn't his damned mother.

TWENTY-FIVE

"WILL MY HAIR COVER THE SCAR?" EDGILY, GERARD REGARDED HIS reflection in the shaving mirror as Lowell arranged his overlong hair.

"I'll part it from the other side, but the marquess isn't a barber. He butchered it in the process of stitching you up. Be grateful you're alive." Lowell snipped a few strands and combed them out. "You'll simply start a new fashion with close-cropped sides until it grows out."

"I don't want to start a fashion. I just don't wish to frighten small children." Or Iona, but that went without saying.

"A new bride won't notice her guests." Lowell scoffed, understanding the direction of his thoughts. "Just put a hat on and smile as if you mean it."

He'd shoot Arthur first. Well, perhaps second—Mortimer was likely to be there. Max had said the old bastard hadn't shown up yet, but the twins were at Calder. Now that their stepfather was out on bond, he would head straight there.

Gerard tugged angrily at his cravat. She was marrying in two days. *Two days.* And he still only had a feeble plan.

"You don't have to go, y'know," his valet reminded him. "You had your chance with the wench and you lost."

The medallion in his pocket snorted. Gerard hadn't decided if he was relieved or not that his wits were still scrambled. Dolts were already calling him Marvelous Malcolm—or Mister Malcolm, which was worse. He'd never live it down. He was an Ives, dammit.

"I'm not losing," he said curtly, although he might lose Wystan if he continued down this path. The reward money was frittering away quickly. "I had things to do. Wellington didn't win by rushing haphazardly into battle."

"Near enough, if you ask me." The valet stood back to admire his handiwork. "You'll pass."

"Good." Gerard grabbed his hat and cane, waited for Lowell to pick up their bags, and hurried down the stairs to join the wedding party heading for the station.

His shoulder was pretty much incapacitated. His head ached when he was tired. But he'd have to be dead before he missed this trip.

IONA TOOK ONE LAST LOOK IN LYDIA'S PIER GLASS. *SOMETHING OLD*—SHE stroked her mother's newly strung pearls. The string was smaller now, but she felt her mother smiling as she touched it. Isobel wore hers too.

Something borrowed—she adjusted the beautiful veil concealing her too-short hair. Lydia had worn it at her wedding. *Something blue*—that would be her garter. No one would see it but her. She'd arranged separate rooms for their wedding night. The bottle of laudanum would take care of both husband and stepfather. She'd be gone by morning. So would Mortimer.

That thought finally brought a smile to her lips.

"You look so beautiful," Isobel said wistfully, handing her the bouquet. "I wish you were marrying someone a little more dashing."

Gerard had been dashing that night he'd saved his friends' lives and almost sacrificed his own. Dashing got people killed.

"I'm a beekeeper. Dashing isn't for me." She'd never dreamed of dashing. Her only thought these last years had been of survival.

She checked to see that the lace and embroidered train of her gown trailed correctly. Between her new corset and the gown's tight fit, with her shoulders and arms bare above a froth of tulle forming her bustle, she almost looked like a mermaid rising from the surf.

"Everyone has arrived and is in the chapel," Lydia called from the doorway. "Oh, you look so *gorgeous!*" She burst into tears.

The librarian had a tendency to weep these days. Prepared, Isobel handed her a handkerchief and tucked a spare up her sleeve. Her twin was wearing a magnificent royal blue silk with bustle and ruffles that Isobel hoped to wear again to visit the queen. A coronet of white roses dangled blue ribbons down her nape and over her short hair.

Iona kissed her sleepy kitten and tucked him into a basket of ribbons with instructions to a maid to look after him. Her heart melted knowing Gerard had sent the perfect wedding gift—one just for her, to keep her company on the lonely nights ahead. She did love the oblivious man. She simply didn't want to destroy his future.

The wail of bagpipes echoed through the ancient stone halls they traversed to the chapel. In an unusually sentimental mood, Iona wished for her mother's tartan, but she'd had to leave it at Craigmore. She could send for it once she reached Wystan. Perhaps Grace could weave another since the old one was tattered and worn after decades of use.

Outside the chapel, Isobel and Lydia kissed Iona's cheeks, then proceeded her down the aisle of the old Gothic chapel. As always for Malcolm weddings, potted rowans guarded the interior, their autumn berries red against dark green.

The bagpipes blew their last note and a solemn piano chord sounded, signaling Iona's entrance. A moment of panic washed over her, and she hesitated. She would be very rich, she reminded herself. Mortimer would be out of their lives. Isobel would be happy. The estate would flourish again. . . *She would not run and hide.* People waited.

She had a kitten now.

Laughing quietly at her foolishness, Iona stepped into the ancient stone chapel with its cathedral ceiling. She concentrated on admiring the pretty ribbons Lydia had attached to the rowans rather than look at Arthur waiting for her at the altar. If she were to have only one wedding day, she ought to remember the lovely details.

She almost walked into the librarian's wide back. Why had Lydia stopped in the middle of the aisle?

Iona tore her nervous gaze from the décor. Around her, she heard worried murmurs beneath the lovely music. In the pews, heads bent toward each other, whispering, then strained to see the front.

The librarian glanced in concern over her shoulder, then wordlessly stepped aside so Iona could view the altar.

Wearing a flower in the lapel of his elegant dark blue tail coat, standing tall and handsome and strong—*Lord Ives* stood where Arthur ought to be.

What in heaven. . . ? The corset restricted Iona's breathing, and all the air swooshed from her lungs. She might faint like Isobel if she didn't breathe soon.

Oh, my word, he was so strikingly aristocratic and stern. . . He'd rearranged his black hair to cover the wound, which didn't help to soften his harsh cheekbones. Did he look a little paler than usual? At sight of her, the earl's mouth softened, and his whole demeanor changed. She could almost smell his lust and happiness from this distance, and she swallowed hard. There was the man she so wanted to love. . .

Taking a deep breath, Iona skirted around Lydia, squeezed Isobel's arm to tell her she was fine, and marched up to confront the obnoxiously arrogant lord. "What are you doing here? What have you done to Arthur?"

"Your groom accidentally took a little too much laudanum." Gerard attempted to look regretful but it didn't match his scent of victory. "He shouldn't have toasted your future with Mortimer. That was a serious mistake."

Iona couldn't unwind her tongue from her teeth. *He* had knocked out her stepfather? She hadn't even found the cad yet. "How? How did you do that?"

Gerard drew her gloved hand through the crook of his arm and turned her toward the gawking preacher. "Tavern in the village, of course. Shouldn't the rest wait? We have an audience expecting a wedding. You look beyond beautiful, you know. I love the way your hair curls about your ears like that, almost like mine now."

She wanted to laugh. She wanted to hug and kiss him for rescuing her from a lifetime of running away. She wanted to punch him—very, very hard, but she was holding his injured arm.

"You can't do this," she hissed through clenched teeth. "It's not legal. You have no license."

That was a stupid argument, but all the others fell by the wayside while she had Gerard this close and could sense his uncertainty and triumph and rage. He had way too many emotions churning away, concealed from the world by his practiced indifference.

"Irregular, yes. Illegal, no. This is Scotland, remember. In your charming country I'll simply pay the fine when we file with the registrar."

Her head spun with so many fears that she couldn't express them all. "What about your duty to your father and to Wystan? I have no money!"

"I have spent a lifetime carrying out the duties of others. What about my duty to *me*?" For the first time, his insouciance cracked, and outrage peered through. "What about your duty to *you*? Are we naught but cogs in the great wheel of life?"

He turned to the preacher. "Mind going straight to the vows? She's likely to run off and hide again until I have a ring on her finger."

"I do not run off," she protested. Well, she did, she supposed, but for very good reasons. She wasn't certain if this was one of them. Joy filled her heart, even though her head said this was insane.

Gerard glared down at her sternly. "You ran off and left me confined to the bed and unable to follow. Hiding is what you do."

"I do not," she whispered as the preacher uncertainly spoke foolish words about sickness and health, loving and cherishing. "I was right here where anyone with half a brain could find me."

The preacher faltered. Gerard signaled for him to continue.

"You do understand that marriage is forever?" he demanded, his dark eyes glaring down at her like midnight while the preacher hurriedly continued the ceremony.

"I do," she retorted angrily. "I'm not—"

Before she could finish, Gerard placed a finger over her lips and faced the preacher. "You heard the lady, she does swear to love me. And I do solemnly swear to take the wench for richer and a damned sight poorer than she wanted, and in sickness and health, in love, honor and equality. May I put the ring on her now?"

"Repeat after me," the beleaguered preacher intoned. "With this ring I give you, as a sign of our constant faith. . ."

Gerard removed her glove and hurried the process. "For so long as we both shall live." He slid a slender band of gold and diamonds over her finger.

Iona stared at it incredulously. "You can't afford this. You're fixing Wystan." She wanted to add *You can't do this*, except he already had. And she loved him so much, tears rimmed her eyes, and she couldn't think of any way of stopping this mockery.

She might have mentioned "in madness and in health" at some point.

As the preacher intoned, "Those whom God has joined together let no one separate," Gerard murmured, "And I may now kiss the bride."

He circled her waist, drew her up against him, and when she gasped and attempted to protest this wasn't part of the ceremony, he covered her open lips with his and tickled them with his tongue. And she leaned into him until he held her off the floor and there was no separating the spiraling passion between them.

Their guests cheered and laughed and clapped. The preacher harrumphed.

Iona wasn't entirely coherent by the time the bagpipes broke into a triumphant march.

Their audience roared and flung flowers when Lord Ives turned her to face the world as his wife. She was too bewitched and bewildered to do more than smile like a fool.

Bewitched. The Earl of Ives and Wystan had magicked her, just like the Malcolm he was.

~

TRIUMPHANT AND TERRIFIED, GERARD LED HIS BRIDE INTO THE ANTEROOM TO sign the marriage papers along with the preacher. Max and Lydia witnessed them. Iona's hand trembled as she added her signature.

She was eerily silent as they continued down the chilly stone corridor to the drafty great hall, but she'd been a full-fledged participant in that kiss. He hadn't abducted her. Was she already regretting what they'd done?

When they reached the wildly adorned ancient hall, Gerard handed her a cup of punch and waited.

"Arthur may sue," was her opening volley.

He could deal with the practical. "I left him in the capable hands of Lady Alice."

His squabble with the lady hadn't been very diplomatic, until he'd listed the great advantages of marrying a wealthy milksop who wouldn't mind her extracurricular activities. Once Alice recognized Gerard's wisdom, Arthur didn't stand a chance. Her father was a powerful lord, after all, one who could pull all the strings needed to obtain a knighthood for his son-in-law if he desired. He even had an ancient barony or two that might be called upon, if needed. Gerard had done them both a favor. He'd left Alice in bed with Arthur, waiting for him to wake up.

Before he could explain any of this, excited voices echoed down the corridor, almost drowned out by the bagpipe's wail. Lady Dare had promised to delay the party with her camera. She'd apparently lost control of the guests.

"And when Mortimer wakens?" Iona tasted her punch and wrinkled her pert nose.

She was so damned gorgeous, Gerard hoped Azmin had photographic plates left. He wanted a picture large enough to frame and hang over his mantel. Iona was the siren of his dreams, the unobtainable goddess he'd never thought to have—and the wicked wit to match his own.

He'd rather carry her off to a bedroom than stand here arguing, but he knew they couldn't escape the festivities this early. Better to soothe Iona's rightful wariness. She had to guess how close he was to the brink of losing everything.

The woman he'd chosen wouldn't fall into a romantic fantasy about knights in shining armor. She knew him too well. Which oddly made him even happier. "Mortimer will wake on a ship sailing to Africa. He might eventually find his way to Egypt or India, if no one kills him for his cheating. Saves him from the thugs here, at least."

To his relief, she nodded agreement. The throng descended on them, and there was no privacy for more.

While Lady Dare set up her photographic equipment, his cousin Max slapped him on the back, ignoring Gerard's wince. "This is the happiest I've ever seen you!"

It was the happiest he'd ever been, he realized. And the most terrified. The den of thieves hadn't scared him as much as Iona's possible rejection. He'd hoped he was doing the right thing. He still couldn't tell.

He'd find out when he took her to Wystan and explained how he'd spent most of his reward and couldn't fix the roof and they'd have to look for a new place for the library.

He watched as Iona's twin wept on her shoulder. Were those good or bad tears?

"The other one can be the Craigmore countess now, since you just made the eldest your countess." Rainford handed him a glass of fizzing bubbles.

Titles had not even counted on Gerard's growing list of concerns. "Does it matter?"

Musicians warmed up in the gallery. Ah, an opportunity to have Iona to himself again.

"It will matter to the queen." Rain insisted on bursting his bubble. "They're scheduled to meet with her and the Lord Chancellor this week."

Well, damn. "Take Isobel. Iona can send a letter politely declining the title."

"You don't think your wife would like to meet the queen?" The marquess studied the happy crowd congratulating the bride.

"They've had a season. They've met the queen. They'll probably only see Old Gruff Face over formalities this time. Besides, the title was for Arthur's sake and doesn't matter any longer." Still, he'd have to ask. Wystan could wait, he supposed.

The important part was prying his bride from her celebrating friends and cementing this marriage so no one could take her away.

"Have you learned how to choose a wife then?" Rainford asked gloomily.

Gerard recalled the night they'd discussed this while watching a ballroom swirling with tempting feminine confections. He considered the question, but it didn't take long.

"You want the woman who will bring out the best in you." He

smacked Rainford's arm and left him pondering this impossible piece of wisdom.

He had a wedding night ahead. He couldn't remember ever anticipating anything so much. For one whole entire day and night in his life, he would say to hell with his family, his estate, and his duties.

TWENTY-SIX

Iona posed again for Lady Dare's camera while nervously studying the celebrating crowd. Was it time to leave yet?

The punch bowl was empty. Dancers teetered precariously as they swung and hopped around the great hall to increasingly raucous music. Their host must be keeping the musicians well-oiled with whisky. Max Ives liked a good party as much as his wife did, apparently.

Iona covertly watched as her groom handed their host's studious son Bakari a coin. The boy grinned and raced off to do his bidding. Her heart pattered a little faster.

She was still furious with Gerard, of course. A woman deserved to know who she was going home with after her wedding.

But the bored earl had disappeared, replaced by a happy fellow who grinned and endured back slaps from his fellows despite his injury. He danced her around the room as if to show the world she was beautiful and all his. *This* was the earl she knew, the one brimming with curiosity, desire, and spikes of temper and delight, all concealed beneath that insouciant, gentlemanly demeanor. She feared breaching his defenses might be a little like opening Pandora's trunk.

But Gerard endured hugs and kisses with good cheer, lifting her twin so Isobel could kiss his cheek, hugging his cousin Phoebe, laughing at

Lord Dare—and he wasn't in the least drunk like the rest of the guests. Iona didn't think he'd even noticed he wasn't holding a glass.

As if by magic, her groom was suddenly at her side. He held out his hand. She took it. He lifted her ring to his lips and kissed her finger just below the symbol of their totally inappropriate marriage. She shivered in anticipation.

"Lady Ives." He gestured at the floor clearing for the last dance.

"Lady Iona," she decided.

"Iona Ives." He chortled, leading her out as the audience formed a ring around them. "I'm heir to a marquess, so sorry, my dear, it's Lady Ives, a farmer's beekeeping wife."

"A historian and parliamentarian's apiarist countess. We'll be very poor."

"I will be rich beyond my wildest dreams if I have you."

She longed to believe that.

He swirled her into the waltz. Her husband's strong arms held her properly. Gerard danced with more skill than she but led her so capably that she felt as if she floated.

She had no urge to run and hide. For the first time in her life she felt beautiful, like a countess, as if the world might actually be filled with miracles just waiting to happen.

She was married—and she most definitely wasn't running from her marriage bed.

Hooting and hollering, their wedding party followed them as Gerard swept her from the great hall. Lydia waited for them near the stairs, handing Iona her wedding bouquet.

Too excited and anxious to think, Iona tossed it from the landing—directly into the hands of her twin.

Leaving their laughing guests, they fled up the main stairs. The old castle was a warren of rooms and corridors carved from larger chambers and partitioned off over the centuries. Iona wasn't entirely certain she could find her way out again when Gerard opened the door to their bridal suite.

While he turned to bolt the door, Iona nervously studied her wedding chamber. Overcome by all the ups and downs of this day, she let tears leak at the carefully prepared sight.

Her meticulously detailed husband had probably found the only room in the castle decorated in her favorite gold and browns. They weren't popular colors, but they reminded her of her bees, and she cherished them. She relaxed a fraction in the warm comfort of her surroundings.

Candles lit every corner—that's what he'd paid Bakari to do. She wiped at more tears.

Hot house roses scented the air. A confection of shimmering gold silk lay across the ivory damask coverlet. On top of it lay a velvet jewelry box. It had been years since anyone had done anything special for her, and even then, it had never been such a grandiose gesture. After he'd given her the beautiful wedding ring, she was afraid to touch the box.

Her new husband circled her waist from behind and leaned down to kiss her ear. "You didn't leave me a lot of time to plan. And just so you know—I'm hoping you'll wear that gown in the morning. Right now, I wish to see all of you."

He removed her veil, kissed her nape, then started on her buttons.

A hot flush heated her better than the fire in the grate.

"We really should wait until we're at Wystan," she said, nervously. "I should consult with my queen before doing anything drastic."

He halted and turned her to face him. Crossing his arms, he raised one eyebrow and waited.

She didn't like that. She squirmed. "I am *not* hiding."

He waited some more. He looked so commanding, so very. . . magnificent.

Iona rubbed the ring on her finger and studied the waves of white lace covering her shoes. "It's not hiding to need confirmation that I'm doing the right thing."

He tilted her chin so she had to meet his forceful dark eyes and taunted. "I can sense it, y'know. Your head and your heart know what is right. Your bees only confirm what you already know. To back away and say you may consult with them is hiding."

"I. . ." But the damned man was absolutely right. All her life, she'd fled to her hives for comfort—and to escape her unhappiness. The bees had been her confidants when Mortimer raged through the house or stole the coins she'd hidden.

She wasn't unhappy now. Mortimer was out of her life. In his place stood an arrogant honorable lord who wanted to please her—who admitted to *sensing* her mood. And she was too stupid to know how to react.

At her silence, he asked worriedly, "Are you sorry we did this?"

Another woman might scold and accuse him of arrogant presumption, but Iona knew better. He'd known she'd never choose her own wants and desires over what was best for others. He understood her, just as she was learning to understand him. He was a man people relied on because he did what needed to be done, no matter how unpleasant or difficult. They were not terribly different.

But this marriage—he was actually doing for himself because he was braver than she was. He was doing it because it *felt* right, not because it was logical or practical or all those things they normally did.

"I am terrified," she whispered as she toyed with the buttons of his waistcoat. Her *husband* had unbuttoned his tailed coat hours ago. "I'm so excited and happy that I may be delirious. And that terrifies me too. Like my queen, I flee when startled and fly elsewhere when threatened. What I feel right now—is overwhelming."

Gerard caught her hand and kissed the knuckles, then picked up the jewelry box and held it out. "I know I was hasty and arrogant in believing you feel as I do. But I *do* know it. You were the one who taught me to heed the energies people emit. And for that, I wanted to thank you."

Uncertainly, she released her hold on his waistcoat to open the box.

"My pearls?" she asked uncertainly, smelling the love on the luminous beads, unable to believe it was possible. "You bought back my *mother's pearls?*"

He closed the box and set it aside while kissing her hair and temple. "I had Max ask your sister. I hope I found all of them."

Closing her eyes, Iona swayed, feeling almost as faint as her twin. She clung to his waistcoat and let the love well up inside her, a love she hadn't felt in so very long. . . And still hadn't the words to say. "I cannot thank you. . . It's too much. Your reward money. . ."

"Money is not as important as convincing you that I am the best husband for you. I didn't spend it all. I can patch the leaks. The library is safe for a while longer. I don't know how else to show you that we will be good together."

His hint of uncertainty pierced her heart. She wanted him to be confident that she could be his countess. "We are attuned to each other, my lord. I never doubted that."

His waistcoat fell open beneath her fumbling fingers, and Iona tentatively flattened her palms against his hard torso, as she'd wanted to do so many times. She drank in his odor of integrity and desire, steadying her quaking nerves.

He covered her hand with his, letting their paired senses read the moment. "Your queen doesn't flee your drones, does she?" He teased kisses across her brow and down her nose. His big hands encompassed her waist and found the ties for her train.

Drones, oh my. That was plain enough. "We've already performed our mating dance?" If they talked, perhaps she wouldn't be quite so aware of the hard beat of his heart.

Her train fell to the floor. With shaky fingers, Iona unknotted his cravat and cast it aside so she might start on his shirt studs. She really needed to see his chest naked again. Joy and desire pushed aside doubt and fear.

"Is that what bees do? Perhaps this can be our mating dance." He spun her around and nimbly started on the tiny pearl buttons at her back.

"A little less. . . primitive. . . perhaps." She suppressed a moan as he let her bodice and chemise fall and released her corset ties.

She tried to grasp all the fabric falling off her, but with masculine strength, he spun her back around again.

Gulping, she fastened her gaze on her husband's face as he unwrapped her like a gift more precious than her pearls. She was nervously left standing nearly naked from the waist up. Gerard's worshipful expression reassured her, along with his scent of lust and. . . expectation? She thought he trembled as much as she did when he pushed aside her gauzy undergarments to lift her bare breasts from her underpinnings.

"I'm feeling very primitive." His voice was a low rumble that stirred all her nerve endings.

He lifted her and put his mouth to the aroused crest of one breast. Iona cried out with the intensity of her need.

He kissed her then, kissed her with such all-consuming passion that Iona was scarcely aware when her gown fell off and the rest followed, all except the gauzy final garment.

But she was very aware when her bare shoulders hit the bed linen, and she looked up to see Gerard fling his shirt and coat to a chair.

Muscles rippled everywhere she looked, and she stopped breathing all over again. When he reached for his trouser placket, she had to force herself to study the bandage on his shoulder so she did not expire of fear and excitement.

GERARD HAD PLANNED ON SEDUCING HIS BRIDE WITH FINE WORDS AND gentle caresses. He knew how to do those things, and Iona deserved all his attention for this night. He knew his duties didn't often allow him the leisure for pampering a wife. But for one night—

And he was ruining it all. He was so desperate to touch her that he nearly ripped off her clothes. She was a virgin, but he'd suckled her breasts as if she were an experienced courtesan. He was fortunate his brave Iona didn't faint.

And now he had her flat on her back, those big golden eyes watching him as if he were Atlas, and she was a sacrifice to the gods. And damned if he didn't feel like a god. If he revealed himself as aroused as he was now, she was likely to flee off the other side of the bed.

He leaned over to turn off the oil lamp on the bedside table. The candles might allow him to see the splendor of his bride—

Her delicate hands halted him. "Don't. I want to see what passion looks like."

"If you've seen animals, then you know it isn't pretty," he said gruffly, hoping to spare her.

"Animals don't know desire. Or love. We just vowed to *love* one another. Doesn't that start with seeing each other for who we are?" She caressed the bulging placket of his trousers. "If I can't hide, neither can you."

"I'm going to regret saying that for the rest of my days, aren't I?" He pried off his shoes.

Trousers still on, he blew out the candles, then lay down beside her in the light of the single lamp. She instantly sat up enough to explore his bare chest, as he'd hoped. This business of going slow was about to cost him a new pair of drawers. He'd been very careful dressing this morning.

"I do not need coddling," she informed him.

"Of course you need coddling. Everyone should be coddled occasionally, and I intend to see that you have your fair share." He desperately wanted to keep that promise, but Wystan's eventual demise loomed in their future.

He'd work something out—just not now, while Iona continued exploring him, and he was gripping the sheet to control his need to roll her under him.

"I have married a barbarian who believes he need only take what he wants." She kissed his jaw and throat to soften her words. "I know better than to believe you'll change. I have insanely agreed to accept your flaws for a lifetime. And because I can sense the man you hide from others, I know you won't hurt me, not intentionally. So let me learn what you really want."

She kissed his chest and suckled his nipples the way he had her. Gerard nearly lifted off the bed.

Apparently responding to what she *sensed*, she carried her kisses down the thread of hairs over his abdomen. He had to dig his hands into her hair and drag her back up to his mouth so he could kiss her—and finally cover her with his weight to prevent further migration to parts she wasn't prepared to see.

She responded hungrily. She let him invade her mouth and maul her breasts like the barbarian she'd called him. He generally paid ladies the courtesy of going slow, but she dug her fingers into his arms and bucked against him and drove him wild with her desire.

He could *feel* her vibrations. Desire apparently felt differently than anger. He'd have to learn all her tunes.

He tore off the final bit of gossamer covering her breasts and nipped the tightly furled peaks. She cried out as she had earlier, then performed the trick he loved so well and wrapped her leg around his buttocks.

Kissing the beautiful bosom that had tantalized him all evening, he unfastened her frail silk drawers and slid his hand over her bare hip. She rose into him, begging for a touch he'd only showed her once.

Daringly, he kissed lower, sliding off her drawers as he went. She dropped her embracing limb and spread herself for him. He growled at the wispy blue garter on her thigh, licked and kissed her there, and compelled by her high keening, applied his mouth to virgin territory.

Holding her rump, he plied her until she came apart in his hands.

Only then did he shed his trousers and drawers, just enough to rise above her and take the plunge that made the beekeeper his countess forever and a day.

Man and wife, lord and lady, richer or poorer, they became one.

TWENTY-SEVEN

Satiated, eager to please Gerard as he had her, Iona clung to the muscled torso of her husband as he entered her. His lust and desire aroused her, but she also felt. . . his concern, like a warm loving blanket. She kissed his shoulders to let him know she wasn't another one of his duties but cried out once he breached her barrier. He hesitated, although she sensed how difficult it was for him to halt.

Her husband. She was holding her husband. She'd never thought to have one. But for Gerard. . . She breathed deeply and raised her hips and took him in, as he needed.

It was painful. It was glorious. And in the end, his wild desire drove her to another shattering climax that left her breathless and spinning.

And in that moment, as he spilled his seed into her, Iona sensed his needs in the same way she understood her queen, sensed what he didn't really understand himself—because he was a man and an Ives. She almost laughed into his broad shoulder. Instead, she kissed his salty skin anywhere she could reach.

He rolled over, removing his heavy weight. She curled against his side, fearing he'd hurt his shoulder. "I'll be a very bad countess," she whispered, not knowing if he heard. "But I'll be the wife you need."

His arm tightened around her, and they drifted off to sleep.

A kitten pouncing on their faces woke them in the early dawn.

Gerard growled and lifted the creature up in one hand. "Tell me I made a mistake gifting you with this creature, and it will go back to Phoebe by evening."

Iona sat up and snatched the kitten from his hand. The sheet fell from her breasts, and her husband instantly took advantage. Cuddling the kitten, she lay back and covered herself again. "You did that on purpose."

"Probably." He eyed her with interest. His mussed hair and morning beard gave him a rakish look that had her heart thumping.

"What do we do now?" she whispered. "I had planned to run for Wystan before dawn."

"It would be foolish to go to Wystan if you need to go to Balmoral. We'll stay here until then. Do I need to take you into the city and buy you pretty gowns? Or maybe just pretty corsets?" He leered convincingly—giving her a lovely glimpse of the raw male behind his proper façade.

Remembering the golden nightgown he'd bought for her, she slid from the bed in search of it. The kitten insisted on exploring while she shimmied into the loveliest piece of lace-edged silk she'd ever known. "I should make this into an evening gown!" She caressed the sheer silkiness in wonder. "I've never owned anything like it."

She held out the narrow skirt and spun around for him to admire.

Propped on one arm, Gerard regarded her dance with appreciation. "I would shower you with silk, if I could."

Realizing she'd just cost him any chance at a wealthy wife, Iona plummeted off her foolish cloud. "I don't need silk. Wystan needs a roof. Your library is far more important than clothes! I hope you did not waste too much on me."

"It wasn't a waste. I'm enjoying every minute of money well spent." He rolled out of bed, drawing the sheet around his hips.

She could still see the bulge of his arousal, but it was what he didn't say that caused her trepidation. He didn't have the funds he needed to save Wystan—because of her. "If you'd married an heiress, you would be honeymooning in Italy, exploring your gift. You need to explore your gift as much as you need to put a roof on Wystan."

That was what she'd sensed last night. He still didn't want to admit to his friends that he was a gifted Malcolm, but it was his only hope now.

"It is a useless gift." He shrugged his still-bandaged shoulder. "Keeping Wystan's library from the damp is more important than Italy. We'll travel someday. It's not as if I'm poor. We'll always have a roof over our heads. You can have silks, if you like." He advanced on her.

Iona stepped back. "Lowell is quite vocal about your refusal to improve your wardrobe. I won't have you buying silk for me if *you* won't buy new clothes. You have given up far too much for me! I hope I know duty as well as you do. Wystan comes first."

She darted behind the dressing screen. "Where is my trunk?"

"In the other room, where the kitten should be." He peered around the screen, completely comfortable with their dishabille and obviously not fretting too much over their pennilessness. "Are you sure you would not like to take breakfast in bed?"

"I've never done anything so decadent. I should think it would cause a great deal of trouble." She had no robe to cover the sheer silk. She'd never lounged about in leisure and didn't know what to do with herself. She tested the water basin. It was chilly.

"You have much to learn about being a countess, my lady." He leaned in and kissed her nose. "Do you even own a robe? I'd lend you mine, but then I'd have to order a tray while wearing a sheet. Hop back in bed and let us pretend we are in a mansion above the sunny coast, being pampered."

Iona basked in that glorious thought, dodged out of the other side of the screen, and jumped back in bed, pulling the covers up. "Dinnae say that you haven't dreamed of a drafty castle overlooking a loch with snow coming through the windows as your honeymoon."

"All right, I won't say it." He pulled on a robe and yanked a rope.

In a short while, a parade of servants arrived bearing trays of tea and pastries, as well as their clothes and warm water—niceties she'd never experienced. Pulling a sheet up to her neck, Iona nervously allowed a tray to be set over her lap. Gerard merely gestured for his to be set on a dresser. He grabbed the kitten before it could butter its nose on toast and handed it to a departing maid.

"Find it—"

"Kingsley," Iona informed him. "His name is Kingsley."

"Please take the king out for nature's call and find him something more appropriate to eat than toast." He turned to the valet and maid puttering about with clothes. "Go find something to iron. I think we'll figure out how to dress ourselves."

"And shave?" Lowell asked, dourly eyeing his whiskers.

"A beard is just the thing. Go on or I may decide to crawl about the foundation like Max and come in covered in filth," her lord and husband commanded.

Wide-eyed with horror, Lowell fled.

Iona sipped her tea and watched him with interest. "You could grow a beard and wear a colorful scarf over your battered head and look like a pirate. Foundation exploring may be just the thing. Didn't Max say it is Roman? We needn't go to Italy to explore Roman ruins."

"I cannot believe I'm spending the first day of our wedded life crawling around in a sewer." Gerard held up his lantern so his dainty bride could avoid sticking her too-large boot into a hole.

"You're not crawling," she pointed out pragmatically. "And I do not believe this part was the sewer. Did you not listen when Lydia regaled us with tales of ghosts and spirits down here?"

"It's Lydia's *duty* to listen to books." Of course, *he* was listening to a Roman soldier chuckling in his head. Iona couldn't know that.

"But Max is the one who saw the ghost, remember? Can there be any better place for us to practice your talent for seeing history? There is no one around to notice. Think of this as my wedding gift to you."

She had him there. Allowing him to explore the peculiar without disapproval was quite a spectacular gift, now that he realized the freedom she provided.

"Here." She lifted her lantern to examine what appeared to be a filled-in archway. "I can sense. . . the oddity. It's not like feeling the knife we found. I can't describe the scent."

"Mold. Decay. Rot." Hiding his exhilaration at this freedom, Gerard found the names engraved on the arch as Max had described. His fingers tingled. He picked up weird. . . sensations. People whispering. Bells tolling. Song. Prayer. A church?

"You're hiding behind cynicism," she accused, hitting the mark dead on. "You're afraid you're weird—like me."

"Maybe I'm afraid I'm *not* weird." That was a stupid retort. The voice in his head cackled agreement.

"You're not insane," she reassured him.

"I didn't think I was." But he did, down deep inside. Ives weren't weird. He was an Ives, a logical, educated earl, someday a marquess. He was meant to be a leader of men—not a madman who stroked stones. His bride was a shade too perceptive.

"I can smell your fear, and I know perfectly well it isn't of ghosts. Tell me you don't feel anything here." She ran her hand over the arch.

Gerard didn't want to open his Pandora's box of fears, but Iona seemed as mad as he was. She hadn't minded his earlier vision. And sensing *vibrations* may have saved his life. He supposed if he were to be labeled a Mad Malcolm, he should at least experiment to see if it was justified.

As if he stroked old stones every day, he removed his leather glove and pretended he was an archeologist hunting for hidden hieroglyphics.

The vibration stung him, almost like a bee. He yanked his hand away.

"I'm not sensing anything painful or I would have warned you." Iona regarded him with fascination, as one might a monster in a freak show.

"And to think, I married you for life. What was I thinking?" She'd given him a *map*, one that might locate a Roman ruin. But he'd need this weird talent to find anything. If there might actually be treasure. . .

He held his palm a fraction above the surface, looking for. . . who knows what. Curiosity and excitement warred with practicality. "Will we spend the rest of our days crawling about Wystan, hunting ghosts?"

"Or treasure," she said with equanimity. "Or just satisfying our intellectual nosiness."

For good or ill, and against all logical sense, he'd married a woman after his own heart. Feeling a little less stifled, he crouched down and flattened his palm against the oldest name carved into the wall.

No church bells. "Chanting Latin," he decided.

Iona crouched beside him. "Bell has been studying her affliction. She says we may be like tuning forks, designed to find a perfect pitch in the energies around us. In our case, that pitch may be the right combination of vibration and smell."

She laid her delicate fingers across his. The connection was instantaneous.

Hooded figures, large and small, male and female. Sorrow. A bier carrying a slender, white-robed woman. A man in primitive leather armor—a Roman soldier?—kissing her cold cheek, laying a circlet of gold on her chest.

The chanting increased. The soldier embraced the shoulders of two weeping girls. "My treasures," he murmured.

The trio wept and watched as the bier was laid inside a vault and sealed.

Warning shouts. With the tomb sealed, the robed figures slipped away.

Immense sorrow and tension. Setting a gold medallion into the seal, the soldier hugged his daughters, then handed them over to another. "You must go south to your mother's family, to safety."

~

IONA LOST HER GRIP AND SAT DOWN ABRUPTLY, SHAKEN. UNDOUBTEDLY ruining his trousers, her husband sat beside her and drew her into his lap, murmuring comforting, if meaningless, phrases.

How did one make meaning of what they'd seen? She shivered in his embrace. Gerard had done this. *Her husband had pulled ancient history out of a stone.*

Once she'd drawn her mind out of the vision and recovered from the shock, she leaned into his broad shoulder and contemplated what they had seen. "Interesting, if not illuminating. Very good for a beginner."

He snorted and dug his square chin into the top of her head. "Minx. Admit, you were enthralled."

"Maybe, just a little." She leaned back and kissed his stubbly jaw. "I could *smell* his grief. I've never had visions until you came along. You could be a very dangerous man."

Gerard fished inside his pocket and produced a small gold coin. "Not necessarily. I may have had guidance. This is one of the artifacts Max dug out of the foundation in his repairs."

She could sense his unease as he handed her the coin. In the light of their lamps, she examined it. "You think it is similar to the one in the vision?"

He reluctantly nodded. "It speaks to me. That's why I picked it up."

He waited for her reaction, as if this were a matter of grave importance. She'd been speaking to bees all her life. She was more curious than amazed. But for Gerard—it revealed so much.

"It is a weird sensation, isn't it?" She phrased her words with care, as if hearing voices in her head was an everyday matter. "I had to learn to accept the buzz and interpret."

He relaxed a fraction. "The soldier in our vision spoke colloquial Latin, like the voice in my head. It's not easy to interpret. He called his daughters his treasures. He used that word when I found the coin."

"I've had some Latin. I wasn't certain. The others weren't soldiers, were they? Even the men plaited their hair, like the woman's. Her hair was gold."

"So was the children's. The voice in my head said there was treasure in Wystan. If it is the same soldier—"

"He sent his daughters to *Wystan*—the original Malcolms! The people in hoods, could they have been a Celtic tribe? Could the one leading the indecipherable chant have been a druid? He had golden hair too. Druids are part of our Malcolm legends." Iona eagerly reviewed the vision, but her knowledge of ancient language was nil.

"Perhaps the legends are based on visions such as these—and our interpretations. It could be their carvings in this arch. I suppose I'll have to take writing my journal a little more seriously."

She pinched his arm through his coat, then kissed his cheek when that brought no reaction. "You should always take journals seriously. We should ask Lydia for books on visions."

"Oh no, you don't!" He stood, still holding her. "I'll not have Max laughing me out of the house. This goes no further than us. An earl with an affinity for dead people does not lead to intelligent discussion."

"You're being ridiculous." She wriggled out of his hold to shake out her dirty skirt. "If you wish one day to write scholarly tomes on ancient civilizations, perhaps it might matter—"

He snorted inelegantly. "I doubt that vision qualifies as research. It's just . . . interesting." He tilted his head as if listening. "The soldier is gone from my head, perhaps to be with his wife now that we've found her."

He pressed the coin into the dirt by the wall and covered it. "But he was right. I found my treasure at Wystan. We'll figure out how to repair the castle together. I had considered closing it and letting it rot, but we need to know more of its history."

"Closing Wystan?" She stared at him in horror. "You'd be cursed into all eternity. Or we both would be, since it's my fault you can't marry an heiress."

"I should be allowed one happiness outside of duty. And that would be you, my love." He hugged her and began an interesting exploration that she wasn't about to allow down here.

His amazingly heroic deeds had proved his love as far as she was concerned, even though he'd never said the word until now. Still, Iona pushed away. "We should explore a little more while we're here."

If she loved him, she had to repay his romantic, fateful gesture in some manner. She hoped, just a little bit, that they might find something valuable. Or at least useful.

"Seeing visions doesn't make your head hurt?" He let her push him away.

"A little, but I'm fascinated. It's hard to quit now. Why did that one stone call to you and not the others?"

Gerard shrugged and studied the arch. "As I said, I apparently have an affinity for dead people. I simply started with the oldest name. Does this wall contain a burial vault for our ancestors?"

"Quite possibly, although isn't it the foundation of Lydia's library? Perhaps the memories were somehow implanted here."

Not rejecting her theory, he studied the arch. "Roman texts claim the druids were literate, but they kept their stories in their heads, handing them down verbally, as primitive tribes do elsewhere."

"But if the druids are the origin of Malcolm gifts. . ." Excitedly, Iona held her lantern to the writing on the arch. "Perhaps they had a gift for leaving their stories in stones? Let us try one more, please?"

"You really believe they had some means of impressing tales into *stone*?" He kept his voice neutral.

She grew more confident knowing her husband did not scoff at one of her wilder theories. "If the bottom stone showed only a crypt without the tower that's there today, could we try one of these middle stones to test if it is a century when the tower existed?"

He held a palm over the middle stones. "I sensed church bells and chants earlier. You may only see more funerals."

"Our vision showed only a stone vault," she argued. "It could mean the original watchtower was built on top of it. Would they still have access to the vault after that?"

He cast a light down the tunnel they'd been following. "Through the passageways beneath here, possibly. Do we have to tell Lydia that the library may be a mausoleum?"

"They buried the previous librarians in a vault beneath the chapel. For all we know, there could be veritable catacombs under the entire castle. Let's try one more, please?"

He glared down at her. Iona grinned back. The earl's scowls might intimidate others into doing his bidding, but not her.

"Which name?" he asked in surrender to her whims.

Iona examined the wall, using her sense of smell more than her eyes. Sadness permeated the stone blocks, but she found whiffs of love and respect.

"I don't think any of them will be terribly enlightening," she decided. "Lydia has journals back to the 14th century, I believe, when the castle was built. Perhaps chose a stone before that point, when it was only a watchtower? I think this is the name on the first journal." She pointed at a block a few feet from the ground. "So we should start before it?"

Gerard placed his palm over the name she indicated. Biting her lip, Iona covered his hand with hers.

TWENTY-EIGHT

"THERE THEY ARE! YOU'VE BEEN GONE SO LONG, WE THOUGHT YOU'D FALLEN into the oubliette!" Max's loud voice echoed off the old walls, penetrating even Gerard's thick skull.

"We never thought even an Ives could fall asleep in this dungeon, no matter what you and your bride might be doing," a feminine voice scolded.

Phoebe?

Gerard rubbed his pounding skull, then realized he couldn't sit up. His heart lurched a beat as fought the very real nightmare filling his head and identified Iona's soft weight on top of him. Had he killed her. . . ? But she stirred at the shouting and shifted to one side.

"For pity's sake, Ives, you couldn't find a better boudoir?" Rainford—sounding amused.

Rubbing his head, Gerard spurted out—"Ives!" He recalled the scene they'd experienced with wonder. "They were everywhere—with crossbows, spears, trebuchets, even a catapult!"

Beside him, Iona rubbed sleepily at her eyes. "The women worked beside them," she added, sounding equally dazed. "They made arrows. They boiled oil. It was terrifying!"

"The books!" Excitedly, Gerard recalled the beautifully illustrated manuscripts the women had hidden. "They were protecting the books. The raiders were well armed."

"But the invaders couldn't climb the bluff," Iona continued excitedly. "And they couldn't break past the wall around the village. It was like watching from the top of the tower—"

Finally heeding their audience, Gerard squeezed Iona until she recognized the stillness too. They'd been speaking to each other as if there were no others to hear. Not very diplomatic of him. And he would never hear the end of this. *Damn.*

Soberly, he climbed to his feet and offered his hand to his wife, who glanced nervously at him. "I love you," he whispered with feeling, still thrilled with their shared vision. "Whatever happens next, know I love you forever and always. Apparently Ives aren't good at expressing that."

She grinned and squeezed his hand.

"Go on." Phoebe gestured impatiently. "Tell us more."

Max regarded them warily. "You both had the same dream?"

"What kind of books?" Rainford crossed his arms and leaned a shoulder against the wall.

"Malcolm journals!" Phoebe cried, poking him. "Lydia has a library of them, if you haven't noticed."

"Defended by trebuchets?" The blond marquess waited. The blasted marquess should be on his way home by now.

Gerard would never live this down. Those were not journals they'd seen.

"Illustrated manuscripts!" Iona cried excitedly when he didn't explain. "The ladies were hiding precious works of art."

"Iona," he said warningly. "You promised."

"Don't make me punch your sore arm." She stepped away from him defiantly. "I love you madly, but you aren't allowed to make all the decisions."

He quirked his eyebrows. His gut clenched, but he refused to let anyone see his fear. If he loved this woman, he had to listen to her. Occasionally. Especially when she claimed to love his worthless self in the process.

She stood on her toes and kissed his jaw. "You can't hide from *me,* my lord. I know you want to find those books. You can't, not without help."

"My decision, isn't it?" he asked, keeping his voice neutral. He really didn't want to explain this to an audience.

His insides knotted more when she glared back.

"Oh, and deciding who I was to marry without asking was your decision too?" she taunted. "How is that, pray tell?"

"She's right, Cuz," Phoebe said gleefully. "Sometimes, it's best if one simply swims with the tide."

"Perhaps we should go upstairs and discuss this over tea like civilized human beings?" Rainford raised his shoulder from the wall and gestured for the ladies to proceed him.

Gerard wanted to stay and explore, not be mauled with questions he couldn't answer.

But he had a wife now, and as she'd so rudely pointed out, they needed to learn to make decisions together. Besides, despite her strength and courage, he'd just put her through a painful and terrifying experience. Even he was still shaken by the violence.

"More than tea." Wrapping his arm around Iona's waist and leading her from the tunnels was the only thing that felt right at the moment. He didn't feel like himself but more like one of those barbarian warriors chasing down the invaders.

"Illustrated manuscripts?" Rainford asked from behind.

"*Books*," Max grumbled. "More blamed books."

Phoebe laughed. He couldn't blame her there. Poor Max couldn't read but he'd married a *librarian*.

"Why the devil are you still here—Cuz?" Gerard asked his long-legged cousin. The woman was striding ahead of them like a jungle explorer with her lamp.

"I'm to help prepare your bride and her sister for their visit with the queen, of course. The aunts insisted." This from a woman wearing split skirts and a porkpie hat.

"That is generous." Iona spoke hesitantly, as well she should. "Do we really need preparation?"

"You are fine just as you are," Gerard insisted. "You'll probably only see the Lord Chancellor anyway. Phoebe's family is just bossy. I'll be there with you."

"If you want to keep the aunts and quite possibly my mother from going with you, you'll take me," Phoebe called back. "Andrew needs to go with us. I believe he's under consideration for knighthood for one of his inventions. We'll make it a party."

"Or a circus," Gerard grumbled.

Iona snickered and squeezed his arm. He hoped she had a way out of Phoebe's machinations.

But if he was to rely on the only person in the world who understood his weird gift—

He had to concede to telling *their* tale, as she'd made clear. The vision belonged to both of them. His duties had become tremendously more complicated. Or perhaps *love* complicated them.

"It can be very simple," Iona whispered, as if hearing his thoughts. "We do what we like unless it affects others. Think about it."

Lydia bustled in to join them once they settled in the small guest parlor with their tea and whisky. "I'm so glad you're safe! You were gone so long! And the books could tell me nothing about your whereabouts. The past isn't always helpful."

Gerard tipped his cup in Iona's direction as if saying, "See, old history doesn't count."

Iona didn't believe that. They could *learn* from experience. That was the whole point of their library. "Does the library mention illustrated manuscripts?"

Lydia looked surprised. "I haven't looked. Shall I?"

"Sit down and drink your tea, put your feet up," Max ordered. "We'll have the tale of the pair before we decide."

"Well, Ives?" Phoebe asked, sipping her tea. "Do we have to pry it out of you?"

"History is *important*," Iona murmured, daringly trailing her fingers over her husband's thigh. She thought Gerard needed more touching. He'd been carrying his burdens alone too long. "Would you leave those books for rats to nest in?"

"After four or five centuries, if they're not already rat nests, they'll last a few more. And there's no proof that they're still hidden or that we can determine where." His cynicism sounded hollow to Iona's ears. He was as eager to explore as she was.

"Illuminated manuscripts are extremely valuable," Rainford noted from his chair by the fire. "If the castle holds them, Lydia stands to make a fortune."

"I couldn't sell *books*," the Malcolm Librarian said in horror.

"As Iona said, illuminated manuscripts are works of art." Gerard added more whisky to his cup, then squeezed her hand. "Ancient, possibly historical, works of art should be shared by the public in museums."

"Or one could charge to see them," Iona suggested. "I should imagine they'd require care and that would be costly."

"Just tell us the tale, for all that's holy!" Max bellowed. "Making up fairy tales is futile."

"Fairy tales are literary parables," Gerard taunted. "Something you would not understand."

Iona pinched her husband's hard thigh. It wasn't easy. In retaliation, he poured whisky in her tea, and she sputtered, setting the nasty stuff aside.

He launched into their tale of barbarian invaders and dark-haired Ives' defenders and most likely blond Malcolm women at their side. The vision had shown them illustrated manuscripts being hidden, but it hadn't told more. What seemed certain was that all this had taken place here, in Calder Castle, as it was being built.

By the time he finished, his audience was enrapt. Like any good lawyer and politician, her husband had a smooth way with words.

Iona knew Gerard was uncomfortable with the questions that followed. Possessing a few more years of experience in discussing oddities with her family, she put a halt to his torment. "Lydia, Phoebe, I know you have experience living with your gifts. I don't know about Max and Rainford. Would anyone like to explain *how* their gifts work?"

The men remained stubbornly mute but interested. Lydia and Phoebe made several false starts and gave up.

"That is why we have journals," Iona pointed out. "We write down what we *experience* because we can't really explain how we do it. There is no sense pestering us for what we cannot tell you."

Iona sensed Gerard relaxing a fraction. She stroked his thigh encouragingly, loving that she had the right to touch him like this. He seemed to respond to tactile sensation the same way she did scent.

She grasped that what they'd done was strange to him, and he hated explaining himself. His position of authority had led him to expect people to take his word as law. That was an enlightening realization.

People wouldn't question an earl, but they were bound to doubt a Mad Malcolm.

"Gifts aren't tort law or contracts." Gerard admitted his inability to explain.

"Where did you see them hiding the books?" Max demanded, going straight for the practical. "We'll hunt them down."

"That's hard to say. The new tower was only partially built and there was no castle." Gerard gestured at the room they sat in, just outside the tower. "The women stayed between what appeared to be an old watchtower and the partial wall of the new one they were building. The old watchtower walls were probably sealed in when they finished the new one."

Ignoring male frustration, Iona turned to the librarian. "Lydia, if you would be so good as to look up references to the manuscripts—and perhaps to mausoleums or catacombs? That might be simpler than tearing down a tower over a vague vision."

The librarian nodded thoughtfully. "Perhaps in the interest of showing how gifts work instead of explaining, I should demonstrate how some of mine works. It's quite hard to describe how books speak to me."

Iona sensed her husband's tension relaxing even more. She had never really used her sense of smell for more than identifying flowers her bees might like or avoiding people in ugly moods. Using it to *help* added an exciting dimension.

Gerard had been right—isolation affected how she learned, not always in a good way.

"Are you inviting us to see your library?" she asked in excitement.

"You and Gerard, not these other heathens who tend to mock what they don't understand. They've seen it." Lydia rose with stately grace and led the way out.

Eagerly, Iona clasped Gerard's hand as they crossed to Lydia's office, where Isobel sat with stacks of books. Her twin glanced up and stood, looking puzzled.

"We didn't tell your sister you went missing," Lydia explained. "She is a little too anxious."

Iona hugged her twin. "We have been exploring. Marriage is quite exciting. You should avoid it."

"I'm sure I shall." Isobel regarded them in her studious manner. "Balmoral will be more than my nerves can handle. I've been thinking you should go in my stead, pretend you're me. Did you need the office? I can leave—"

"No, dear, I'm showing your brother-in-law that history is important." Lydia opened a hidden door behind the desk and gestured for them to enter.

Iona gasped as they stepped inside what had once been an ancient watchtower—the one in their vision?—and saw a stairway spiraling to the roof.

Around the stairway, books were almost leaping off shelves, jiggling as if in anticipation.

Thrilled, Iona practically danced in delight. "It's magical! They're so eager to see you, Lydia!"

The librarian smiled shyly. "It's more like, I'm so happy to hear them speaking to me, that they want to leap into my hands." She pulled one out from one of the lowest shelves. "This would be the lady who lived here while the fortress was built. I only read her earlier journal that described her new home when I was helping Max. I think she may be trying to tell us about manuscripts."

Gerard took the tome and the others Lydia handed him that mentioned mausoleums, crypts, and—visions.

"It will take weeks to translate all these," Iona protested, opening one of the journals. "I think this one is French."

"I can take the French and Latin ones." Gerard juggled the stack trying to open pages. "Gaelic is beyond me."

Lydia pulled out a few more books from further up the stacks. "I can hear what the journals say, no matter the language. And they'll open up to where we need them, so we needn't read everything."

"A much more useful gift than talking to bees," Iona said in admiration.

"But it means I can never live anywhere else. It's difficult, because Max loves traveling and can find jobs in exciting places—" Lydia opened the study door and led them out.

"Our gifts have downsides," Iona agreed. "My mother was tied to her hives. But with the new frames, I can carry my queen wherever I like." She glanced up at Gerard. "That is fortunate, since not everyone enjoys drafty castles in the north."

"I'd follow you anywhere but there," he whispered into her hair.

She poked his ribs and followed Lydia out of the library, into the study where Isobel waited with interest.

Even her twin followed as they carried the stack of books back to the parlor. Lydia held up the oldest one. "Manuscript first?"

After a general clamor of agreement and ordering a new round of refreshments, Lydia opened to the appropriate page and began to read aloud, translating as she went.

Silence ensued after she finished. Iona studied her husband worriedly. She sensed a slight odor of excitement, but his gentlemanly layer of duty was more pronounced.

"If I am understanding correctly—a Malcolm bride carried the books from Wystan as her dowry?" Gerard asked cautiously.

Max grunted. "Aye and that would figure. Books as riches—as if we can eat the blamed things."

Iona chuckled. Rainford glared. Lydia intervened. "They were Bibles. She'd learned the art from a priest in her household. She had a gift for art. They could have earned income from her talent."

"Except it says she occasionally inserted passages that weren't in the Bible and her artwork tended toward prophesy," Rainford said dryly. "Both could have her burned at the stake. Her husband might have been an ignorant brute, but he was right to protect her by refusing to show them."

"I want to see those books," Iona cried. "Max, does the description of the hiding place tell you anything?"

"That she was furious with the lout and didn't want him to find them," he grumbled.

Lydia held up another tome. "This one was written by her sister and was written at a later date."

"The sister she left the manuscripts to?" Gerard squeezed Iona's hand.

Now, she could sense his excitement taking over.

"The sister who understood the prophesies, yes." Lydia read the passages where the younger woman described moving the precious but dangerous manuscripts to her sister's burial vault in the newly-constructed chapel.

"We can probably find that." Max lumbered to his feet.

Lydia pulled him back down and waited expectantly.

"Does the sister say who she meant to have those books?" Gerard stroked Iona's hand as he spoke. She didn't recognize the scent surrounding him but she thought it might be hope. "Or did she mean to leave them buried?"

Lydia flipped a few pages. "She was quite angry with her brother-in-law, who never learned to read." She shot a knowing look at her husband. "He apparently remarried soon after his wife's death but refused to send his sister-in-law back to Wystan as she asked. Her ability to read and write was too valuable."

Iona leaned forward. "So the sister died here too? And the knowledge of the books went with her?"

"Until now," Lydia said in satisfaction. "This is the last mention of the manuscripts in the library. She wrote her request in excellent French, in a clear hand: *I bequeath the dowry we never used to Wystan and its inhabitants, the only ones who might find these words and appreciate our gift.*"

TWENTY-NINE

WHILE EVERYONE ELSE PREPARED FOR DINNER, GERARD AND MAX DESCENDED into the chapel crypt.

"I can't believe I'm desecrating a graveyard for *books*." Max shone his lamp at the vaulted ceiling of the underground chamber. "Look at this! Someone knew how to build for eternity."

"The same someone who didn't appreciate his gifted wife? I think the women are telling us he was a bone-headed Ives." Gerard had seen the dynamic between his mother and father long enough to know how it worked.

"A man needs to be single-minded if he's to accomplish anything," Max grumbled. "If this place was built four hundred years ago, the engineer was brilliant."

Gerard ran his hand above the plates marking names and dates. Without Iona to help him focus, he only received mild vibrations that he translated as grief and loss, with the occasional sharper pangs of what might be greed or anticipation. He had no practice at actually defining different oscillations.

The fact that he thought in terms of oscillations and not spirits proved he was still his father's son. "I'll remind you that I'm not you. Only some of us are single-minded."

Max snorted. "Fine then, the brute couldn't read or write, so building was all he could do. Let me know when you find the right date." Max might not be able to read the lettering, but he knew how to open a vault without bringing the ceiling down on their heads.

"If I'm remembering Roman numerals correctly, this is the oldest section." Gerard indicated a plate with several names on it—all female if he knew anything of medieval French.

"All right then, let's see where this goes." Using chisel and hammer, Max pried at the crumbling seal. "If I see any ghosts, they'd better speak English."

"If they mean to curse us for interrupting their rest, I'd rather it be in a language I don't recognize." Gerard tried not to expect too much.

The manuscripts had been left to the *inhabitants of Wystan*—currently, that would be his family.

The metal plate clattered to the stone floor. The crypt was so old that little more than a hint of must and dust emerged.

Max grimaced at the black hole. "The honors are yours."

The lantern light barely reached the interior. Gerard wasn't wearing his gloves. Preparing himself for a shock, he extended one hand into the opening.

Happiness. Contentment. Singing. Without Iona, he had no real vision. But as other artifacts had, a box spoke to him. He couldn't hear the words, but he sensed relief and encouragement as he fumbled around among the caskets—until he encountered a square metal box that shouted *Yes*. Finding a handle, he drew it out, praying it wasn't a child's coffin.

"Do we open it here?" Tools in hand, Max studied what appeared to be a small, elaborately embossed brass casket. "I'd hate to take a pile of bones to the ladies."

Gerard held the box in his palms and shook his head. "This is it. I feel Wystan on it. It's very strange. I didn't know Wystan had a feeling until now."

"It's called *home*, old boy." Max slapped his back. "I knew it the moment I saw Lydia."

For a man who thought only in terms of duty, who knew the law inside and out, Gerard was torn in two as he carried the box to the great hall. This business of allowing emotion to speak hampered logical decision making.

Just watching Iona sweep in, wearing one of her new dinner gowns, carrying her kitten, looking more like a countess than any beekeeper should, Gerard knew what she would say. It would be the same reaction as all the other ladies of Wystan—of his entire Malcolm family. His own mother would side with Iona.

But he was a practical Ives. The box held the answer to his dreams: a refurbished Wystan, income for travel, a cushion against disaster. Even his family should concede it was more important to protect the Wystan library and provide a home for the women who lived there and had nowhere else to go. He could send Aunt Winifred to her son—

They would never allow him to sell books.

After setting the kitten down to sniff delicately at the treasure, Iona caught his arm and studied the darkened casket. "You found it."

She said it with confidence. Only she understood that he wouldn't mistake bones for books. How could he disappoint a woman like that? How could he not? Gerard covered her hand with his filthy one. She didn't even notice his dirt but kissed his cheek, nicely removing the chill of the grave with a surge of warmth.

The entire household gathered in expectation. Iona made her vaporish twin sit down and pet the kitten. Even Phoebe's husband appeared from the depths of whatever he'd been taking apart. Servants lingered in the doorways.

Max didn't wait for permission but slammed a pick into the ancient lock, then stood back for Gerard to open it.

The leather-bound books looked as new as the day they'd been placed inside, centuries ago.

"Oh, my, do we dare touch them?" Iona breathed in delight.

She vibrated with awe. Gerard was learning to interpret his wife's emotions—a truly terrifying prospect. "I think the Librarian should do the honors. As I understand it, Lydia is a Malcolm from Northumberland, so it was likely her ancestors who created them."

That was one of the many arguments pounding in his skull. After so many centuries, the Malcolms of Wystan might number in the thousands.

With reverence, Lydia held her hands over the manuscripts, then shook her head. "We need gloves. I know how to tend our journals, but these. . ."

"Are extremely valuable, possibly priceless," the lanky marquess said with a pragmatism that overruled all the flowing emotions. "The value to scholars alone—"

"For *women* scholars." Iona's quiet wren of a sister spoke decisively.

Since Isobel seldom spoke, Gerard regarded her with curiosity.

"I doubt there are many female art scholars," Rainford argued. "Why women?"

"Because that's what the lady says." Isobel's eyes rolled back in her head, and she crumpled to the sofa. The kitten licked her lifeless hand.

Iona held Gerard back when he would have gone to help. "No. She's fine. She's learned to stay away from sharp objects and sit in soft places. She's already coming around."

"She hears voices on objects too?" he couldn't help asking.

"No, Iona hears spirits. This lady must be exceptionally strong if she's come back from centuries ago to reach Isobel. I'm almost afraid for us to touch the book. Lydia, are you hearing anything?"

The Calder librarian frowned and shook her head. "It's not a Malcolm journal. If they're Bibles, then there is nothing for them to say to me. I think they're simply treasures for what they can show of us of that era and for the art. The gold leaf alone must have cost a fortune."

And there it was. Riches untold awaited in that box. Gerard knew the law. Legally, he could defend the argument that they belonged to the *inhabitants of Wystan*, not their descendants. But Malcolms thought in terms of generations—hence the libraries. The creator of these Bibles wanted them for all Malcolms. At the time, only Malcolms had inhabited Wystan.

"Could we eat first?" he asked in resignation. "I'd like to spend a lovely hour or two imagining gold pouring into my coffers."

Climbing to her feet with Rainford's assistance, even Isobel looked sympathetic.

~

DAYS LATER, IONA FLAUNTED HER MOST FASHIONABLE GOWN, BUSTLE, AND petticoats—for a hunting lodge. "Balmoral is draftier than even Craigmore," she whispered to Gerard.

She could feel the rumble of his laughter, but he dutifully faced his diminutive queen. Even Iona felt tall next to the monarch, but she lacked ruffles and jewels and would never possess Victoria's regal presence.

"You do not mind that your wife is surrendering her claim to her grandfather's title and estate, Ives?" the queen asked after the chancellor explained their request.

"No, your majesty. The expense of my own estate is quite sufficient."

Iona bit back an inexplicable giggle at the queen's complacent nod. Had her majesty even listened to what he'd said beyond "no"? That the queen had asked Iona's *husband* and not Iona if she wished to give up her title had not escaped her.

Dismissing the rest of the affair, Iona studied the lofty chamber of the queen's vacation home. She felt no loss as Isobel was appointed countess and caretaker of Craigmore. Isobel was her other half, after all, the one connected to the land.

Only when the queen addressed Gerard directly did Iona return to the conversation.

"I have been told you are in possession of a national treasure, Ives. Is this correct? You have uncovered a priceless medieval Bible?"

Iona almost bit off her tongue. They'd spent these last days arguing over what would be best for the relics. They'd even consulted the Marquess of Ashford, Gerard's father, confidant of the queen—ah, of course. He'd told her.

"We are certain the Bible is genuine, Your Majesty, but we are still debating who should be chosen to verify it."

Iona heard his wariness. Surely the queen could not appropriate personal property?

He was talking *Bible,* singular. There were two of them.

"A Bible of that significance should belong to all, should it not?" the queen suggested with a hint of steel. "We would find the finest experts to examine it and see it properly tended. It should be on display in the royal collection."

Iona would like to object, but the Bibles belonged to her husband's

Northumberland side of the family, not her Scots one. And Lydia wasn't here to present her arguments as a librarian.

"We would be honored if our family treasure could enlighten the minds and souls of many," Gerard said in his best diplomatic tones. "But it would come at great cost to the women of my family, to whom it was bequeathed. They prize it greatly and wish to learn from it and pass on their knowledge to future generations. You have children of your own, Your Majesty. You'll understand the desire to improve their souls."

Oh my. Under that layer of diplomacy, Gerard roiled with so many emotions, Iona feared he'd explode. How could any one man contain so much energy without a sign of it appearing in his voice or features?

Practice—a lifetime of practice. He knew precisely what he was doing. She squeezed his arm in reassurance. His stew of emotions steadied into a scent of. . . determination?

She murmured so only he could hear, "I love you, my lord. You are my heart and soul."

His arm jolted a little, and then he covered her hand with his while the queen spoke.

"Of course, we are prepared to offer your family free access to the treasure at any time and reimburse you for your loss. There is a marquessate. . ."

Gerard bowed, effectively cutting her off. "If I may, your majesty?"

She gestured irritably. "You will tell me the expense of one marquessate is sufficient."

Iona stifled a giggle. So, the queen had heard.

"Yes, your majesty. As is the upkeep of Wystan. The ladies there are rightful owners of the book. They are the ones who should be reimbursed, not me."

The queen sighed heavily and turned to the chancellor. "I believe you have discussed what the royal coffers can afford?"

Iona's jaw dropped at the sum named.

THIRTY

GERARD ASSISTED HIS FLUSHED WIFE WITH REARRANGING HER RUMPLED travel garments as his new carriage rolled down the rutted drive in the final leg of their journey. His *carriage*—a wedding gift from the marquess. His father had declared a wife needed one. Then the old nip-farthing had given Gerard his old growler and bought himself a sleek new brougham.

Gerard appreciated the sentiment. The marquess traveled about London and needed to flaunt his position. Gerard was taking up residence in the middle of nowhere and could have lived with a mule-drawn cart.

"I think I can come to appreciate this mode of transportation." He helped Iona button up her bodice. "Having a wife as travel companion has proved most—enlightening."

Iona laughed. He loved hearing her laugh. She'd been much too serious for too long.

"I appreciate any transportation at all. And having a husband is most —*exciting*. Look, the ladies are gathering on the portico!"

"In this gale?" Gerard peered around her as the coach rattled into the courtyard. "There will be no arriving unannounced anymore, will there?"

Strangely, he did not mind. Yes, his tenants were odd, but then, so was he. Now that they had the wherewithal to make improvements, he was eager to make changes—if the women approved. "I don't think I even mind that you and the others are allowed to question my decisions. I'll have someone else to blame if the choice is wrong."

Iona laughed again and kissed his cheek, heating his blood even though they'd just christened the new carriage in satisfying fashion. "Your ancestor prophesies a land of milk and honey. The Bible illustration shows a man surrounded by bees being saved by such a concoction. We may cause harm, but we do strive to repair it."

"Prophesies are so very illogical. Milk—we should buy more cows? We should fix the roof with leather from the cows and glue it with honey?" He laughed when she poked him for his rudeness.

"Despite all logical sense, I love you," she declared. "I have not told you enough, I think. I love the way you think. I love your sense of duty. And I love waking up with you in the morning."

As soon as the carriage door opened, Gerard handed out the kitten's basket to the post-boy. Stepping out, he reached to lift his wife down. "And I love your sauciness and the way you make me see all sides, even when I know I'm right. And I love it when you. . ." He bent over and whispered in her ear.

She blushed and shoved him away, taking his arm to properly greet Wystan's inhabitants. Gerard wasn't worried about this prim reaction. He had learned that his bride was as adept at learning bedplay as she was everything else she set her mind to. She would apply herself to his preference with enthusiasm the instant they retired to his own private tower.

"You brought the Bible?" Little Mrs. Merriweather asked excitedly as they approached.

Iona laughed. "His lordship is bringing enough wealth to fix the roof, improve the chimneys, start another orchard, and give you each a stipend. And you ask about an ancient Bible?"

"Of course." Aunt Winifred gestured for everyone to return inside, out of the chilly wind. "It was exceedingly generous of the Calder librarian to cede ownership to Wystan. We are isolated here. Malcolms will have to travel some distance to study it. It must have been difficult for her to give it up."

"We could charge room and board if travelers wished to stay beyond one night," Mary Mike mused. "That will allow us to refurbish more rooms."

Gerard chuckled and hugged Iona, who listened with equal amusement if he judged her vibrations correctly. "The beekeeper and I found the lost treasure, so we request our fair share of the reward for repairing the roof first and our share of any profit for improving crops after that. And I demand the deciding vote in any other decision since I'm the one who takes the blame. And why is Ceridwen wailing?"

He liked to establish his authority, but the banshee cry echoed through the halls, disrupting his planned arguments. The wail did not sound quite as mournful as he remembered from earlier.

"She's weeping in happiness," Grace decided. "Let us see the book."

So much for prepared arguments.

Lowell carried in the trunk. Gerard gestured and the valet opened it while the ladies gathered around. "Mrs. Merriweather, if you will do the honors?"

Reverently, the librarian lifted the box from the trunk shelf. "It's talking to me already," she said in awe.

Iona looked up at him expectantly. Gerard shrugged, then bowed his head in acknowledgment. "Actually, since we reached Northumberland, the book has not shut up. Our ancestor has a great deal to say."

Isobel had apparently woken the lady's spirit, but it was Gerard she'd chosen to enlighten. Now that he no longer had a Roman soldier in his head, he had a harridan who spoke medieval French—*if* he held the book. He didn't think he'd do that often.

The women turned their stares to him. "You hear her?" they all asked at once.

There, he'd admitted it to one and all. There was no turning back. He was one of them.

"She's just one more female scolding me," he said with nonchalance. "Mrs. Merriweather, I hope you have a nice chat, but please don't recite all my foibles to her. My first rule is that I don't follow the orders of dead people. Live ones are more than enough to test my patience."

Leaving his astonished tenants spewing questions, Gerard swept his giggling wife from the hall and back to the privacy of his suite—and that immense bath designed for two.

"Let's shed a little travel dust, shall we?" he whispered as she hurried beside him.

"Together?" Her tone was decidedly wicked.

"I don't think I've told you enough—I love the way your mind works." Reaching the back hall, Gerard lifted her in his arms and carried her over the threshold to his tower.

Her laughter christened the old walls with hope.

And he still had a map to a possible Roman fortress. Who knew, maybe his talent would find more treasure to keep Wystan in good repair for his children and his children's children.

They'd have a jolly good time finding out.

CHARACTERS

Gerard Ives, Earl of Ives and Wystan, heir to Duncan, Marquess of Ashford

Lady Iona (Nan) Malcolm Ross, heir to Countess of Craigmore

Lady Isobel (Belle) Malcolm Ross, Iona's twin

Jasper Winchester, Marquess of Rainford, heir to Duke of Sommersville

Avery, Gerard's steward at Wystan

Great-Aunt Winifred, Gerard's relation, writes articles

Grace, weaver at Wystan

Simone, spiritualist at Wystan

Ceridwen, ghost/banshee

Mrs. Faith Merriweather, Wystan librarian

Mary Michaela Wilson (Mary Mike), lives at Wystan

Ralph Mortimer, Iona and Isobel's stepfather

Arthur Winter, Iona's suitor

Lydia Wystan Ives, librarian of Calder Castle

Maxwell Ives, Lydia's husband

Lady Alice, duplicitous widow

Lowell, Gerard's valet

Zane, Lord Dare—doctor, professor, viscount

Azmin, Lady Dare—photographer
Lady Phoebe Blair and Andrew Blair—friends of the School of
Malcolms

Entrancing the Earl
Patricia Rice

Copyright © 2020 Patricia Rice
First Publication: Book View Cafe, May 2021
ISBN ebook - 978-1-61138-950-0
ISBN print - 978-1-61138-951-7

Published by Rice Enterprises, Dana Point, CA, an affiliate of Book View Publishing
Cooperative
Cover design by Kim Killion

Book View Café
304 S. Jones Blvd. Suite #2906
Las Vegas NV 89107

ABOUT THE AUTHOR

With several million books in print and *New York Times* and *USA Today's* bestseller lists under her belt, former CPA Patricia Rice is one of romance's hottest authors. Her emotionally-charged contemporary and historical romances have won numerous awards, including the *RT Book Reviews* Reviewers Choice and Career Achievement Awards. Her books have been honored as Romance Writers of America RITA® finalists in the historical, regency and contemporary categories.

A firm believer in happily-ever-after, Patricia Rice is married to her high school sweetheart and has two children. A native of Kentucky and New York, a past resident of North Carolina and Missouri, she currently resides in Southern California, and now does accounting only for herself.

ALSO BY PATRICIA RICE

The World of Magic:

The Unexpected Magic Series

MAGIC IN THE STARS

WHISPER OF MAGIC

THEORY OF MAGIC

AURA OF MAGIC

CHEMISTRY OF MAGIC

NO PERFECT MAGIC

The Magical Malcolms Series

MERELY MAGIC

MUST BE MAGIC

THE TROUBLE WITH MAGIC

THIS MAGIC MOMENT

MUCH ADO ABOUT MAGIC

MAGIC MAN

The California Malcolms Series

THE LURE OF SONG AND MAGIC

TROUBLE WITH AIR AND MAGIC

THE RISK OF LOVE AND MAGIC

Crystal Magic

SAPPHIRE NIGHTS

TOPAZ DREAMS

CRYSTAL VISION

WEDDING GEMS

AZURE SECRETS

AMBER AFFAIRS

MOONSTONE SHADOWS

THE WEDDING GIFT

THE WEDDING QUESTION

THE WEDDING SURPRISE

School of Magic

LESSONS IN ENCHANTMENT

A BEWITCHING GOVERNESS

AN ILLUSION OF LOVE

THE LIBRARIAN'S SPELL

ENTRANCING THE EARL

CAPTIVATING THE COUNTESS

Historical Romance:

American Dream Series

MOON DREAMS

REBEL DREAMS

The Rebellious Sons

WICKED WYCKERLY

DEVILISH MONTAGUE

NOTORIOUS ATHERTON

FORMIDABLE LORD QUENTIN

The Regency Nobles Series

THE GENUINE ARTICLE

THE MARQUESS

ENGLISH HEIRESS

IRISH DUCHESS

Regency Love and Laughter Series

CROSSED IN LOVE

MAD MARIA'S DAUGHTER

ARTFUL DECEPTIONS

ALL A WOMAN WANTS

Rogues & Desperadoes Series

LORD ROGUE

MOONLIGHT AND MEMORIES

SHELTER FROM THE STORM

WAYWARD ANGEL

DENIM AND LACE

CHEYENNES LADY

Dark Lords and Dangerous Ladies Series

LOVE FOREVER AFTER

SILVER ENCHANTRESS

DEVIL'S LADY

DASH OF ENCHANTMENT

INDIGO MOON

Too Hard to Handle

TEXAS LILY

TEXAS ROSE

TEXAS TIGER

TEXAS MOON

Mystic Isle Series

MYSTIC ISLE

MYSTIC GUARDIAN

MYSTIC RIDER

MYSTIC WARRIOR

Mysteries:

Family Genius Series

EVIL GENIUS

UNDERCOVER GENIUS

CYBER GENIUS

TWIN GENIUS

TWISTED GENIUS

Tales of Love and Mystery

BLUE CLOUDS

GARDEN OF DREAMS

NOBODY'S ANGEL

VOLCANO

CALIFORNIA GIRL

Urban Fantasies

Writing as Jamie Quaid

Saturn's Daughters

BOYFRIEND FROM HELL

DAMN HIM TO HELL

GIVING HIM HELL

ABOUT BOOK VIEW CAFÉ

 *Book View Café* Publishing Cooperative (BVC) is an author-owned cooperative of over fifty professional writers, publishing in a variety of genres including fantasy, romance, mystery, and science fiction — with 90% of the proceeds going to the authors. Since its debut in 2008, BVC has gained a reputation for producing high-quality ebooks. BVC's ebooks are DRM-free and are distributed around the world. The cooperative is now bringing that same quality to its print editions.

BVC authors include New York Times and USA Today bestsellers as well as winners and nominees of many prestigious awards.

CPSIA information can be obtained
at www.ICGtesting.com
Printed in the USA
LVHW032328140721
692684LV00003B/235